THE STREETBIRD

Also by Janwillem van de Wetering

FICTION

The Grijpstra-de Gier series:

Outsider in Amsterdam
Tumbleweed
The Corpse on the Dike
Death of a Hawker
The Japanese Corpse
The Maine Massacre
The Mind-Murders
Blond Baboon
Rattle-Rat
The Sergeant's Cat (short stories)
Hard Rain
Just a Corpse at Twilight
The Hollow-Eyed Angel

Other:
Inspector Saito's Small Satori
The Butterfly Hunter
Bliss and Bluster
Seesaw Millions
Murder by Remote Control
Mangrove Mama

AUTOBIOGRAPHY

The Empty Mirror: Experiences in a Japanese Zen Monastery
A Glimpse of Nothingness: Experiences in an American Zen Community

BIOGRAPHY

Robert van Gulik: His Life, His Work

CHILDREN'S BOOKS

Hugh Pine
Hugh Pine and the Good Place
Hugh Pine and Something Else
Little Owl

THE STREETBIRD

Janwillem van de Wetering

Published by
Soho Press, Inc.
853 Broadway
New York, NY 10003

Library of Congress Cataloging in Publication Data

Van de Wetering, Janwillem, 1931-
The streetbird / Janwillem van de Wetering.
p. cm.
ISBN 1-56947-093-6
I. Title.
PS3572.A4298S8 1997
813'.54—dc21 96-37388
CIP

PRINTED IN THE UNITED STATES OF AMERICA

for Morgan McNeven

THE STREETBIRD

I

Adjutant Grijpstra slept, tucked between army-surplus sleeping bags wrapped around a foam-rubber mattress, all brand new. Except for the camping gear and Grijpstra's snoring bulk, the room was empty. Although the apartment on the Amsterdam Oilmakerscanal was old, and rented by the adjutant a great many years ago, the room looked new. Its walls had been recently whitewashed and the floor sanded, removing all traces of much wear and tear. The other upstairs rooms of the small gable house had also been worked on, mostly by Grijpstra himself but also by his friend and assistant, Sergeant de Gier. The sergeant had moved in immediately after Mrs. Grijpstra and the little ones left, squeezed into a van that also contained the family's furniture and countless odds

The ranks in the Amsterdam Municipal Police are constable, constable first class, sergeant, adjutant, inspector, chief inspector, commissaris, chief constable. An adjutant is a noncommissioned officer.

and ends. Only the adjutant himself stayed, just about forgotten, left to his own devices and work: the tracking of evildoers wanted by the Murder Brigade or the Department of Serious Crime of the Amsterdam Police.

Now de Gier had left too, after a long and busy weekend, leaving his superior almost unburdened of possessions and in a happy frame of mind. The adjutant's happiness had continued into his sleep and was about to be broken now, at 3:30 A.M. on Monday.

The telephone rang. The adjutant's left eye opened and his right hand began to pat the floor. It came back holding a pistol. The adjutant ordered his hand to put the gun down and try again. This time it gave him the phone.

"Now what?"

"I was asleep too," de Gier's voice said accusingly, "but it seems there has been this murder."

"Why tell me about it?"

"I'm not only telling you, I'm coming to fetch you—in a minute, because right now I'm still in bed."

"Umptssjteh."

"I didn't quite get that."

"I smacked my lips," Grijpstra said patiently, "in order to manufacture a little spittle because my mouth was dry, as it often is when I've been asleep. Where is this murder?"

"Olofs-alley, corner Seadike."

"You exaggerate," Grijpstra said. "As you often do. Maybe a bit of manslaughter, sergeant, and I will not be joining you. Try Cardozo, he likes little stuff like that. Do a good job. Good-bye."

"Hey."

"I'm about," Grijpstra said kindly, "to replace this phone."

"Whoa!" de Gier yelled. "Murder, I say. With an automatic weapon. Not just one misplaced small-caliber bullet, but a complete spray of killing fire. A deadly rattle, and you'll love the corpse."

"I know the previous owner?"

"Of course you do."

Grijpstra's toes were feeling for the floor. "Who?"

"Luku Obrian," De Gier said triumphantly.

Grijpstra, if fully awake, might have shouted. But he was partly awake and merely mumbled louder. "The prince of the quarter? Assassinated? Damn his black soul!"

"Wouldn't we have liked his soul too," de Gier murmured wistfully. "It got away," he said in a loud voice, "and so did the killer. But *he* is still about and if you would get dressed and step outside, we might catch him."

Grijpstra dropped the phone and put on his shirt, back to front. He put it on again, front to back. Exhausted, he sat and thought until the disruptive clash of a garbage can, stumbled into by a drunk outside, reminded him of the sergeant, now surely halfway there.

De Gier arrived in a new-model Volkswagen, already rusty and liberally dented. Grijpstra folded himself into the car. "The commissaris should be on his way too," the sergeant was saying. "The station in the red-light quarter called him directly. He will have picked up Cardozo. Lovely murder, adjutant, it will be very useful."

"For who?"

"For us." De Gier adjusted his mustache, modeled after the Queen's Cavalry of the previous century. His large brown eyes glanced at his passenger. De Gier's strong after-shave made Grijpstra crank open a window. The sergeant looked neat, in narrow freshly laundered trousers and a tailor-made wide-lapeled jacket adorned with a loosely knotted silk scarf.

Grijpstra sat stolidly, his hands intertwined on the waistcoat of his pinstriped suit. The car whined on, at twice the legal maximum speed. De Gier, foot down, while artfully turning the wheel, talked about riddance and rubbish and six black holes in a chest of the same color, in a cheerful manner.

The car raced through Amsterdam's old inner city. Grijpstra looked up, to avoid flashing lampposts and the feverish sweeping of tree branches. He yanked at the sun roof and prayed to the sky that was steadier than blurring objects.

"No!" yelled de Gier.

Grijpstra groaned. "No what?"

"That couldn't have been real," de Gier said. "Even in Amsterdam. Did you see what I saw?"

"What could I have seen?"

The three men, far behind the onrushing car, roller-skated on. They were perfect gentlemen, properly attired, in spotless white shirts under three-piece suits, with well-knotted ties, and proper hairstyles, not too long, not too short. They carried new briefcases and swung their free hands in unison, riding easily on the smooth tarmac, heading for the Dam square and the National Monument, intent perhaps, on circling it three times to honor the country.

"What did you see?" Grijpstra insisted. "What *is* there to see at four in the morning?"

De Gier explain. Grijpstra grunted.

"Really," de Gier implored. "Three gentlemen roller-skating soberly on their way to where?"

"To their office. Staggered hours? Who cares? We are going to the Olofs-alley. Over there. Make a right. Avoid the cyclist."

The Volkswagen avoided the cyclist, but he fell over anyway and the car stopped. Grijpstra got out. "Are you all right?"

"No," the drunk said. "just fell off my bicycle."

Grijpstra got in again. "Gentlemen," de Gier muttered. "On roller skates."

Grijpstra fumbled with a cigar. The Volkswagen jumped

away. The cigar broke. Grijpstra threw it out of the window. "Why not? There are gentlemen and there are roller skates. The ideas can be combined."

"At four A.M.?"

"Anything can be combined," Grijpstra said. "Just give it a chance. And there has to be a time. What's wrong with early in the morning?"

The car found the Seadike and was parked. The detectives strolled into the alley. No one was waiting for them, but their arrival seemed acceptable. The commissaris extended a small hand and allowed it to be shaken, first by Grijpstra, then by de Gier. The commissaris was old, an insignificant shadow next to the large uniformed sergeant with the red hair. "Hello, Jurriaans," Grijpstra and de Gier said simultaneously. "Hello, Cardozo." Cardozo stood on the sergeant's other side and also contrasted with the martial figure, for Cardozo was young, loosely fitted together, untidily dressed in a well-worn velvet coat and crumpled corduroy trousers. The young detective's nose curved nobly and his eyes, too large for his face, gleamed inquisitively. He couldn't keep still and pulled Grijpstra by the sleeve. "Come along, adjutant, the corpse is over there."

The corpse welcomed its visitors with a wide grin, between drawn lips displaying strong white teeth, perfectly repaired with much gold. The dead Obrian was as imposing as he had been alive. His tightly buttoned linen jacket was stained with blood that had dribbled down to his trousers, followed the immaculate lines and reached his polished white leather boots.

"A marksman got him," Jurriaans said, and squatted down to point out bloody tears in the jacket. "Six shots, all in the chest. A machine pistol, the experts think. To aim an automatic weapon correctly isn't easy. A splendid job, colleagues."

The narrow alley was crowded and the police were everywhere, both uniformed and plainclothed. Grijpstra and de Gier were nodding to acquaintances. Two constables appeared to study the dead man. The constables looked alike; they were of the same size, that of the commissaris, and of Cardozo.

"Hello, Ketchup," Grijpstra said. "Hello, Karate."

"Hello," said de Gier.

"Got the bastard nicely, didn't they?" Karate asked.

"Who?" The commissaris shuffled forward, leaning on his cane. "*Who* got him, constable?"

"Hard to say, sir. And so close to our station. We heard the killer fire but we thought there was trouble with our furnace again, we haven't had hot water in the station lately—bubbles in the tubes. Or maybe a car with a busted muffler."

"And you?" the commissaris asked Sergeant Jurriaans.

"I wasn't aware anything was wrong either."

"So how did you find out?"

"Crazy Chris told us, sir."

"And who is Crazy Chris?"

"A methylated-spirits drinker, sir," Ketchup said. "The old codger had been watching Obrian's car. Crazy Chris sells vegetables and stuff off his cart by day and can't sleep, so he's around at night too. One of Obrian's retainers, sir, unpaid of course and dumb enough to do odd jobs like guarding the Porsche, brand new, with all the options."

"Crazy Chris saw the murder?"

"Not quite," Jurriaans said. "That would have been too good. He heard shots and saw Obrian fall, so far okay, but Chris never thought of ascertaining where the bullets came from. Lost his cool and whirled about for a while, took him a little time to understand that he should call us." Jurriaans pointed. "That's where the killer stood, sir."

The commissaris looked at the top floor of the corner building. "The burned-out ruin?"

"A sex shop unable to pay its bills. Valid insurance, a match and an old newspaper. Last week, sir. It will be pulled down shortly."

"Traces," the commissaris said. "The trail is fresh. There'll be plenty of charcoal inside, and charcoal holds good prints. We've got prints?"

Cardozo wanted to dart off. Jurriaans restrained him by lowering a large hand. Camera flashes could be seen inside the building. "You don't want to go in there now," Jurriaans said kindly. "You might be in the way."

"Machine pistol?" the commissaris asked. "Why?"

Jurriaans turned ponderously to face the old man. "A rattle, sir, according to Crazy Chris, and also to an old lady farther along the alley. The weapon was heard, not seen. *Turrám.* A powerful weapon, for the bullets went through the body, we found all six of them. Nine-millimeter."

"A heavy caliber," the commissaris agreed, "possibly too heavy for a revolver or a pistol, although there are army sidearms of that size, I believe. Machine pistol? Any particular brand? The Germans had a nine-millimeter, I recall." He thought, carefully touching the tip of his small nose. "A Schmeisser perhaps?"

"Or a British gun, sir, the Sten."

The commissaris nodded. "Where was Chris when Obrian got hit?"

Jurriaans paced about. "Here stood Chris." His arm extended accusingly. "There lives the old lady, you can see her now. It's a great day in her life. And there was the killer. All he had to do was run down the stairs and leave by the Seadike, to the Dam Street and a maze of alleys on the other side, to be lost forever."

The commissaris leaned on his cane and studied the corpse's face. "Quite, sergeant. Now, who benefited by this man's death?"

"The competition, sir, the exploiters of the quarter."

"The dead man was a pimp?"

Jurriaans smiled. "Pimp of all pimps. Prince of the quarter. Bottom of the line, sir, close to the devil."

The commissaris' weak eyes blinked behind his small rimless glasses. "So the competition would be pimpish too. Anyone in mind?"

"Lennie," Ketchup said.

"Gustav," Karate said.

The commissaris' cane slipped on a bloody cobblestone. Helped by de Gier, he regained his balance. He rubbed his hip.

"In pain, sir?"

"Yes," the commissaris said. "And I shouldn't be here. This is the worst time for my rheumatism, and I'm on sick leave anyway. Tomorrow I leave for Austria, there's some slimy hot water there they say, and I will sit in it for a week. If I don't get home quickly my wife will kill me before I can be cured. This murder is badly timed."

The remark caused silence, respectful and compassionate as expressed by Grijpstra, de Gier, and Cardozo; respectful and slightly amused in the half-smiles of Jurriaans, Karate, and Ketchup. A thrush, perched on the corner of a roof gutter, framed the pause with clear powerful notes, stridently lowered at his audience. Hoarse singing interrupted the bird. An undisciplined crowd of inebriated seamen or degenerate tourists, arms around each others' shoulders, appeared in the delicate light of the early morning, staggering forward. Karate and Ketchup, gesturing with their truncheons, attempted to head it off.

The group lowered its many chins.

The constables advanced. The group split up into strategically placed individuals, fists swinging. Sergeant Jurriaans stretched to his full length, de Gier spread his legs and bent, ready to jump. Cardozo sneaked ahead. Grijpstra froze. The commissaris stepped back.

The commissaris hadn't really seen the enemy. He was interested in the thrush. He ruminated, leaning on his cane again, and raised his small head sparsely covered with neatly combed hair. The thrush obliged and a fresh arpeggio tinkled down but broke once more, as a large shadow winged over the gutter and made the songbird falter and flutter away. "My," the commissaris muttered as the shadow wheeled away and disappeared behind the gables. "What on earth . . . ?" The commissaris mumbled. "Blacker than a crow? Larger than a falcon? A wide tail kept up by stiff yellow legs? A sharp bent beak?"

"Sir?" Grijpstra asked.

"Talking to myself," the commissaris said. "Old men, you know. That's what they do." His cane touched the corpse. "Pity."

Grijpstra looked down. "An evil sort of chap, sir."

"How evil?" the commissaris said. "And why? I would like to know, but I've got to sit in slime. Don't want to, really. Nevertheless."

The enemy had linked up again, but retreated in ominous silence, surrounded by Ketchup and Karate, running in opposite circles and waving their nightsticks. "Don't hit them," Jurriaans shouted. "There's enough trouble," Sergeant Jurriaans said to no one in particular. "Sir? Can the corpse be taken away?"

"By all means." The commissaris touched the sergeant's sleeve. "A simple case?"

Jurriaans shook his head. "No. Tricky, I would think. It takes a clever man to do away with the prince himself. And a bad man. Truly bad. Like Lennie. Like Gustav. War between the big pimps, hard to figure out their moves, from the outside."

"There's an inside too," the commissaris said. "Grijpstra?"

Grijpstra was looking at the sky. His mouth hung open. Jurriaans tapped his shoulder. "The commissaris wants you."

"Sir?"

"You're in charge, adjutant, since I won't be here. Find a

place to live, close by if you please, and Cardozo can join you, de Gier too. But de Gier should work in uniform, I think."

De Gier had listened in, and protested, but the thrush returned and sang away the sergeant's comments.

"Lovely," the commissaris said, smiling at the bird's turned-down head and little beady eyes. "Sergeant Jurriaans?"

"Sir?"

"I want you to lead the frontal attack while my detectives slither in from underneath. I will communicate with your chief so that you may be released from your routine. De Gier can serve as a sort of in-between. Would that be all right?"

"Sir," Jurriaans affirmed.

Karate and Ketchup came marching back and stood at attention.

"Did you hit them?" Jurriaans asked.

"They were Germans," Ketchup said.

"You aren't allowed to hit Germans either."

"You see?" Ketchup asked Karate.

"You were right," Karate said sadly. "But it's hard to believe."

"I'm often right." Ketchup smiled proudly.

"You hit them too," Jurriaans said. "When you were out of sight. You shouldn't have."

The commissaris turned away after saying good-bye. De Gier walked along toward an old but well-kept Citroën parked half on the sidewalk of the Seadike. "Shall I drive you home?"

"No," the commissaris said. "It doesn't hurt so much once I sit down. It's getting worse, Rinus, and the pain is reaching my neck. I'll have to give in soon, my wife is right."

The others were watching the ill-matched pair—the tall, wide-shouldered detective sergeant, bouncing on his long legs, an example of virile awareness, and the little old chief, leaning on the arm of his protector, dragging his almost useless leg.

"About to retire?" Jurriaans asked.

Grijpstra frowned. "Never."

Cardozo jumped up and down. "A murderer, a real murderer, haven't had one for years. A true killer, who has thought it all out, and he used a *machine gun*. Are we going to get him, adjutant, are we?"

"Of course," Grijpstra said.

Jurriaans removed his cap from under his arm and placed it carefully on his head. "I admire your optimism. Any idea what you're getting yourself into?" He adjusted the cap with both hands. "This is not your regular murder, politely planned by nice suburban types. Here everything is sick, rotten."

"Good," Cardozo said.

"A cup of coffee?" asked Jurriaans.

"And an apartment," Grijpstra said. "Close by, available immediately so that we can move in at once." His lower lip protruded sadly. "Not that I want to. I have a nice house myself now."

"You?" Cardozo asked. "Where? You always say you don't like your house. Did you move?"

De Gier had come back. He smiled at Cardozo. "Things don't have to move to change, you know. They can stay where they are and be different."

"So soon?" Cardozo flapped his hands. "The adjutant was still complaining last week." He puckered his nose. "About the smell." He covered his ears. "The noise." He held his throat. "The lack of space."

"Shshsh," Grijpstra said. An ambulance had arrived. The attendants placed the corpse on a stretcher. Obrian's long arms dangled and were tucked away. He was still smiling, in all directions now, as his head lolled about. The policemen followed, automatically falling into step, Jurriaans next to the adjutant, de Gier with Cardozo, Ketchup with Karate. They lined up, waiting for the attendants to close the doors of the ambulance.

"Prince of the quarter," Jurriaans said. "I thought he would never leave."

"We are the Crown."

Jurriaans looked at Grijpstra. "What?"

The adjutant reached up and took off the sergeant's cap. "Here, the crown, the supreme emblem, on your own hat."

Jurriaans nodded. "One almost forgets here."

De Gier talked to Cardozo. "A little while ago I saw three gentlemen roller-skating." He put one hand on his back and made his legs slide. He dangled his other hand in front of Cardozo's face. "Carrying briefcases. Can you imagine."

"Do I have to?" asked Cardozo. He thumped de Gier on the arm. "Murder! I had almost forgotten. We've got a murder, sergeant. Hey ho!"

"For five years," Ketchup said, "Obrian fucked us over. Made idiots out of us, had us by the neck, played with us like rag dolls. And now he's off forever." He shook his head. "Hard to believe."

Karate was shaking his head too. "Can't believe it either, liberated illegally, we can't even thank the killer."

The two constables ran up the stairs of the station together.

"Stupid little buggers," Grijpstra said.

"You think so?" Jurriaans asked.

Grijpstra prodded the sergeant's stomach with his stubby finger. "Yes. They were right here, fifty paces away from the killing, and they didn't even bother to come out to see why someone might be firing a machine gun. Bubbles in pipes! Faulty exhaust!"

"I was in there too," Jurriaans said. "It must have been a very short rattle. Machine pistols fire at a rate of five to six hundred rounds per minute, but they don't carry more than thirty or so. Six hundred rounds a minute, that's ten per second. Six rounds take about half a second. Bang." He flicked his fingers. "That was all."

"*Turrám*, you said just now. Not bang."

"Adjutant," Jurriaans said pleasantly, "I often hear bangs. But they aren't shots. This is a bad district but it isn't a battlefield. There's bad sex here, and bad dope, and theft and blackmail and mugging. All bad. But hardly ever bad bullets."

De Gier stepped up. "Coffee?"

"Cake?" Grijpstra asked.

"Be my guests."

Jurriaans led the way. Grijpstra followed. Cardozo was still in the street, watching a lithe black cat, high on its legs, with a dainty small head.

"Coming?" de Gier asked.

"Yes."

"What's with the cat?"

Cardozo stroked the cat's back. "I saw her before, hanging around the corpse. Chased her away, as I thought she might lick the blood, but she came back and just sat there staring."

"So?"

"Bad luck."

"Really," de Gier said. "Cats are never bad luck. Get into the station." He grabbed Cardozo by the arm and pushed him up the steps. A loud squeak made him look up. On a TV antenna poking out of the burned-out corner house's sagging roof sat a vulture. The bird wasn't particularly large but at least twice the size of a big crow. Its yellow claws were wrapped around the antenna's top bar and a sharply curved beak stuck out of its hairless gray head.

Cardozo had gone. "I've lost my mind," the sergeant whispered. He waved at the bird. It rose slowly, flapping awkwardly. Gaining height, it flew easily, gliding low over the tiles, changing direction by effortlessly bending thin fingerlike feathers at the extreme ends of its wings.

2

"NO," SAID THE COMMISSARIS' WIFE.

The commissaris, holding his knife loosely and eyeing his boiled egg, looked up to smile. "The money, dear? You mean we lose the deposit at the travel agency? It isn't that much, and Austria will wait, its healing mud bubbling forever. I do think I will have another chance to soak my bones."

"A waste."

"You know," the commissaris said, "I don't really mind losing a bit of money now and then. Remember those mutual funds your brother talked us into? They've been going down ever since I bought them." He decapitated the egg fiercely and stabbed the contents with his spoon. "But what is money anyway? Paper printed with funny faces. One needs it, of course, for food and so on, but after a certain point one is done with it. Fortunately you never wanted fur coats or jewels, and the children are doing well. No, money . . ."

She got up and pushed the garden doors open. She turned. "Yes, money . . . It isn't that. I care about your health. Those baths have cured a lot of patients. If only you would take a rest and leave some work to others. The papers say that there are over three thousand policemen in the city. You're not really that important, are you, now?"

"The chief inspector has a migraine."

She arranged lettuce leaves on a dish. "Turtle?" The weeds below the steps moved and the small reptile showed its face. "Here, breakfast." She put the dish down and watched Turtle grab and chomp. "The chief inspector? I think he's faking again. And the inspector?"

"He's learning Turkish. Now that we've caught all the unwanted Chinese and flown them back to Singapore and Hong Kong, we have Turks. Their heroin is even better, it seems. The inspector is doing good work."

"And Grijpstra? I'm sure Grijpstra can deal with a pimp."

He pushed his chair away from the table. "That was an excellent egg." He drained his cup. "And splendid tea." He stroked her back. "I'll have to go now, I think. Will you help me find suitable clothes?"

She pushed silver hairs back into her bun. "No. You're trying to be smooth again. I know what you're up to. It's madness. I won't have any part of it." A tear dribbled down her cheek and she wiped at it impatiently. "You're old now, Jan, you've got to rest, the doctor keeps saying that. Do you really expect me to accept your getting into that filth? By yourself? How often have I sat up nights worrying about you, but then I knew that Grijpstra was with you, or de Gier, although he's crazy too. Where will you be? Floating around that lawless district? In a canal maybe?"

He put his arm around her narrow shoulders and pushed his nose into her neck. "I'll phone you. This is Amsterdam, dear,

I'll be nearby. I won't be in Beirut. I'll just walk about a bit, to see what's going on, and if anything goes wrong, I'll call a constable. There are hundreds of them in the district."

"And if the pain bothers you? What if you fall, won't you be mugged?"

"I won't be mugged, and I can call a cab."

She took his hand in hers and followed a blue vein with a gentle finger. "You like going there, don't you? Those women? Some of them are beautiful."

"Really, dear, at my age."

"You haven't changed, Jan. On the outside, perhaps, a little. But not really."

"I have been faithful."

"Since when?"

"Since a long time."

Her hand slid up his sleeve and patted his shoulder. "Yes, because of lack of choice."

"Because of much love. Will you help me now?"

"No," she said in the bedroom. "That jacket is worn through the elbows. I don't even like to see you wear it in the garden. Can't you take the gray suit? That is worn too, but at least it hasn't got holes."

"And this hat?"

She had to laugh. "That used to belong to my father."

"It fits." The commissaris looked at the mirror. "And it has a good wide brim, to hide my face. Do you know what happened to those round glasses I used to have?"

"The spectacles for the retarded?"

He found them in a drawer. "You do exaggerate. Not the retarded, the *tough*. I bought them when I was learning unarmed combat. I always got beaten up, but the spectacles didn't break."

"Take this." She offered him his pistol, carefully, on the palm of her hand.

"Too big," the commissaris said. "Why we had to change over to that monstrosity is still beyond me. The Walther P5, worth its weight in gold, bought in bulk without a discount, hits anything at two hundred meters, doesn't rust because most of it is plastic, is quite impossible to hide." He opened his jacket and held the gun under his armpit. "Even a long-gone junkie can see it from the other side of the street."

She crossed her arms. "I won't let you go unarmed."

The commissaris waved his cane. "But I *am* armed, dear. The handle is weighted with lead. The sergeant of the arms room has been teaching me. Watch this."

He turned the cane around and swished it a few times. "See that ashtray?"

"Don't, Jan."

The cane struck. The ashtray exploded. The glass plate under the ashtray cracked. "Ha," the commissaris said. He looked at his wife. "I'm sorry, dear. More deadly than I thought."

His wife left the room and came back with a dustpan and a brush. He helped her, by indicating shards with his cane. She got up, pressing the small of her back. He caressed her arm. "I beg forgiveness, dear. I know you shouldn't bend down, but my leg is so stiff."

"And you shouldn't be fighting muggers with that silly stick. You really think they'll allow you to hit them? They'll throw a knife at you."

The commissaris narrowed his eyes. "I'll catch it between my teeth. Now all I need is that bag. The bag I took fishing once and dropped into the lake. Grijpstra retrieved it hours later. Thank you, dear. It looks suitably disreputable."

She helped him into a coat. "That was my father's too. It's too large for you, but it'll keep you warm."

"But it's summer, dear."

"The nights are chilly. Where do you think you'll sleep?"

He examined himself in the corridor's mirror, bag in hand, leaning on his stick. "In a nice room. I'll find a hotel. I'll let you know where."

"Can I come and see you?"

"If you must." He peered at her from under the hat's turned-down brim. "But I'd rather you didn't. Grijpstra and de Gier will be about, they might see you. Cardozo too."

"They won't recognize *you*?"

The commissaris shuffled through the corridor, bent, prodding the rug with his cane. "Like this? They're not looking for me, they're looking for a despicable character who can mow down a brother in crime with automatic fire. Why should they look for me? I'm in Austria, with my bum in a bath."

"Oh!" She stamped her foot.

He pushed up his hat with his cane. "You said 'oh'?"

"Oh, Jan. Why can't you behave like a normal police chief? Sit nicely behind your desk? Why sneak about?"

He straightened up and presented his cane. "Because this is a sneaky case. It has too many sides."

"You look ridiculous."

He nodded. "Yes, a ridiculous case, too."

She embraced him, cane and all. "Don't grin at me. Will you behave? You're a father figure now and young women will find you doubly attractive. They'll try to hold on to you, maybe they'll pull you over."

"They will?" the commissaris asked.

"You're giggling," she said.

He liberated himself gently from her arms. "No, I was squeaking. I smoke too much, makes me wheezy at times."

About an hour later, a small poorly dressed old man dragged himself through one of the side alleys of the Seadike. A worn and discolored leather bag dangled from his narrow dry hand.

Round minute glasses glistened under the wide rim of his old-fashioned felt hat, protecting colorless eyes that studied an indifferent locality in a curious but somewhat sheepish manner. His cane tapped on the cobblestones energetically until he noticed the cheerful ticking and slowed down, dragging the stick.

3

"THIS STATION," SERGEANT JURRIAANS SAID, "HAS BEEN recently restored and we have everything here, including a conference room for those with stars on their shoulders, who never arrive before eleven A.M., or later, because they are busy. Please come in."

The room was vast, had a high ceiling and narrow old-fashioned windows. An antique table was surrounded by straight, leather-upholstered chairs. "You can sit at the head," Jurriaans said to Grijpstra, "seeing you're in charge."

"I'm a guest," the adjutant said, and frowned at Karate and Ketchup, who were sitting down noisily. "Is this our work group?"

A good-looking female constable brought coffee. De Gier studied her and smiled. "A woman," de Gier said, "and this is the whore's quarter. Shouldn't our group have a woman too?"

The constable eyed him coldly. De Gier got up and bowed from the waist. His smile widened. The constable frowned.

Jurriaans coughed. "Allow me to introduce these colleagues to you." He mentioned names. "And this lady is Constable Anne, but she hasn't been fully trained yet. Our regulations say that one-stripe constables may not be led into dangerous situations."

"But to serve you with coffee is okay," the constable said, left the room, and closed the door behind her with too much force.

"A woman," Grijpstra said. "Yes."

Jurriaans pulled a telephone toward him. He leafed through his notebook and dialed a number. "Hello, adjutant. I know you were still asleep, but there has been a murder and we have initiated an investigation. Do you think you might assist?"

He replaced the hook. "She'll be here, Adjutant Adèle, in fifteen minutes I would guess, since she lives around the corner. Do you know the adjutant?"

"I have admired her looks," de Gier said.

"I have been impressed by her brain," Grijpstra said, "the first female to rise from constable to adjutant, with straight A's and music on the lawn."

"I have met her on the shooting range," Cardozo said. "She sort of passed, but I was excellent that day."

"We know her very well," Karate and Ketchup said. "A splendid addition to our team," Karate added. "I often dream of her," Ketchup said.

"Shall we begin or wait?" Jurriaans asked.

"To wait shows better manners," Grijpstra said.

The adjutant arrived, a stately woman with the face of a Madonna as painted by masters of the primitive school, but softened by freckles, subtly placed, to make her human. She shook hands and was given a chair. The constable brought more coffee, and cake, at Grijpstra's request and de Gier's expense.

"What do we have here?" Jurriaans asked. "A dead pimp.

Who? Luku Obrian, black, born in Paramaribo, Surinam, formerly Dutch Guiana on the South American east coast, thirty-eight years ago. Who his father was is unknown, but we may assume that his grandfather, in any case his great-grandfather, was a slave, originating in Africa. Our contemporary corpse arrived five years ago at Amsterdam airport, before independence, but not out of fear for the potentially shaky future of his country or because of small-minded greed, knowing that he could apply for social security and never work again, but because of spite. He wished to avenge the fate of his forefathers. He told me so the night of his arrival, when he was dragged into this station, accused of unruly behavior. Drunks do not always speak the truth, but Obrian wasn't lying when he predicted that he would *disconcert* us. The expression is his, for he spoke perfect Dutch, better than we do, and phrased his thoughts accurately, using excellent grammar. He *did* disconcert us, during five long and terrible years, us and the civilians, and last night he was finally taken away from our midst by means of six nine-millimeter bullets fired from an automatic weapon." Jurriaans looked at Adjutant Adèle. "Corner of Olofs-alley and Seadike. Did you hear anything?"

"I was asleep," Adjutant Adèle said.

Jurriaans telephoned. He thanked the other party and replaced the receiver. "That was headquarters. The sergeant of the arms room said that the weapon must have been a Schmeisser."

Cardozo crooked a questioning finger. "I'm not familiar with the term."

Jurriaans held his hands apart at a distance of sixty-five centimeters. "That long." He diminished the distance to twenty-five centimeters. "This is the size of the clip, perpendicularly inserted into the chamber. The clip holds thirty-two cartridges. An antique machine pistol, Second World War vintage, used by SS and Gestapo, well-known from concentration camps and street raids, reputed to work well and shoot accurately. When the German Army surrendered, its weapons were supposedly handed over, but we didn't get them all, every now and then another one pops up, and is used improperly, like last week when the Turks held up a bank."

Adjutant Adèle got up. "The weapon is still in this station. I'll get it so that you can see what we are looking for."

De Gier watched Adjutant Adèle leave the room. She wears the uniform well, the sergeant thought, which is surprising, since they usually look a trifle homely, our policewomen. I wonder why that would be? Because she has such long and slender legs? And wriggles a little in the hips when she moves? Does that make her so watchable?

Cardozo was thinking too. He thought that he would like to put his hands on the adjutant's calves and move them up slowly to the point where stockings end and pink flesh starts. The pensive desire startled him. He looked at his watch. It was far too early for carnal lust. But it's her fault, Cardozo thought. She may be my superior and well respected, but she is also tall and lusciously shaped. Just the sort of woman to trip up and jump upon. Why do I think that? I'm not that way at all. I'm polite and thoughtful in female company. Why is she provoking me? Why isn't she dumpy and silly like other policewomen? What's getting into me anyway?

Adjutant Adèle returned and placed a machine pistol on the table. She spoke softly but clearly. "This is a Japanese imitation of the German original. It doesn't fire and is meant as a model, for collectors. Sold to a Turkish migrant worker who bought the instrument in London. He smuggled it in because our law says that models like these look too real and can be misused. Said Turk misused it—he pointed it at a bank teller. The Turk is no longer with us. He was shot twice in the belly by a colleague who was in a hurry." She looked at Karate.

"Yes," Karate said. He picked the model up and put it down. "Looks real enough, doesn't it?"

"Our own weapon," the adjutant said, looking at the tabletop that hid Karate's pistol, "is meant as an instrument of prevention, not as a means of immediate destruction. A suspect, even a Turk who handles a toy, could possibly be warned first so that he has an opportunity to surrender and maybe answer some questions."

"Luku Obrian," Jurriaans said, "was black and moved in black circles, hard to get into for us, but I do not think he was killed by a representative of his own race. Obrian was an example of a man who knows how to organize his resources, a rich and successful entrepreneur, owner of an expensive car and a luxurious apartment on the Emperor's Canal, of at least two local bars, of—"

"Wait," Grijpstra said. "If you knew all that, you could have alerted the detectives of the Internal Revenue. Pimps are known not to declare their income. If a pimp is the owner of expensive property—such as a Porsche convertible and an apartment in the best area of the city—that fact is taken as proof of tax fraud. He could have been arrested and his property confiscated."

"Besides, it's a good way to get suspects into debt," de Gier said.

"Because," Cardozo said, "the fine is more than what their property will be worth."

Grijpstra picked up his saucer, tipped it, watched the cake crumbs slide into his cupped hand, and poured the contents of his hand into his mouth. He chewed and swallowed. "Well?"

"How easy," Jurriaans said. "What a pity Obrian wasn't an easy man. The Porsche has a foreign registration and we can't trace its rightful owner. Officially, Obrian rented his apartment, but he didn't pay rent. The bars he owns are operated in the name of his employees, who gave him eighty percent of the profits in cash. Obrian declared what he couldn't hide, which was something, sufficient to pacify the tax hounds."

Grijpstra produced a cigar from his waistcoat. "May I?"

"Rather not," Adjutant Adèle said.

"May I say something?" Ketchup asked.

"Could I perhaps smoke a cigarette?" Grijpstra asked.

The adjutant ducked a strand of hair back behind an ear. "If you blow the smoke the other way."

"Listen," Ketchup said. "You know what Obrian did? There was a whore here by the name of Madeleine, a most extraordinarily beautiful woman who acted like a lady and worked for her own account, from the best-placed display window of the entire quarter. She could unlock her door electrically and would only push the button if the client looked well-heeled enough, and she earned a daily fortune."

"With exaggerated but still aristocratic boobs," Karate said, "and legs like you see in private movies made for oil dealers."

"Yes," Ketchup said, "and she kept all the dough she earned, right? No pimps dragging it from her, man, and the gents were bringing it in, a wheelbarrow a day. Cold frog, like the best of them, but with soft mysterious eyes and a smile that just begs a little, a comedian with character in her soul."

Karate's small fists banged on the table. "And Obrian couldn't touch her, that's what we all thought."

Ketchup's fists banged the table too. "Even if he had every hooker in the quarter, even if they all slaved for him and got the tremors when he happened to pass their windows, our Madeleine was made of steel, he would never get our Madeleine."

"Never would get near her with his sooty grabbers." Ketchup was standing up.

Karate was also on his feet. "You know how he got Madeleine?"

"By glancing at her," Ketchup shouted, "sideways, when he passed her window."

"And you know what he made her do?" yelled Karate, "on a

beautiful Sunday morning, with the weather as bright and fresh as today? On a lovely summer day, when we were all out in the street, to keep a quiet eye out and make sure everything went the way we wanted it to go?"

"He made her come to the small green bridge," whispered Ketchup, "the cast-iron bridge on the Oldside Canal, pedestrians only, with lions' heads on the railing, many centuries old, a cherished antiquity the tourists gape at."

"They were gaping too," Karate whispered, "and so were we, and everybody else as well. Obrian looked too, but he was quiet, like a cucumber."

"He wasn't doing anything in particular, Obrian wasn't."

"Just standing there, high on the bridge."

"In his linen tailor-made suit, worth a thousand or so, and under his panama hat, and with a Cuban cigar between his gold-rimmed teeth."

"And with his silk handkerchief hanging from his pocket."

"And unarmed, clean as a whistle."

"Unseizable; a civilian is allowed to stand on whatever bridge he likes."

"And there Luku Obrian stood, and there she came, our Madeleine, in her new lovely dress, with the skirt not too short and the cleavage not too visible. Our *lady*."

"And she knelt for him."

"And she opened his fly."

"I don't want to hear it," Grijpstra said.

"And then?" Cardozo asked.

"Now, what do you think?" Karate asked. "Eh? At her leisure, softly and firmly, as if there was nothing she'd rather do. As if she were grateful for the favor he bestowed."

It was quiet around the table. Adjutant Adèle looked at her nails, transparently lacquered, perfectly filed. Grijpstra killed his cigarette in the ashtray, slowly, ferociously. Karate and Ketchup sagged back into their chairs and sighed. Jurriaans drew a circle with a sharp pencil on a fresh page of his notebook. De Gier waited for his blush to fade away.

"And Madeleine?" de Gier asked.

"She continued to work," Jurriaans said, "but not for long, because Obrian soaked all her money out of her and the heroin he supplied her with was never enough. She hung herself from the lamp in her room. I still have her file, complete with photographs. I'll show it to you whenever you have a spare minute."

Grijpstra felt in his pocket, produced the cigar he had put away, made it crackle near his ear, smelled it, and put it on the table. He watched the cigar. He mumbled.

De Gier mumbled too.

"You two sound surprised," Adjutant Adèle said.

"I'm always surprised," de Gier said, "if I don't pay attention. That's because I believe in certain limits, which I must have made myself, since reality makes fun of limits. Take this morning, for instance—three roller-skating gentlemen carrying new briefcases, and it wasn't four o'clock yet and now this Obrian again, on a cast-iron bridge, sucking his Communist straw while the lady whore sucks him, in full view of everybody."

"Never mind," Grijpstra said. He took a deep breath. He scraped his throat. "Look here. The number of whores is not unlimited. If Obrian got more, others got less. It is a human habit to become angry when something is taken away. I have heard names; Gustav and Lennie. How angry did those pimps get, and what would they be likely to do once something made them angry?"

Jurriaans smiled. "That's the way to go, adjutant. A cause deducted from its effect, via the relentless logic with which every policeman has been suitably equipped. I am glad you're with us." He drew two circles. "Who are our suspects? All criminal types out in these streets. How many remain once we have applied discernment to our thoughtful structure? Two."

He pricked centers into his circles. "Who are our suspects now? Gustav and Lennie. The cheerful satisfaction of Obrian was the biting pain of his rivals. Do we acknowledge the right motivation in our suspects Gustav and Lennie? We do. Did they have the opportunity? They did. Do we grab them?" His pencil stabbed the circles. "We certainly do."

Jurriaans bent over to Grijpstra. "This, adjutant, is our opportunity. We will clean out the quarter so thoroughly that our streets will be clean forever. We have the blessing of your commissaris, the chief of detectives who—could it be better?—has left on sick leave at once. In his name we will slash away in, under, and above. Thank you, Karate."

He took the handkerchief that Karate was offering and dabbed at the spittle that was bubbling in the corners of his mouth. He leaned forward again and extended his hands. His index fingers became pistol barrels. Soundless bullets streaked past Grijpstra's ears. "Do you realize the power we have been given? Our power added to yours? Our station joined by the Murder Brigade? Without any restrictions from above?"

"Attaboy," said Adjutant Adèle.

"We will bust them all and kick them down the stairs," shouted Karate.

"We'll pound them into the floor of our worst cell," shouted Ketchup, "and never feed their remains."

"That's about how I would like to see it," said Jurriaans, wiping the sweat off his forehead. "With due regard for proportions and decency. We must try to remember that we have no skulls and bones on our caps and that even Gustav and Lennie belong to the shadow created by our own light. They have to be cut to slivers, of course, by the sword of justice, but with just a wee touch of love and kindness, as is our wont."

De Gier got up. "I'm going home, my cat has to be fed. I'll be back."

"In uniform," Grijpstra said, "and wait for me. I have to go home too."

"Please, adjutant."

"You object to my company?"

"If you insist on my uniform."

"I don't insist on anything," Grijpstra said, pushing himself out of his chair. "The commissaris insisted. Uniform, he said; uniform, it will be."

"Take your time," Jurriaans said. "This is a reasonable station and it doesn't only accept the needs of its staff, it understands them too. Feed your cat, put on your uniform, and come back at once. There is work to do."

"Got to pack a bag," Grijpstra said. "We are expected to work from the quarter itself. We even have to live here."

"One apartment," said Jurriaans, "for our appreciated colleagues."

Adjutant Adèle had left the table but turned. "It's available. A suspect, now in one of our cells, a burglar by the name of Kavel, resides on the Seadike but he won't be able to go home for a while. The owner of the property has asked if we'll keep an eye on the apartment because even burglars' homes are burglarized these days. I'll fetch the keys."

"Ha," Cardozo said. "The three of us together, that'll be nice."

"That'll be terrible," de Gier said, forcing the Volkswagen through thick traffic. "That'll be sickening. Why do we allow ourselves to be part of idiotic situations?"

"Why shouldn't it be nice?" Grijpstra asked. "We'll do the best we can and keep at it until it's behind us so that we can get into the next situation, which'll undoubtedly be better."

De Gier drummed impatiently n the steering wheel. "And you won't even be allowed to smoke cigars during meetings."

"Adjutant Adèle," Grijpstra murmured. "A handsome woman. I like working with handsome women."

"And the number of suspects has been reduced to two. We can't even reason for ourselves."

"We'll catch the two first and the others later."

De Gier stamped on the gas pedal. "That Obrian must have been a most exceptional specimen. Imagine that prostitute on the bridge. I wouldn't have minded seeing that, although it's despicable. Revolting." He braked and swerved around a bus. "Amazing."

"Whoa," Grijpstra said. "Park over there and let me go. I'll go home from here, and you don't have to fetch me either. I'll walk back to the station, once I have my bag."

"But do you understand what happened there?"

"I understand it in detail," Grijpstra said, "but I have learned to live with evil, which doesn't mean that I'm without a taste for battle. Now, will you park or won't you?"

De Gier chopped liver for his cat and dissolved plant food for his geraniums. "Tabriz," the sergeant said, "Grijpstra doesn't realize the misery we got ourselves into. The quarter provides nothing but smut. Slimy muck up to our ears. We have been misplaced."

Tabriz studied the contents of her dish and swept the floor with her short striped tail. She folded her chubby front legs and grunted while she ate.

"Remember your manners."

Tabriz looked up. "Maybe you're somewhat fat and ugly," the sergeant said, "but that's no reason to behave like a piglet."

Tabriz slobbered on. The sergeant waited until the cat was done, picked her up, and carried her to his balcony. He sat down on a wicker chair and put his feet on the railing. The cat burped on his lap. De Gier opened his eyes. "Burp the other way."

The cat purred and put a paw on each side of his neck. De Gier slept and dreamed that nothing mattered while he engaged himself in racing a Mercedes sports car through empty Amsterdam alleys, caressed Adjutant Adèle's milk-white limbs, and turned into a condor, flying above the English Channel. He woke up because Tabriz hooked a claw into his lower lip.

"Easy, now." He pushed the claw out of his mouth. Tabriz jumped off his lap and began to butt her dish.

De Gier got into his uniform and stood at attention in front of the mirror. Tabriz left her dish and stood next to him.

"What's on display here," de Gier said, "is a madman, in the queen's coat, about to be released to wreak havoc amongst the perverted." He tightened his belt and rested his hand on the butt of his pistol. "A lunatic, armed to the teeth, who will slay the insane." He put on his cap and saluted. "A nut who sees roller-skating gentlemen in the small hours of the night, and a vulture on a TV antenna."

Tabriz pushed herself against his leg. "Keep your multicolored hairs to yourself," de Gier said. "Sit on the balcony and catch insects until I come back." He pushed the cat with a polished boot. "To report on how I worsened a situation that was already hopeless to begin with."

4

GRIJPSTRA SAT DOWN SUSPICIOUSLY ON A COUCH UPHOLSTERED in red vinyl and tried to rest his eyes on fading wallpaper printed with a design of dead flowers. Cardozo ran into the small room holding an imitation bamboo tray on which two chipped mugs wobbled. "Tea, adjutant. Do you think we're about ready now, or do you want to clean out the loft too?"

"As ready as we'll ever be," Grijpstra said, "thank you." He stirred the pale fluid. "Is that real milk?"

"Powder, adjutant. Just as good. Tastes the same."

"Plastic milk," Grijpstra said. "Why do I bother walking around in a real body? Can't I have one molded, and swallow a tape recorder?"

Cardozo sat on the windowsill next to a bowl filled with paper flowers. Grijpstra pointed. "Throw those out."

"But I dusted them."

"Away with the rags."

Cardozo carried the torn bouquet out and came back with a sponge. He knelt and wiped tea drops off the cracked linoleum floor. "Please, adjutant. It took us eight hours to get this place clean."

Grijpstra nodded. "Criminals are dirty buggers. We've got six bags of debris in the corridor; if that chap ever gets back here, he won't recognize his hole. What was it again that we have him for?"

Cardozo arranged a set of polystyrene elephants on a shelf, ranging from the size of a large rabbit to the measurements of a small mouse. "Burglary."

"Simple or complicated?"

"Complicated. He crapped on the carpet too. Same suburb where de Gier lives. Hardly a professional, this Kavel. They've got new cars out there and he arrived in a junker. But he had telephoned first, to make sure that his mark wasn't home. Lugged all his tools into the elevator and was seen by a neighbor who was good enough to phone us. Kavel forced the door, filled his bag with plated silverware and the owner's worthless collection of Nigerian stamps and didn't forget the child's piggy bank. A curtain moved in the draft, and he took fright and crapped on the rug, just as the cops came in. A habitual offender, he'll get a few years this time."

"Crapped, eh?"

"That's what they do, adjutant. Part of the pattern. Always in the best room and always on the Persian rug."

"Disgusting." Grijpstra bit into his cigar and spat. Cardozo glared. The adjutant groaned, bent down, and picked up the shreds of tobacco. "Now what?"

Cardozo held out a paper. "Put it here, adjutant. Don't do it again." The bell rang and Cardozo pulled a rope. He greeted de Gier, who ran up the stairs.

"In time for tea but much too late to help out," Grijpstra said. "Why aren't you in uniform?"

Cardozo stood in the open door. "Sugar, sergeant? Milk, sergeant?"

"Please," de Gier said. "I'm not in uniform because I left it in Adjutant Adèle's cupboard. A uniform draws unwanted attention. You can't even cross the street against the light without being admonished."

"By the authorities?"

"By a black toddler." The sergeant looked about. "Was the previous occupant convicted on a charge of bad taste?"

Grijpstra spilled more tea. Cardozo set to work again. Grijpstra pushed the sponge away. "You're staining my trousers. The sergeant has been goofing off while we worked, and now the sergeant is tired. Why don't you take the sergeant to his nice clean room?"

De Gier joined Grijpstra on the creaking couch. "The sergeant was doing his job. He now knows something."

"Share it," Grijpstra said. "I will draw the correct conclusion and go out to make a proper arrest, so that we can get out of here. I have a pleasant place of my own now and want to make a painting, of an exotic bird. What does the sergeant know?"

"That the killer was wearing size thirteen shoes."

"No," Grijpstra said. "I don't want to fight giants."

"Rubber soles?" Cardozo asked.

"New?" Grijpstra asked.

De Gier nodded.

"Galoshes," Cardozo said. "Now in one of the city's garbage boats, under ten tons of goopy glop."

"What else does the sergeant know?" Grijpstra asked.

De Gier looked at his watch. "That lunch time has come and gone. Are we eating?"

"We'll go to a Chinese."

"Lennie," de Gier said, "one of the two other superpimps, has had a trying time since Obrian got busy here. I have admired

Lennie's photograph and read his file. He's an ordinary-looking man, which probably helped him toward his success. Forty-three years old and a native of the city, like his father, and his father was no good either. Another pimp, making out on a few whores placed here and there. The father had little brains but he sent his son to school and Lennie was studying mathematics when his father was arrested on a charge of buying stolen property and had a heart attack in jail."

"Mathematics? University? And he still became a pimp?"

"Why not, Cardozo? Numbers go both ways. Some numbers are lucky. Lennie inherited seven whores. He relocated them to the most popular alley and extended his operation from there, moving his headquarters to a floating brothel for the select on the Catburgh Canal."

"Outside the quarter," Cardozo said. "A quiet area."

"The select don't want to be seen, but they know the way."

"Dope?" Grijpstra asked.

"A lot of dope, more and more, especially since Obrian pushed him out of the alleys."

"And where was Lennie supposed to be last night?"

"On his boat. The bouncer, the ladies in residence, and the barman will confirm his alibi. This morning, at twenty past three, when machine-gun fire hit Obrian in the Olofs-alley, Lennie had just stepped into bed. His Mazda sports car was on the quay—this much is true, because a local cop saw the car there at the fatal time. But Lennie could have used another car, or walked. Catburgh Canal is close by."

"And was he pleased that Obrian is now under refrigeration?"

"Delighted," said De Gier.

"Did he say so? Not to you, I hope."

"He told one of the detectives of the station."

De Gier placed his mug on the floor. Drops of tea danced across its edge. Cardozo jumped up.

"Stay here," Grijpstra said. "You worked from this station

for years, as a uniformed constable. How can it be that a floating brothel is tolerated outside the quarter?"

"Just a minute, adjutant. I take pride in my work." Cardozo brought the sponge and rubbed the floor clean. "How can it be? Indolence, adjutant."

"No more than that?"

"Well," Cardozo said, "Lennie wholesales heroin. Heroin is costly material. It comes in small parcels. Money comes in small parcels too. The parcels are easily opened and the top bills may float away." He checked the floor, holding his sponge ready. "Or so I have been told."

"And Jurriaans?"

"An incorruptible official." Cardozo looked into Grijpstra's eyes. "King of the quarter. Jurriaans has long arms but I don't know whether they reach as far as Catburgh."

"The local station employs a few hundred able men," de Gier said. "How about a little raid across the border once in a while?"

"Yes."

"So?"

"When they get to the boat, the lights are out and there's nobody home. The station here has a large number of telephones. I imagine most of the colleagues know Lennie's unlisted number."

"That was Lennie," Grijpstra said. "What about Gustav?"

"Lunch first," said de Gier.

"You can't eat here, adjutant," Cardozo said, and pulled Grijpstra's sleeve.

Grijpstra pointed with his other arm. "Is that sign in Chinese or isn't it?"

"That's a gambling joint, adjutant. The characters are different. We can eat across the street. See?"

Grijpstra turned his hand. "Same scribbles."

"No, adjutant. See the ones on the sign across the street? Meaning 'Eating House'?"

"Scribbles."

"Look at the scribble at the left. See the little running legs sticking out of it? It means 'eat.' And the one on this side, see, with the uncombed beard hanging underneath, says 'gamble.' "

Grijpstra narrowed his eyes. His hand weighed heavily on Cardozo's shoulder. "Since when can you read Chinese?"

"I worked here, adjutant. I had to learn what is what. I got to know the signs to know what goes on inside."

"The boy is intelligent," de Gier said. "He can't help it. Can we go to the eating house now, or do you prefer to play Mah-Jongg?"

Grijpstra crossed the street. He still held on to Cardozo. "Constable first-class?"

Cardozo's chin rested on Grijpstra's hand. "Yes?"

"If gambling is illegal, how come the slit-eyes have the sign on their door?"

Cardozo squeaked. "But this is the *quarter*. Anything goes here."

"Too far," Grijpstra growled. "You too."

A middle-aged black man squatted on the sidewalk, leaning against the restaurant's gable. He wore a heavy sweater in spite of the heat and was rolling up his tattered sleeve. The man wasn't interested in the portly gentleman in the pinstriped suit who was observing him. He was intent on the point of his hollow needle, sucking milky fluid out of a bent teaspoon. When the needle was full it emptied itself again, into the man's arm, after having found a spot of skin between running sores. The needle yanked free and the man looked up, grinning inanely, then sighed and closed his eyes. Grijpstra closed his eyes too. De Gier pushed the adjutant's shoulder. "Come eat. Mandarin cooking. Very special."

Grijpstra studied the gleaming dark red naked carcasses dangling from a sagging string behind the restaurant's dirty window.

"Birds," Cardozo said. "Exotic birds."

"Yecch."

"Duck is good," de Gier said. "Ugly duck is good too. Come along, dear."

The waiter brought the menu.

"Don't take forever," de Gier said. "I'm hungry."

Grijpstra was still staring through his half-glasses. "I wanted fried rice, with a fried egg on top, can't find it on the list."

"You can eat that everywhere."

"So I can eat it here too."

The waiter covered the table with dishes. They weren't Grijpstra's. Grijpstra got a small bowl heaped with dark brown rice topped with a fried egg the size of an overcoat button.

"Small egg," the adjutant said.

"Duck's egg," said the waiter.

"Bald duckling's egg," said Cardozo. "Will you tell us about Gustav, sergeant? Is he still driving a Corvette? He did in my days, always the latest model."

Grijpstra jabbed at the egg with a chopstick.

"Hold them like these, adjutant," Cardozo said. "One fixed and the other like a pencil. Like this. You can do it."

Grijpstra pressed the bowl against his mouth and inhaled the egg. "What's a Corvette?"

"American," de Gier explained. "Flat. Like an iron without the handle, hollow inside. Goes fast, costs money."

"How much?"

"What you and I make a year."

"But he has other cars too," Cardozo said. "Gustav likes cars. He likes women too, he's got lots of them, in my time anyway. Look, adjutant, it's really quite easy. Hold your chopsticks like this and you can pick up anything. See that bit of meat next to de Gier's bowl? I'll pick it up."

Cardozo inserted the meat between his teeth and chewed.

"There's a bone in it," de Gier said. "I've been chewing it for a while too. Okay, Gustav. Still drives a Corvette. No alibi for last night. He doesn't like women, he only likes the money they give him. He sleeps alone, in his seventeenth-century city-funded restored gable house on the Old Mint Canal."

"Bust him," Cardozo said with his mouth full of noodles.

"Beg pardon?" Grijpstra asked.

Cardozo swallowed. "Handcuffs. Drag him to the station. He's got the motivation and the opportunity, so we've got serious suspicions. I say Gustav is our man. He likes to hunt big game, in Africa with a cannon, so why shouldn't he hunt competitors here with a machine pistol? Sergeant Jurriaans is right, we're the Murder Brigade and this is the quarter. Anything goes. The local cops scare easy, but we're from outside. Bust him, I say, and—"

"Right," de Gier whispered fiercely. "Disengage the buzzer in his cell. Nail a board over the window in his door. Forget to feed him. Fill his jug with sea water. Beat the bastard."

"No, no," Grijpstra said.

Cardozo stopped slurping his stew. "Why not, adjutant?"

"Because that isn't the way."

"And what if we do it a little bit?"

"I've got to sleep at night."

"Heaven is waiting for us," de Gier said. "Gustav and Lennie. How many enemies did Obrian have? Just those two? What about the prostitute on the cast-iron bridge with the lions' heads? She may have a friend, a relative, a son even. Revenge, you know. All we think of is greed and jealously. A black soul brother Obrian had kicked into the gutter? Some heroin merchant who Obrian never paid? Or plain indignation? Some good guy fired the gun?"

Grijpstra paused in his effort to shovel the rice with the fat ends of his chopsticks. "We haven't even begun to think. We don't know the corpse either. He had a house. The house will still have his smell. I want to go and sniff. Now, maybe? After Cardozo has paid the bill?"

"Later," de Gier said. "I went to bed late and got up early. A nap."

Cardozo paid. "We have to go to Hotel Hadde too, tonight maybe. It's open all night and the bar is a hangout for pimps. Maybe we'll hear something."

"A nap."

"And the morgue," Grijpstra said. "They'll have looked into Obrian's pockets by now. Thank you, Cardozo. I didn't like the food. And because you took me here, you can spend a few hours on your own now. Look around. Do more than we can expect of you."

"And you?"

"I will go for a walk," Grijpstra said. "I tried earlier on but I felt disturbed then. I feel better now. When I come back, I'll wake up the sergeant."

"That way we all do something," de Gier said.

De Gier got through the door first, tripping over the threshold. He bumped into a little old man who shuffled along on the narrow sidewalk, leaning on his cane. The old man managed to stay on his feet.

De Gier apologized.

The little old man, his small head tucked away under the wide brim of his felt hat, walked on slowly. Grijpstra stood next to de Gier. "Can't he get a better coat? Social security is getting fatter every year. I thought moldy rags were out by now."

"Old drunk," de Gier said.

"An alien," Cardozo said. "They get no welfare. Maybe I should go after him and take him to the Salvation Army. Sir?"

The old man had reached a mud puddle and slithered on, jabbing his stick ferociously into the tiles of the sidewalk.

"Leave him alone," Grijpstra said. "It's not your job to save old bums."

5

THE COMMISSARIS TURNED A CORNER AND SLOWED DOWN again. The good weather hardly improved the quarter's mental climate; the alley he found himself in was gray and smelly, a sewer, the commissaris thought, through which the lower lusts slide along by night and dribble by day.

Older women pushed wet rags along grimy windows, the squealing of dirt against dirt matched the shrill voices that argued or complained. Hung-over clients left dingy one-night hotels, staring from red-rimmed eyes at the lack of possibilities that another day would offer. A hawker pushed a cart, yelling hoarsely out of a toothless mouth between sunken stubbly cheeks: "Radishes and smoked eel."

A cat on high legs rubbed itself against the commissaris' cane and looked up, squinting from bright yellow eyes. The commissaris scratched the animal's gleaming fur. "Haven't we met?"

The cat howled softly.

"Yes. In the Olofs-alley this morning." The commissaris shivered violently, reacting to a stab of pain that had burned up his thigh and found the bone in his hip. He concentrated on the cat, stroking its neck, feeling its soft body vibrate under his hand.

"Not enough love?"

The cat slid away and ran ahead, stopped and looked back before it turned the next corner.

"Love may be hard to find around here," the commissaris mumbled, following the cat.

"Hi, Gramps," a female voice said. The commissaris looked up. A young woman, a girl perhaps, leaned out of a window on the second floor. He saw her breasts bounce. "He's got me from the rear," the girl said, "and I've got to wait till he's done. Want to talk to me meanwhile?"

The commissaris couldn't see the man but he could hear him groan. He walked on, his cane tip scratching on the alley's cobblestones. The girl called after him, "Come back later, Gramps, I'm cheap today."

"Radish and smoked eel."

A bit to eat, the commissaris thought, and then an hour's worth of quiet contemplation in a clean room. He turned the corner the cat had taken before. The cat was waiting, sitting on the edge of the sidewalk, licking a paw. She jumped up when she saw him and ran on.

A guide, the commissaris thought. The alley ended at the wide Eastern Canal. He followed the waterside, walking under huge elms and their proud load of small newly green leaves. An old woman, wrapped in plaid, crumbled bread for noisy ducks, who splashed each other to reach their free lunch. The commissaris watched. Two small boys, one white with long blond hair and one black, bright-eyed under a frizzy crest, paddled a plastic bathtub. The cat stood next to him, stiff forelegs pressed on stacked bricks, chattering at the quacking ducks. "Not quite your size," the commissaris said. "Try a sparrow." There were sparrows about too, hopping at crumbs.

I really need lunch, the commissaris thought. His original plan—to be a tramp in the Salvation Army dormitory and listen to the gossip—faded out. He saw a stone jug with a silver spout, tinkling coolly while cold *genever*, the juniper flavored gin the Dutch favor so much, filled a long-stemmed tulip-shaped glass. He also saw hot toast, thickly buttered, spread with slices of white and pink eel, circled with cut radishes and artfully placed gherkins. He glanced about, searching for the sign of a suitable establishment, but saw only freshly painted windows of tall gable houses, leaning against each other in age-old confidence. He lifted his hat and addressed the old woman. "A small hotel? Where the food is good?"

The woman looked doubtfully at the leather bag, cracked at the seams, dangling from his gesturing hand. "Can it cost a few pennies?"

"Oh, yes."

She pointed. "The Straight-Tree Ditch. Ask for Nellie. Third house on the right."

"Much obliged."

"Rooms," the sign said in four languages. The sign was elegantly lettered and hung from a freshly painted heavy rod, ending in a copper ball. The commissaris admired the narrow house, five stories high, with wooden planters holding pink geraniums attached to each window. The dark brown bricks shone and the white trim of sills and posts set off the pink of curtains. A rather fleshy pink, the commissaris thought, but what's wrong with flesh? The cat had lost interest and danced away, tail up, legs straight.

The commissaris leaned on his cane and tried to remember why the house was familiar. Had he been here before? There had been a murder in the street, some years back, but on the other side, he thought, across the water and farther along. Pink? What had been pink in that case, properly solved and conveniently forgotten. He tried to activate his slow brain and worried about cells lost through age and never replaced.

Eel on toast.

I don't want to think of food now, the commissaris thought. But why shouldn't he? The pinkness of whatever it was would come to him later. He rang the bell. The door clicked open.

"Come in," the mature voice of a woman called out. "I'm in my office, on the left, come in."

The commissaris dragged himself along, tired of the long walk and the increasing weight of his bag. The point of his shoe hit the threshold of the room and he had to force himself to lift his foot. He took off his hat. "I'm looking for a room for a few nights."

She didn't answer at once, and he looked at her quietly, hat in hand, the other clawed around the handle of the bag. The woman's breasts, caught tightly in a pink jersey, seemed abnormally full; he felt as if the massive mounds pointed at him, with their aggressive nipples, surging through the thin material. She smiled and he saw the whiteness of her strong teeth, growing firmly out of healthy gums. "This isn't a cheap place, Gramps."

"I don't mind."

"Are you sure? Are you in town to visit relatives? There are more reasonable rooms available, not far from here." Her hand touched the telephone. "Shall I try to get you one?"

"I've got cash." The commissaris put down his bag and took out his wallet.

She pointed at a chair. He shook his head. "Can I see the room? I would like to lie down for a minute and then eat something perhaps." He stepped forward, put the wallet on her desk, and brought out his tin of cigars. "Do you mind if I smoke?"

She struck a match. "You can do what you like, as long as

you pay in advance." Her breasts were close and he had trouble looking into her eyes. He knew who she was now and wondered if he'd remind her. She had been trustworthy then, so why be squeamish now?

"Nellie?"

She smiled. "Did someone tell you my name?"

The commissaris sat down. "Try to think back. Five, no, it must be six years ago. A street hawker on the other side, living with his sister, killed by a lead ball at the end of a fishing rod. There was trouble in the streets then and the police fought the rioters, so my adjutant brought me here, but you didn't have a hotel, the place was a kind of bar."

She clapped a hand over her mouth.

"You made coffee for us. Adjutant Grijpstra had a bad cough and you made him drink syrup."

She got up and walked around the desk. "And I just let you stand here, and called you Gramps!"

"Well." He touched his shabby coat. "I look a bit strange maybe. Can I stay here? If I do, you can't tell anyone who I am. There's been another murder, in the Olofs-alley, and I'm working on my own for a while."

She dropped her voice. "I know. Luku Obrian was shot. Nobody knows you're here?"

"I'm supposed to be on holiday." He missed the ashtray. "I'm sorry. Only my wife knows I'm not. I'd better phone her."

"Henk doesn't know either?"

"Henk?"

"Your adjutant. Henk Grijpstra. Surely you've told him."

Right, the commissaris thought. I thought so at the time. Henk and Nellie, a romance. And Nellie was a prostitute then, entertaining clients in a cozy bar without a license. Not quite the thing to do, but even an adjutant has a private life.

"No, Grijpstra doesn't know."

"You don't trust him?"

He nodded. "Yes, of course I do, but it isn't a simple case and I prefer us looking at it from different sides. We'll meet later, when suspicions firm up a little. I need a few days, longer maybe."

"I never!" Nellie said. "And me worrying whether you could pay."

He smiled. "So you should. This hotel is far too good for bums, but I'll try to keep out of the way."

She hid her nose and mouth under her hand. Her eyes twinkled.

"Yes?"

"Some bum." She laughed outright. "A top official earning a yearly fortune. You're quite an honor to have around, sir."

He laughed too. "I'm glad you got rid of your bar. How do you like running all this?" He gestured about him. "Such a pleasant-looking place."

She pushed out her lower lip. "I was making out but it got harder every night. Bah." She shook her head. "I was taking ten baths a day in the end and throwing up too. All those hands, all over me." She patted her hips. "I was losing weight too, made me look better but I was crazy inside. Had to give it up. The money went into the hotel but it's coming back again and most of the customers pay cash so it doesn't show on my forms. Henk feels good about it too. Not that he was complaining, but a woman who makes a business of it isn't quite what a big shot like Henk should take out, or, well . . ." She rubbed her cheek. "I'm his girlfriend, you know."

"I know."

"Commissaris?"

"I think you shouldn't call me that now."

"No, because you're working, right? Gramps?"

He put up his hand. "I'm not that old."

"Dad? But we look so different."

"Jan," the commissaris said. "That's my name, but only my wife calls me that. Uncle Jan? From Utrecht? Visiting his niece? How would that do?"

"Good," Nellie said. "Uncle Jan, and about the money, I would rather that you didn't pay me. Henk wouldn't like that, I'm sure."

"No." The commissaris opened his wallet. "I have to pay. What do you charge per day?"

She mentioned the price. "But you can give me half."

"No." He counted the bills. "Here you are, three days in advance."

The room was on the second floor, spotlessly clean and with a large comfortable bed covered by a pink crocheted spread and a pink rose in a slender vase on the night table.

"You prefer that color, don't you?"

"The color of what I used to do, so that I won't forget." She squeezed his arm. "Retired whores get uppity, you know. Henk doesn't like that. He wants me to be quiet, so that I can listen to him. There's a bathroom next door. Henk put in the tiles and we painted it together and it has its own tank. You can have as many baths as you like, the hot water is included."

"Beautiful," the commissaris said. "I had no idea Grijpstra was a handyman. Can I see the rest of the house too? You wouldn't have a rear door, would you? So that I can get in and out without anybody seeing me?"

Nellie held on to his arm, and the commissaris had himself guided down the stairs, through the kitchen, and into the small rear garden. "Is that the door?"

"No, it leads to the garden of my neighbor." She giggled. "Another uncle. He calls himself Wisi. He's black, but we're good friends and I'm sure he will let you use his exit."

The commissaris admired lettuce plants and tomatoes growing against the wall. "My wife should see this. We never have much luck with ours. A black man, you said? From the west, you mean?"

She picked a small tomato, washed it under the tap, and gave it to him. "Yes, but he didn't come with the others. He's been here a very long time, he came before I was born. He is old, he says he doesn't know how old. You may know him, he used to sell herbs in the street market."

The commissaris felt the earth with his cane. "Let me see. White hair? Wears a robe and a little skullcap made out of beads?"

"That's him." She laughed. "You do know everybody, don't you, Uncle Jan?"

"Fortunately," the commissaris said, "you exaggerate. I have seen the man, however. Didn't he have a houseboat before, on the Prince's Canal? And keep animals? I think I recall seeing a donkey, and a fox or a wolf, and birds. I distinctly remember birds."

"Yes, but that must have been a while back. And he still keeps animals, but not too many now."

The commissaris glanced at his silver pocket watch. "A little lunch, I think. Would there be a restaurant you can recommend?"

"Yes. Right here." Nellie swept an arm in the direction of her kitchen. "I'll make lunch and you can sit here in the garden if you like and enjoy the sun." She brought him a chair and got a small table from the house. "Henk likes to eat outside too. What would you like? I don't have too much choice today. Fried eggs maybe? On toast with some roast beef? Or smoked eel? With a salad, yes?"

"Yes." The commissaris rubbed his hands while she laid the table. "Radishes—would you have those too? And some cold genever, to encourage the digestion?"

Why do people complain so much? the commissaris thought

as he ate. Life isn't all that bad really, and with a bit of patience you get just about anything you can wish for. I thought that I would have to hang round the streets and be thoroughly uncomfortable, and look what fate has pushed my way. But one has to be able to frame the exact desire, like smoked eel on toast, so that fate knows what to give.

"You seem happy," Nellie said.

The commissaris raised his glass. "I am. Your very good health."

"Henk likes to eat too," Nellie said, "and he loves the garden. I'm fond of men who know how to enjoy themselves. But he doesn't come too often. How is his wife doing?"

The commissaris pointed at his mouth that he had just filled with lettuce leaves. He chewed diligently.

"Do you know his wife?"

"From a distance."

Nellie became interested in the hem of her little apron. "Isn't she rather fat?"

The commissaris stuffed his mouth again.

Nellie's fingers plucked away at the hem. She looked down. "I have that problem too, but Henk doesn't like too much of me, so I'm careful." She made gymnastic movements. "Every morning, with the radio, there's a lady who says what to do, and music. I get all twisted up sometimes. Pity in a way, I like pie, with cream on top." She patted her hips. "But the cream makes me puffy. But why bother, eh? He doesn't come too often anyway."

"His sense of duty," the commissaris said. "The children, they need a father around the house."

"But aren't they growing up now?" Nellie fetched a chair from under the kitchen stairs and unfolded it energetically. She sat down at the other side of the table. "I don't want him to come and live with me, although that would be a good idea too. He wouldn't even have to work anymore, he could ask for early retirement. He always says he wants to paint but that his house is so full that he hasn't got the space. He could have my basement, or sit outside if the weather is like it is now."

The commissaris lit a cigar. "A most excellent meal, Nellie, I do thank you."

"Another drink?"

"No, thanks."

"Coffee? It should be done perking by now."

The commissaris looked at her slender well-cared-for-hands playing with each other on the tablecloth. "I'm working, Nellie, although you wouldn't think so. About Obrian, now, the man who was shot early this morning. Did you know him at all?"

"I'm glad," Nellie said, "I'll never have to know him again. It's a sin, of course, but if I think it, I may as well say it. I hope Luku Obrian goes to hell. He was worse than the worst types one sees around here. If that bastard looked at a woman with those large moist eyes he had, then she could forget her future, and everything else as well. All *he* wanted to do was have your guts and then throw away the skin."

"A pimp, wasn't he?"

Nellie's fingers cracked as she contorted them. "Right. I know all about pimps, had one myself when I started out. He talked nicely enough, but he was just like the others, after the money to spend it on others. Once you get into their hands, you'll never get out again, and when mine caught a knife in his lovely flat belly, I swore I would never have another one."

"Obrian was after you too?"

She looked up. "Whatever makes you think that?"

The commissaris crumpled his paper napkin. "Well, he was a pimp, wasn't he, and he knew you, and you're a very attractive woman. I'm just asking. Policemen ask. I didn't want to offend you."

Nellie laughed. "You're a cop, aren't you? Who would ever think so?" Her hand slid across the table and touched his.

The commissaris smiled. "Grijpstra is a cop too."

"Yes, I'll never believe it. Such a sweet man. The ideal father, and you would be the right grandfather."

"Now now."

"Only when you dress up funny. Old clothes make you look old, but without the coat you look much younger already."

The commissaris waited.

"And you're right," Nellie said. "Obrian was after me."

"Could you resist?"

"I had Henk."

"Of course," the commissaris said softly. "I hadn't thought of that."

"And Sergeant Jurriaans," Nellie said. "He's a very strong man and he sometimes drops in for coffee here, always in uniform."

She was holding his hand. The commissaris pulled it back and stretched. "So quiet here, and yet we're in the midst of the city."

"Shouldn't you take a nap now? Henk always rests after a meal."

"No," the commissaris said, "but you know what I would like to do? Have a hot bath. I'm somewhat rheumatic and hot water soaks the pain away."

"Go right ahead." Nellie began to clear the table.

"Yes?" the commissaris asked from the tub.

Nellie's hand appeared, holding a silver tray."I thought you wouldn't mind another cup of coffee."

"Please."

"Do you mind if I come in a moment? I won't look."

She sat on a stool next to the tub, and the commissaris pushed himself up carefully, concerned about keeping his cigar dry.

"I'm lonely sometimes," Nellie said. "It's nice to know

there's someone in the house. The guests don't count and there aren't any right now anyway. Is the water hot enough?"

"Cooling. Would you mind turning the faucet?"

Nellie reached to the tub's other end. "The tank is enormous, you can have baths all day."

"Good to know," the commissaris said. "Hot water is about the only thing the pain reacts to. I say, Nellie, I was thinking about Obrian again. He was shot with a machine pistol. Would you have any idea who might have used such an unusual weapon?"

Nellie rested her chin on her hand. "Another pimp, who else? Luku was taking it all, the others couldn't accept his grabbiness. To live and let live—Luku never heard about that idea."

"With a machine pistol," the commissaris said. "Strange, eh? Who would have a gun like that?"

"Hard to handle. They jump in your hands."

"You know about shooting?"

"Yes," Nellie said. "I'm a farmer's daughter. My brother and I had to shoot crows, to save Dad's chicks. And I have used a machine pistol too. We had German soldiers on the farm during the war. We were only little kids then, and I hardly remember the soldiers, but my brother found their gear, years and years later, where my father had hidden it. Rifles, hand grenades, ammo. The grenades were fun, we used them for fishing. You just throw them in and there's a fountain, that high"—she pointed at the ceiling—"and then the dead fish float. We used a machine pistol on a crow. There was nothing left of him afterward but broken feathers."

"My, you were a dangerous girl. How old were you then?"

"Fourteen, I think. My father was all upset and the local cop came and took the guns. My father would have been fined, but he called the cop himself, so it was all right."

"Shouldn't have guns about."

Nellie smiled. "No? With all the mugging going on? In this neighborhood?"

"You have a gun?"

She handed him a towel. "Shouldn't you get out? If you stay in too long you get all wrinkled. Look at your fingers now."

"Yes," the commissaris said. He raised himself with difficulty and wrapped himself in the towel. Nellie looked away. "I'm all covered now," the commissaris said. "Tell me, do you have anyone in particular in mind?"

"Who could have shot Obrian? Lennie, I would think, or Gustav. They hated him most. Here, let me dry your back."

"No," the commissaris said, turning away. "What if Henk were to suddenly come in and see us like this?"

She grinned sadly. "I wish he would. It's his own fault. Staying away doesn't do much for our relationship." She followed him to his room and folded the sheets open. "Nap time, Uncle Jan."

"No. I'll lie down and think."

She walked to the door. "That's what Henk says he does too, and then he snores for hours."

"Not me," the commissaris said to himself. "It's a matter of self-discipline. Keep sleep back by force of will and enter the in-between dreamscape where all facts connect." He sighed, closed his eyes, and fell asleep.

6

DE GIER SLEPT ON THE RED PLASTIC COUCH IN THE burglar's apartment. He had closed the curtains before lying down. Dripping spittle was cooling his mustache and he was turning on his side when he heard the door squeak. He was still too far gone to wake up completely, or perhaps fear crippled him; that possibility occurred to him later, although he never bothered to confirm it.

Whether he was dreaming was to remain unclear too. He saw a black shape that he interpreted as a bird, a vulture. The vulture did not walk, but hopped. Each hop brought the bird closer to the couch. The vulture looked like the bird that he saw in the early morning, on the antenna in the Olofs-alley, but this vulture was considerably bigger, bigger also than the birds of prey in the zoo, hunched-up sad feathery bodies staring morosely at a hostile world.

The vulture wasn't in a hurry. The sergeant heard its claws scratch on the floor's linoleum. He saw its wings, flapping clumsily. He also noticed the sinister hooked beak and the evil eyes, surrounded by dry folds of skin.

The dream's backdrop changed. The sergeant was lying in a white-yellowish desert, under a scorching sun, and the vulture fluttered closer, bent over his prostrate body, and stared down curiously. Vultures don't wait until you're dead, the sergeant thought, they get right into you, chisel into your skull, tear out brains, hack away.

He was also thinking that the bird was an aspect of himself, representing his own evil, the solid poison that had accumulated because of wrong living and that now was strong enough to split away and take its own form.

That he was frightened was certain. The impulses emitted by his brain did not connect. Paralyzed by dread, he tried to concentrate on the wet sensation in the lower extremity of his mustache, the only part of his body he was still aware of. His fear was somewhat comical. It was funny that he could do nothing to protect himself. Here I am, the sergeant thought, judo champion of the Amsterdam Municipal Police, with the world's most deadly pistol tucked into my armpit, and I'm ready to be torn into slivers.

The dreadful bird stood next to him, stretched out, its head bent back in order to be able to strike down more forcefully. The sergeant wanted to scream but couldn't produce more than the weakest squeak, drowned immediately in the vulture's awful screech. The biting impact numbed his head. The furious bird shuffled away; the door banged closed.

The painful and, in spite of its lengthy introduction, still rather sudden attack broke his sleep-induced overall paralysis and the sergeant groaned, sat up, and even managed to force himself to his feet and stagger over to the windows to open the curtains. He saw that the couch was covered with soppy white worms, which were also stuck to his shoulders and slithered down his jacket. The worms burned his hands and he yelled as he tried to flip them away. The couch looked too disgusting and he staggered to a chair. He heard the door open again and tried to get up, to defend himself against the returning bird.

"What's all this?" Grijpstra asked.

"Adjutant," babbled de Gier. "Adjutant. To arms!"

"What on earth for?" Grijpstra was about to sit down on the couch.

"No!"

Grijpstra studied the white worms on the red vinyl. "What's the mess?"

"My brains."

"Looks more like spaghetti."

"Look, my blood too."

"Spaghetti with tomato sauce?" Grijpstra smeared a finger with the warm fluid. "Still hot. Tastes okay. Why did you throw it out?"

"Attacked. By a vulture. While I slept."

"You got sick," Grijpstra said. "Unwell. Puked, I imagine."

"No no no." De Gier grabbed his head. "I was hit. *Beaked.* By a bird." He knelt in front of the adjutant. "Feel my head."

"Never," said Grijpstra, in the bathroom watching de Gier shower, trying to follow the sergeant's stuttered explanations. "All that happened is that someone knocked you on the noggin with a pot." He made a fist. "Clear case of assault. Shall I contact the station? We need a fingerprint man."

"No."

"And how is your head now? Want me to take you to a hospital?"

De Gier dived into a clean shirt. "No." He followed the adjutant into the living room.

"Let me clean up at least, before Cardozo comes back, or we'll have that again. Get a bucket with hot water and I'll handle the rag."

Grijpstra mopped. De Gier sat at the table and tried to roll a cigarette. His hands trembled. "I must have been dreaming."

"Yes, but the actual violence was no dream or you wouldn't have a lump on top of your head. Where did you get the vulture idea?"

"It was a vulture."

Grijpstra carried the bucket out and came back. He sat down next to the sergeant, placed his notebook on his knee, and drew a bird.

"That's him," de Gier said. "How did you know?"

"Because I saw a bird like this, in the Olofs-alley, just after the drunken seamen lost the war. I looked up and saw a vulture fly above the rooftops. But as there are no vultures in this country, and never have been any, I assumed I was mistaken. A falcon maybe—there are falcons in the city, hunting pigeons."

"A vulture, with yellow legs and a yellow beak."

"Quite. But vultures have never been seen here."

"This one was seen," de Gier said. "Very much so, and he came after me too, and waited on the roof until I was asleep, and sneaked in and beaked into my head with his infested mouthpiece."

"Why not?" Grijpstra said. "After all, anything is possible. I've seen camels in town too, advertising trips to North Africa, and elephants trumpeting about a circus. But why would the vulture be carrying a pot of spaghetti?"

De Gier tried to roll another cigarette. Grijpstra took the paper and tobacco out of his hands. "Let me do it for you." He inserted the cigarette between de Gier's lips and flicked his lighter. "Here you are." De Gier inhaled and coughed. Grijpstra patted his back. "You're still not all there. Poor Rinus. Quietly asleep, minding your own business, and look what happens. How about a nice cup of nice coffee?"

Grijpstra brought the mug. "Here, half a spoon of sugar,

seven drops of milk, just as sir likes it. Stirred lightly from the wrist."

De Gier stared at the coffee.

"But you have to drink it yourself. Shall I steady your hand?"

Cardozo came in. "Is the sergeant being fed?"

"I always say hello when I enter a room," Grijpstra said.

"Hello," Cardozo said. "I have news. I found Crazy Chris, pushing a cart filled with eels and radishes. Crazy Chris did see the suspect, but his memory is a bit faulty, due to intake of alcohol, which, as we know, does not stimulate the intelligence. I shook him a bit and he managed to remember."

"What did he remember?"

"That the suspect was large, black, shapeless, and creepy. He wore a black cape and a floppy hat. He walked west, following the Seadike, away from the station. Gait somewhat jumpy, and he almost stepped out of his shoes."

De Gier lowered his mug.

"You're spilling," Cardozo said. "Please. We try to keep it clean here."

"Did the suspect resemble a bird?" de Gier asked.

Cardozo looked at Grijpstra. "He must have carried the Schmeisser under his cape, and he certainly looked odd. I do think we should try to catch him. A mad murderer, in the possession of an automatic weapon." He nodded at de Gier. "What *is* the matter with the sergeant?"

"The sergeant dreamed that he was attacked by a large bird, right here in the room, while he was napping on the couch."

"Are you sure he didn't happen to be awake?" Cardozo asked. "Earlier on he saw three roller-skating gentlemen. I'm sure the psychiatrist can recommend suitable therapy."

"Come here," de Gier said. "Feel my head."

Cardozo felt. "A lump." He felt again. "Biggish."

"Hit on the head," Grijpstra said, "with a potful of spaghetti and tomato sauce. Someone's hot dinner. I cleaned up the mess and *you* will find out who harassed the sergeant."

Cardozo sat on the couch, elbows on knees, chin on hands. His head nodded violently. Grijpstra looked at Cardozo's bobbing curls. "What are you doing?"

"I'm concentrating, adjutant. If the spaghetti was still warm, the perpetrator of the crime came from close by. He also had a key."

"Very likely true."

"Neighbor?"

"Possible," Grijpstra said. "The previous occupant lived by himself. He could have given the neighbor a duplicate key."

Cardozo pointed at the floor. "There are only neighbors downstairs. The house has cafés on each side, nobody lives above the cafés."

"Think more."

"Shall I visit the neighbor?"

Grijpstra smiled encouragingly.

Cardozo jumped off the couch.

7

"AHA," GRIJPSTRA SAID. HE STOOD ON A LARGE MOROCCAN rug, cream-colored between patterns of stylized flowers. The carpet covered a small part of a gleaming parquet floor. The room was furnished with a large leather couch and matching easy chairs and a low table with a top of brick-colored tiles. A slender alabaster vase filled with fresh lilacs stood on a table. An antique cylinder desk had been placed against a white plastered wall. The room occupied the entire second floor of a patrician house in the fashionable bend of the Emperor's Canal. Century-old elms could be seem through high curved windows of lightly stained glass in front and a well-kept garden through a glazed veranda in the rear. The porch contained man-high exotic potted plants growing from earthenware pots. A grand rosewood piano mirrored a bamboo bush in its raised lid.

"Would simple good taste, refined by grandeur, make Obrian smart?" de Gier asked.

Grijpstra strolled about, his hands on his back, his half-glasses on the tip of his nose. He interrupted his walk to look at a painting. The narrow silver frame held a dancing black couple; the man with his arms raised, jiggling his tight waist, the delicate woman tripping around her imposing lover. The figures weren't ornate and consisted merely of colored segments—bright red, tropical blue, white, and dark brown. The dance moved about the yard of a quickly sketched house, shadowed by trees with slightly bent trunks and joyfully waving leaves. "Good," Grijpstra said. "I always add too many details, but this fellow has learned how to avoid the spurious. To catch the essence only, not so easy."

"How long did Obrian," De Gier asked, "owner of this extraordinary but tastefully arranged environment, live in our country?"

"Five years."

"And how much is the house and contents worth? Now add the Porsche, with all the options. A great wealth, don't you agree?"

"I do, and collected without labor."

"The labor of weak women," de Gier said. "If intelligence is the ability to react to ever-changing circumstances in such a way that the manipulator obtains optimal profit, I would say that Luku Obrian was a very clever fellow."

Grijpstra had found the couch and rested both his head and his feet. "But he was shot and killed, which was kind of stupid."

"A moment of unawareness?"

"An unlucky moment," Grijpstra said. "Moments like that occur from time to time. Let's see. A criminal crosses our border five years ago, without a cent to his name. But he knows the language and has friends. The friends take him to a bar, the company becomes drunk and is disorderly in public. Patrolling cops arrest the merrymakers, and Obrian meets with his opposite, our Sergeant Jurriaans. Jurriaans represents the law and order of the fatherland, Obrian the rebellious chaos of the colony. We're on Jurriaans' side. What does Luku tell us? That he is about to *disconcert* us. He does, too. How?"

De Gier's long arms swung, indicating all parts of the spacious room. "Theft," the sergeant said. "Everything here is stolen. We are disconcerted, because we have been robbed. He even took our women, enslaved the poor creatures we cherish."

Grijpstra swung himself off the couch and faced the sergeant solidly, immovable on his heavy shoes sunk in the carpet. "I do not believe that colonials are stupid, but I do think that Obrian was lucky. And as luck has to originate somewhere, I would like to know where it came from. What else can we study in this house?"

"Here," de Gier said, and opened an upstairs door. "What do we have here?"

Together the detectives, hands in pockets, observed odd objects displayed on a trestle table of rough-sawn boards.

"Rats' skulls," Grijpstra said. He counted. "Thirteen of them, in a half-circle of seven and a concentric half-circle of six. Both numbers and the way they are arranged should have meaning. And those are colored rags, also placed for a purpose. I mean, he wasn't showing samples of textiles, was he, now?"

"And that little statue represents J. Christ," de Gier said. "Couldn't be anybody else, even if he is dressed in a skirt and his face painted pink."

"A drum," Grijpstra said. The drum had been made out of flattened cans, tightly covered with skin. The adjutant hit it with his knuckles. "Don't," de Gier said. "Please."

"Penetrating sound," the adjutant said, replacing the drum gingerly. "Bit high." He waved a finger to the right side of the table. "How would you describe that conglomeration?"

De Gier stepped back. "Picture of a naked woman, obtaining

sensuous pleasure by embracing a large bottle of tomato ketchup. Glued to a bit of driftwood found in a canal and framed with shells stuck into the edge. An altar, it seems to me, because what it all sits on is a slab of marble that looks like rubble taken out of a wrecked church. That penis and balls is a root, grown accidentally and now pointed at the performing woman. The bones came off a bird and form a complete skeleton, once holding up a vulture of the species known to us by now. That copper bowl filled with sand is an incense burner."

"Religious?"

"Sure," de Gier said. "Spiritual symbols, combined in a meaningful way, also tastefully arranged; the entire table would be a prime exhibit in a museum of modern art."

Grijpstra picked the drum up again. "Don't," de Gier said. "I don't like the vibrations, they pierce my lump."

"I won't hit it hard." Grijpstra scratched the skin. "Can you imagine how this room worked? Obrian, in ritual dress, at daybreak or sundown, or maybe at midnight with candles burning? His body swaying, enveloped in incense clouds? Evoking . . ."

"Luck?" de Gier asked.

"Exactly. He manufactured his luck himself. A strong variety, but not quite bulletproof." Grijpstra put the drum down again. "And now I want to see his corpse."

"I saw it already. In the alley."

"There was too much going on then. Quiet-like, I mean, but you don't have to come along."

The car got itself stuck behind a furniture van being unloaded. A new Mercedes was stuck too, between the truck and the detectives' Volkswagen. De Gier pulled the microphone from under the dashboard. "Headquarters? Car three-fourteen."

"I'm listening, three-fourteen," a female voice said.

"Could you find me the highest available member of the Drug Squad, please?"

"I'll do my best. Is that you, Rinus?"

"It is. I'm waiting."

"Car three-fourteen? Ober here."

"Mr. Ober," de Gier said. "A dark blue automatic fuel-injected Mercedes, I'll give you the registration number."

"Got it."

"A black man at the wheel, in his forties, wide-shouldered, Afro hair, gold earring on the left, accompanied by a young blonde woman, dyed hair, fur coat, jaguar."

"I got that too."

"Do we know them?"

"Just a moment."

"We'll be here awhile," Grijpstra said. "They've only just started. I would say there are just under ten thousand objects in that van, and they'll all have to be carried up several sets of stairs."

"We don't know them," the radio said. "Do you want to arrest them?"

"I'd rather not, sir. We're on a job."

"I'll send out a car."

"Emperor's Canal, sir, corner Bearstreet. The suspicious car is caught between us and a van."

"Understood."

The driver of the Mercedes got out and walked toward the Volkswagen. De Gier wound down his window and smiled. "Could you reverse, please?" the man asked. "Then you can get away too. If we wait here, it'll be forever."

"No."

The man raised his eyebrows. "Why not?"

"I'm not good at reversing."

"You want a fight?" the man asked.

De Gier closed his window. The man knocked against the glass. De Gier stared straight ahead. The man tried to turn the Volkswagen's door handle. The door was locked. The man walked to the waterside, looked about, and picked up a brick. He showed de Gier the brick. De Gier got out.

"Either you reverse," the man said, "or I wreck your car."

Two young men dressed in faded jeans and leather jackets walked toward the man. "What's going on here?"

"This gentleman," de Gier said, "is threatening me with this brick. He wants me to reverse, but I'd rather wait here."

"You mind your own business," the man said.

The young men showed their police cards.

"So?" the man asked.

"You're under arrest."

"Watch it," de Gier said. "Sir is rather short tempered."

The young men stared at the man until he dropped his brick. They grabbed his arms, turned him around, and handcuffed his wrists.

"Watch it," de Gier said. "The lady is leaving us."

One of the policemen ran after the woman and brought her back.

"She dropped something," De Gier said. "I'll get it for you." He returned with a plastic envelope filled with white powder. The policeman weighed it on his hand. "Ten grams." He addressed the black man. "You're arrested because I suspect you of harassment of a civilian and trafficking in drugs." He looked at the woman. "You're also under arrest."

The other policeman frisked the man. He showed his colleague a stiletto. "One more charge. We can confiscate his car."

"Your car is confiscated. I'll drive it to headquarters. The key is in the ignition?"

The man didn't answer.

"All set?" de Gier asked.

"Yes, sir. Thank you for your cooperation."

De Gier reversed. "Do you know," Grijpstra asked, "that what you just did is discrimination? Since when do we suspect a black man, unknown to us, and driving a new Mercedes?"

"I was jealous," de Gier said. "You see, that bum got here a few years ago, without a penny to his name, flown out of his hellhole in a government plane financed with my tax money, and look at him now, driving a brand new supercar and with a bit of juicy flesh leaning against his pock-marked skin. I mean, isn't it *terrible*?"

"Exactly," Grijpstra said. "A textbook example of low-class discrimination. If the suspect had been white, he would still be free."

"But he's no good, adjutant."

"No, no, you can't reason that way."

"No?" de Gier asked.

"No."

"And if I tell you that what I just said consisted of platitudes specially formulated to see if you'd go for it and that I saw that same suspect leave a house in the Fishhead-alley two days ago and that that house is known as a meeting place for junkies? And if I tell you too that the same suspect was dressed poorly at the time and riding a rusty bicycle?"

De Gier parked. Grijpstra rang the bell.

"Nobody home," de Gier said.

The adjutant rang again. "They are home, but the trouble is they're dead." He looked about him. "That such a dainty-looking place, surrounded by blossoming bushes in which songbirds chant, can be a morgue is hard to believe."

The door opened. "Hello, Jacobs," de Gier said.

The old man pushed his skullcap to the back of his head and peered over his steamed-up glasses. "Ah, sergeant. Welcome. Hello, adjutant."

Jacobs shuffled ahead. He looked over his shoulder. You'd be after Obrian, I imagine."

"We are," Grijpstra said.

Jacobs pushed against a metal door. "Not a good corpse. Go ahead. Number eleven." The detectives shivered. "I know,"

Jacobs said. "Rather chilly in here, but with this heat they tend to smell and the cold slows their spooking."

De Gier yanked a drawer. "Sticks a bit," Jacobs said. "Here, I'll give you a hand. One, two . . . Hop." The tin box slipped free and Obrian moved about within it, head nodding, arms flapping. De Gier looked away. Grijpstra bowed down to the grinning head. He frowned. "Nothing to laugh about, friend."

De Gier touched Jacobs' arm. "Can I see what they took from his pockets?"

Jacobs brought a bright-yellow plastic tray. Under his gray linen coat his folded trouser legs were visible, tucked into his socks and fastened with nickel-plated clasps. One sock was brown, the other blotched red. "Cigarettes," de Gier said. "Gold lighter, clean handkerchief, wallet." He looked at Jacobs. "The money went to headquarters, I suppose. How much was it?"

"A lot. Big notes."

"So no robbery," de Gier said. "Why not? Corpses are always robbed, even by well-meaning murderers. No time, maybe."

Grijpstra pushed the drawer back into the wall. He felt his chin while he studied the tray. "Big notes? Still there? Curious."

"Big holes in the chest," Jacobs said. "Must have been big bullets. What was it? An army revolver?"

"A machine pistol. A Schmeisser. You know what that is?"

"Wouldn't I know what a Schmeisser is?" Jacobs asked. "Didn't the gentlemen of the SS have Schmeissers strapped around their chests? Didn't I see them a hundred times a day in Dachau? Liquidation tools. Specially designed to do away with the lower type of humanity."

Grijpstra shook his heavy head. "Can't say I approve of the term."

"Aren't Negroes part of the lower humanity too? Or used to be?"

"I wouldn't say that," de Gier said.

"I can say it," Jacobs said, "because I belong to a minority myself. Didn't you guys use to catch them in the jungle? And didn't you use to chain them to each other, in the smelly holds of slave ships?" He nodded. "You certainly did, and six out of ten croaked on the way, but what did that matter? The loss was calculated in the price. Am I right?"

"I think I'll be on my way," Grijpstra said. "You are thanked, Jacobs. Coming, sergeant?"

De Gier felt in his pocket and gave Grijpstra the car keys. "I'll be back shortly, adjutant. There's something I want to ask Mr. Jacobs."

The front door closed behind Grijpstra. De Gier smiled at Jacobs. "Don't look so worried, I just want to talk with you a little. We haven't seen each other in a while."

Jacobs smiled hesitantly. "Friendship?"

De Gier put an arm around Jacobs' shoulders. "Friendship it is."

\\\\ 8 ////

CARDOZO FACED THE SEADIKE'S DREARY AGGRESSION, YAWNing at small bars, peep shows, and fast-food holes-in-the wall.

"Hashish?" a young man whose festering ears were covered with cola-bottle tops asked.

"Be my duck?" asked a small fat woman, balancing painfully on worn needle heels, pulling up her skirt in passing so that sickly white flesh was on view, restrained somewhat by fishnet underwear.

"Ramón?" asked a man who stopped and sought Cardozo's gaze mournfully. The man was brown-skinned, his long hair had matted, and his drooping mustache hardly hid his missing teeth. He wore no shoes. "Are you Ramón?"

"Not today," Cardozo said. The man pulled a rusty knife. "You pay the money?" Cardozo scratched his stomach. His gun-belt showed. The man walked on, hoisting his worn pants, belted with fraying rope. A loose-jointed black woman appeared, carrying a shopping bag. "I do believe I live over there," the woman said, and stepped off the sidewalk.

Cardozo ran after her. A moped sped between him and the woman. "Careful, now," Cardozo shouted, taking her arm.

The woman scowled. "Get away."

He bent down and talked into her ear. "It's dangerous here." He smiled helpfully. "Let me guide you, ma'am."

"Morons," the woman said solemnly. "All of them. Crash right into you and think nothing of it. They've hit me before, and my daughter too." She fumbled in her coat.

"Shall I hold the bag, ma'am?"

She showed her teeth and wrinkled her nose. "Keep your dirty hands to yourself. Grab my stuff and make a run for it, hey? Filch my expensive genever?" She shook the bag. Bottles clanged.

"But, ma'am, I'm your new neighbor. Neighbors never steal from each other, do they now?"

She put the bag down. "And a liar too. You think I don't know my own neighbor? That's Kavel, and Kavel is in jail."

"So now *I'm* your neighbor, and I saw you come from your house a while back and now you're back again." Cardozo patted the woman's thin arm. "Me and my mates took over Kavel's apartment."

"Show me."

"What do you want to see?"

She pointed. "That's your door. Let's see your key."

Cardozo produced the key, opened the door, and closed it again.

"I never," the woman said softly. "And I didn't believe you. That's not nice, is it, now? Care to have a drink with me, neighbor?"

"Right," Cardozo said.

He waited patiently until she had dislodged her own key from a pocket stuffed with her change purse and a crumpled scarf and followed her into a narrow corridor. The living room was small and stuffy. "We'll need glasses," the woman said. Cardozo walked with her into the tiny kitchen and saw a row of pots hung above the sink. The pots were all yellow and one hook had been left open. The missing pot sat in the sink with some spaghetti baked into its bottom. The woman stumbled about and lost her footing. He caught her before she fell. "Easy, now, ma'am."

"I'm drunk," the woman said. "But I'll have another drink to steady myself. Your health, neighbor."

"Your health, ma'am."

She smacked and put the glass down. "So you're a friend of Kavel's, hey?"

"No, ma'am."

"So how did you get the apartment?"

"From the owner."

"You live up there but not by yourself?"

"No, ma'am, I have two mates."

"And you work?"

"Sometimes, but there isn't any now, so we're on the dole."

"Doesn't know Kavel," the woman told herself, as if the conclusion surprised her. Her eyes suddenly glared. "Kavel is bad."

"He is, ma'am?"

"Oh, yes," she sang, "Oh yes . . . oh yes." She squinted and her hand danced toward her glass.

"So why is Kavel bad, ma'am?"

"Because he made my daughter pregnant and then kicked her. Now she's in the hospital, and I think she'll die." The woman began to cry.

Cardozo got up and gave her his handkerchief. She grinned through her tears. "I got him today, yes sir. On his head, with my pot."

"But isn't Kavel in jail, ma'am?"

The woman drank, put the glass down again, closed her eyes, and shook her head.

Cardozo had sat down again. "You had the key, your daughter gave it to you, and today you went upstairs to see how he was doing and Kavel was asleep, so you hit him, right?"

"I hit him?"

"Because he was asleep. If he'd been awake, you would have given him some good spaghetti."

"Yes?"

"I think so," Cardozo said.

She opened her eyes. "That's right. I went to feed him, but then I got angry. Because he kicked my daughter."

"And you were drunk."

"Yes," the woman said. "I was drunk yesterday, too. Uncle Wisi doesn't like that. I went to visit him this morning, but he wouldn't talk to me, because I was drunk."

"Uncle Wisi?"

"Holy holy," the woman sang. Her eyes tried to focus. "Uncle Wisi *knows*."

"Knows what?"

"You name it, or don't name it. Uncle Wisi still *knows*." She drained her glass. "And now you better go. You're too white for an honest women like me, and if you don't go, I'll call the lukuman."

She followed him to the door. "And when I'm sober again, I'll bring some obeah, for your mate."

"What's obeah, ma'am?"

She giggled. "Medicine. Medicine for the sleepy man with

the lump on his head." She pinched Cardozo's arm. "Or did I kill him?"

"No, ma'am."

"Fine," the woman said, "because once you're dead, obeah is no good."

"And the lukuman?"

"He's dead too," the woman said.

9

NELLIE SQUATTED BETWEEN HER ROWS OF LETTUCE PLANTS. She looked up. “Did you sleep well?”

“Yes,” the commissaris said. “I do believe I dropped off for a few moments while you were working so diligently. Pulling weeds?”

Nellie dropped more grass into her bucket. “Yes, I can’t stand weeds. Everything has to be neat, I think, but Uncle Wisi says that I’m overdoing it. He allows most of his weeds to grow—that’s better, he says, because everybody attracts his own plants around him, and whatever you attract is good for you.”

The commissaris sat down and looked about contentedly. “He would approve of my garden, I think. I’ve got all sorts of weeds. Some of them grow quite high, and all of them flower. You have to look for them, but they’re always there. I like weeds, and so does the turtle.”

“You have a turtle?”

"My friend," the commissaris said. "He hasn't got a name and he doesn't achieve much and usually I can't even find him, but if I wait he'll show up and be with me for a while."

Nellie cleaned her hands on her apron. "Yes, I remember. Henk told me about your pet. He often talks about you, you know. I once asked him if the two of you were friends, but he says that you only socialize with your turtle. And with your wife of course. You have a good wife."

The commissaris rubbed his thighs. "I'm glad the adjutant approves of her. I do too. She takes better care of me than I of her. Maybe I'll have time to make it up later, when I don't have to gad about anymore."

"Are you in pain?" Nellie asked. "Would you like to lie in the hammock? Henk uses it too, and then he likes to swing a bit, and I've got to push."

She brought a rolled-up bundle from the house. "Here, I just have to hook it into these rings. Why don't you stand on your chair, then it's easy to get into."

Like a fly in a spider's web, the commissaris thought, helplessly cradled, surrendered to fate, quite a pleasant feeling really.

"Tea is about ready," Nellie said. "You look good like that, you know? And you fit better than Henk. He always rather bulges, and it's the biggest hammock I could find."

The commissaris slurped his tea. Maybe I should do some work, he thought, ask a few clever questions. Or shall I just lie here and admire the sky? To look up is more enjoyable than to look down. There's an excellent cloud, artistically afloat in the divine nothing. Not quite nothing, of course, for it's still blue. Good shade of blue. And there are some vines creeping along the reddish bricks. The smell of flowers. Even horizontally the view is pleasant because I see cookies and cake, pleasantly arranged, and behind all that there's Nellie's bosom, heaving softly. If I could only keep it this way forever after.

He took a slice of cake she offered and nibbled. "Delicious. Now, tell me, Nellie. Gustav and Lennie—where could I find these suspects?"

Nellie pulled a face. "If you don't find them, you haven't missed much. Late at night, I would think, Gustav anyway, since he still has a few women in the quarter and he's got to collect. Lennie hangs out in his luxury boat on the Catburgh Canal. He only comes into the quarter to have a drink at Hotel Hadde, on the Eastern Canal. I saw him there last week, whispering to Gustav. They were talking about Obrian, cursing him again."

"Hotel Hadde. I think I know where that is. An after-hours place, illegal I daresay."

"Most everything is illegal here." She pushed the hammock softly. The commissaris sat up. "Maybe I should see Uncle Wisi now."

"I haven't heard him come back, but I'm sure he wouldn't mind if I showed you his garden. It has a glass roof that he can close in winter so that it turns into a hothouse. He burns a wood stove then, to keep his tropical plants alive."

"I think I need some help."

She reached out to him, but he slipped through her arms and fell against her. She clucked worriedly. "Didn't hurt yourself, now, did you?"

The commissaris freed his head from the pressure of her chest. "Let me sit down a moment."

She held his hand. "That wasn't such a good idea. I'm sorry. Henk never gets out of the hammock easily either. Perhaps you should ask Uncle Wisi about your pains. All the blacks around here call on him. He can cure almost anything."

"Was Obrian his patient?"

"Luku came to see him too."

"Is Uncle Wisi a real doctor? He holds a degree?"

She shook her head. "No, but he was a doctor when he came. He must have studied over there."

The commissaris grimaced and felt his legs. "An herbal doctor?"

Nellie laughed. "You mean like that ugly lady on TV? With the dandelion tea? Uncle Wisi isn't like that. That's all silliness I think, stuff that tastes bad and makes you burp." She sat down next to him. "Here, let me tell you. Like a year or two ago, when I was trying to get my driver's license. I failed and I failed and I thought I would never be done. I told Uncle Wisi about it and he gave me the juice of one of his plants. Kaykay-kankan, I think it is called. It made me very quiet and he held on to me and sang—just before the exam, that was—and I didn't care about anything at all and during the test I heard his voice and I never thought about whether I would pass or not, but I did."

"A drug?"

She smiled. "Nah. Not the stupid stuff they sniff in the quarter. The man who gave me the test didn't even touch me, he always used to before, because I was so nervous I suppose."

"Did you drink the juice again?"

She shook her head. "Uncle Wisi said it was just for once. And that time I was losing things, that was a misery too, and Uncle Wisi gave me some little flowers to put in a vase. There was a girl working for me, and I heard her yell. I ran upstairs and the girl just stood and gaped. My gold bracelet was on the floor and she had my money in her hand, taken from my purse. She gave it to me and ran out of the house and I never saw her since. And another time again, when a man who stayed here was after me, banging on my door at night because he knew what I had been before, and wanting a discount on the room price, that time Uncle Wisi gave me some crushed leaves that I had to smear on the fellow's coat and he ran away too and stayed away."

"Magical herbs?"

"Yes, but they don't do any harm."

The commissaris grinned. "They don't do *you* any harm, you mean. This Obrian, now, you thought he was harmful, didn't you?"

Her eyes narrowed. "I certainly did."

"And you say he visited Uncle Wisi regularly?"

"Aren't you cold?" Nellie asked. "Shall I get you a scarf?"

"No, I'm quite comfortable."

"I'm cold."

"Put something on," the commissaris said. "I'll wait for you here."

She went into the house and put on a jacket. "Now, that fellow, the fellow I mentioned just now who wanted a discount and so forth, as soon as I'd put that ointment on his coat, you should have seen him. He was looking for everything that day, his bag, his hat, his razor, and he kept on phoning and dialing the wrong numbers."

"Poor chap."

She shrugged. "But maybe he just had a bad day. He was a button salesman and he had these hundred thousand samples, all in a suitcase, always mixed up of course. Maybe it got too much for him, sorting those buttons."

"And Obrian?"

She buttoned her jacket. "What do you mean, Obrian?"

"Well," the commissaris said, 'I don't quite understand. I saw him this morning and he didn't seem at all out of the ordinary to me. Now, what could have been so special about the man that he could dominate anybody?"

"You really don't get that?"

"No," the commissaris said.

Nellie sighed. "Maybe because you're not a woman. All pimps know that trick. They pull at you. I don't know what it is, but you can't resist it. They sort of look at you sideways and half-smile and then you get all warm and moist inside and you want to go with them, and do everything they like."

"A kind of power?"

"Yes," Nellie said. "And it works on women, but also on men sometimes. Take Crazy Chris, he's got his cart and he sells good stuff and makes a living. I always thought Chris was his own man, but when he saw Obrian, he followed him like a dog. He could never do enough for that black, and Obrian wasn't paying him, Obrian never gave a cent to anybody."

"Herbs that carry power," the commissaris said. A butterfly landed on his knee and slowly flapped its translucent wings. He watched the delicate insect. "Or insight, that might be a better word." He looked up. "Herbs do work. Take coffee, for instance, a very stimulating fluid, and cocoa, just before going to bed, but made with water, not with milk, never fails to give me good thoughts." He moved his hand slowly toward the butterfly and smiled when it stepped onto his finger. "Cocoa, constipating of course, but clarifying when taken in small quantities."

"Cocoa is an herb?"

He got up. "Grows on a plant." The butterfly was still on his hand and he blew softly until it flew away.

"He didn't want to go," Nellie said.

"Like the cat," the commissaris said. "I had a cat after me today. Strange, one would expect that the senses diminish when one grows older, but when I look at animals, or birds, insects even, I seem to see far more than before, like I can identify with their being . . . well . . ." He watched the butterfly land on a tomato plant. "Lovely creature."

"Go on," Nellie said. "Men don't often talk to me, except Henk of course, he does mumble away a bit every now and then. The being, you said, of animals?"

The commissaris leaned on his cane. He became aware that he was looking at her bosom again, raised majestically inside the tight jacket. " 'Being' is a big word. I don't want to exaggerate, but I do think that I'm closer to nature now. Insight, maybe, more than intellectual understanding. Most miraculous, that butterfly just now, and the cat earlier on. I'm an animal myself, hunting, yes." He looked away when he noticed her motherly smile.

"Yes," Nellie said. "You do talk like Henk, but he only says things like that when he tells me about his painting."

"You go ahead," the commissaris said when she had opened the garden door. "You know Uncle Wisi."

She called out, but there was no answer. "He must be out. I don't really want to go into the house, not with him not there. It's creepy in there."

"Then we'll wait here." A cat slept in a straw-filled basket. It yawned when it saw the commissaris and stretched a leg that flopped lazily over the basket's side. The commissaris scratched its soft fur. "That's the cat I mentioned just now. Look at that. She doesn't even withdraw her paw. You're not going to scratch me with your claws, are you?"

He felt the claws edge along his skin and the pressure of a velvet sole. The cat began to purr.

"That's Tigri," Nellie said. "She's always here when she isn't on the roofs. 'Tigri' means 'tiger' in the language of the blacks."

The commissaris withdrew his hand. "Isn't this garden just like the greenhouse in the zoo? That must be a mulberry tree. I have seen trees just like that in southern France. What's in the dishes? Does Uncle Wisi have other animals?"

"Only the bird." Nellie smiled. "Uncle Wisi says that the god of the garden lives in the tree. In that dish is some fried rice with banana, and there's rum in the other. He buries the food every evening, but he drinks the rum."

"The god?"

She laughed. "No, Uncle Wisi."

"Very practical. That plant also looks familiar. Wolf's claw, I think, but this one is twice the size of what grows in my garden. And it's a lot warmer here, too." He looked up. "That's quite a construction, that glass roof."

Nellie pointed at steel cables that led along the walls and connected to a winch. "At first he just covered it all up with plastic, but it always tore and the blacks from the neighborhood came and made the roof for him. You always hear people say that the blacks here can only collect unemployment and mug old ladies, but some of them can make anything you like. Uncle Wisi says that they had to work too hard on the plantations and were whipped too much. That's why they will never work hard again, but that doesn't mean that they aren't clever."

The commissaris picked a leaf. "I'm sure this is wolf's claw. Contains poison, I believe."

"That's what he gave me to put on that fellow's coat."

"The man who wanted to abuse you?"

"Yes, the fellow who never came back."

The commissaris touched the plant's stem with his cane. "Ah, I remember now. My wife was saying that I should pull it out because it destroys love. I made a joke about it, said that she should put it in my bath, to be rid of all the trouble I cause her."

"Do you often tease your wife?"

"Only when she nags."

Nellie turned away. "I wish I could nag at Henk, but I don't dare to whine. If I do, he might never come back again."

The tip of the commissaris' cane shot up. "What's that squeaking?"

"Opete does that. He lives behind the bushes over there. Do you want to see him?"

The commissaris was hardly surprised. Neither was the vulture. The bird was perched on a stick, stuck through holes in the sides of a crate. It leaned forward.

"He's quite tame," Nellie said. "Right? Opete?"

The bird squeaked.

"Does he ever get locked up?" the commissaris asked.

"No, but he can't get out in winter because then the roof is closed. He doesn't mind that, I think. It'll be too cold for him then."

"I thought vultures were much larger," the commissaris said to the bird. "I mistook you for a crow at first when I saw you this morning, and it's your fault that I'm not in Austria now. A black vulture flying above a black corpse in my own Olofsalley is too much. Do you know that you're an unsuitable apparition?"

The bird bent its head sideways and moved its claws on the stick.

"Poor thing," Nellie said. "You don't like to be scolded, do you?" She ran off and came back holding a bit of meat. "Steak. Not too much, because the price has gone up again."

The vulture took the meat carefully from her fingers and closed its eyes while it swallowed. The commissaris grinned. "Wherever did Uncle Wisi find him?"

"Under Luku Obrian's armpit," a dry voice said behind him. "Incubated in a Jumbo he was, but born here."

The commissaris turned his head. "Uncle Wisi," Nellie said. "I hope you don't mind that we're here. The, eh, Uncle Jan is staying with me and he wanted to meet you, but you weren't home."

Sunlight reflected in the beads of the old man's headgear. He put out his hand. "Hello, *opo*."

The commissaris felt the bones in Uncle Wisi's hand, covered by brittle skin. "They call me Uncle Jan."

"*Opo*," the black man said. "That's what *I* call you. Opo makes *tapu*, but you don't speak my language."

"No," the commissaris said. "And I don't know your country, either, which is a pity. You have a lovely garden, sir."

The vulture hopped out of its crate and walked, wings spread, to Nellie. Its beak touched her skirt.

"Don't beg, Opete," Uncle Wisi said. He put a finger under the bald little head and pushed it up. "Do try to behave, even if you're called a streetbird in Surinam."

Nellie stroked Opete's wing. "Because they keep the streets clean, isn't that right, Uncle Wisi?"

"In the cities?" the commissaris asked. "We should import a few thousand. They would do a better job than the sanitation lads we employ now."

Uncle Wisi laughed. Strong even teeth gleamed between his thin lips. He touched the commissaris' cane. "Are you lame, opo?"

"Rheumatism," the commissaris said. He touched his hip. Uncle Wisi's hand brushed over the indicated spot. The wide eyes above his thin curved nose closed.

"They had you in jail, opo?"

"Yes," the commissaris said.

Uncle Wisi's eyelids fluttered. He shook his head. "Opo in jail. They had me too, but too long, and my cell wasn't flooded. Jews and niggers, the caps and boots didn't care for our sorts. But you had a cap too." His eyes opened fully. "And you still have one."

The commissaris' cane ground in the gravel of the path while he looked into Uncle Wisi's dark pupils, floating in deep ponds of bloodshot white.

"Yes?" Uncle Wisi asked.

"Of course not," Nellie said. "Uncle Jan doesn't wear a cap. He's got a hat, a nice old-fashioned hat with a wide brim."

"Did you once live on a houseboat?" the commissaris asked. "I think I remember you. You kept animals. A donkey, wasn't it? And a wolf?"

"Only a fox, but the German soldiers shot it because he bit them when they picked me up. But they weren't clever, those Germans. Didn't pay attention, so I could escape from their jail."

"A while ago, sir. How old are you now?"

"There's no figure," Uncle Wisi said. "My mother couldn't count too well. But I'm older than you, much older. You're too young to use that cane. Cup of tea, opo? What about you, Nellie?"

"No, thank you," Nellie said. "I have to do some cooking. I'm sure Uncle Jan would love some tea."

She left, half-running. Uncle Wisi grinned. "You can still get away, opo."

The commissaris had to make an effort to face Uncle Wisi. He smiled halfheartedly. "No, I'll stay."

Uncle Wisi turned and led the way. "That's good, we do have to make firm decisions at times. But I don't think I'll give you tea after all." He cackled. "Too weak for the likes of us. Don't you agree?"

10

"This is hardly a place for friends to meet," Jacobs said, looking at the clock above his desk. "It's about closing time. I think I can lock up and leave the dead alone. The sun must be out. What do you think about joining a live crowd on a terrace?"

"Sure," de Gier said. "And some cold genever. No, perhaps not. Iced coffee rather."

"Are we walking?" Jacobs asked. "I think I've walked enough in my life. What about my bicycle?"

"You ride, I run?"

"On the baggage carrier," Jacobs suggested.

"Of course," de Gier said. "It can be done even if I haven't done it in years." He pointed at Jacobs' trouser legs. "Is that why you wear those clasps, so that your trousers won't get into the chain? Ever heard of a chain guard?"

"I live in other times."

"You certainly do," de Gier said, pulling at the baggage carrier."You sure this thing won't break?"

"Sit down. I have a respectable bicycle that doesn't fail. About as efficient as my body. I shouldn't really have my body anymore. Hey!"

A little black boy roller-skated across the cycle's path. Jacobs braked, the cycle veered to the left and almost hit a passing streetcar. De Gier shook his fist at the boy. The boy stuck out his tongue.

"Nasty little boy," de Gier said.

"Why?" Jacobs asked.

"Because he doesn't look where he's going and sets up dangerous situations for others."

Jacobs looked over his shoulder. "Come off it. Don't you read the papers? I wouldn't be surprised if that was the little boy featured in the article. That boy was black too, roller-skating along the sidewalk. *Zheef zhaf*, not a care in the world. He should have a care, of course, since the sidewalk is for pedestrians, but a Turk was mugging a lady on the same sidewalk, grabbing her bag and hitting the poor thing in the face, which wasn't so nice either."

"I read that," de Gier said. "And the boy roller-skated on, following the terrible Turk until a patrol car showed up, whereupon our boy performed some crafty antics, right in front of the cops, who tried to run him down so that they could beat him up, but he told them all about the Turk and the cops caught the mugger instead. A good little boy. A commissaris shook his hand and he would have gotten his portrait in the paper if he hadn't been worried about running into the Turk again."

"What'll you have?" de Gier asked when he leaned back in the easy chair next to Jacobs.

"A double genever."

"Two?" the waiter asked.

"No, no. Iced coffee for me. I say, Jacobs . . ."

"You're really going to ask me now?"

"I think I will," de Gier said. "When the adjutant and I were visiting your cozy establishment earlier on, you said something that I didn't quite follow. You said: 'When *you*,' *you* being me and the adjutant, 'caught *them*,' *them* being black fellows, 'in the jungle and put them in ships, and chained them in the holds . . .' You did say that, didn't you?"

"Yes."

"But I," de Gier said, sipping from his glass, "have never in my life, and neither has the adjutant I'm sure, caught no black fellow in no jungle."

"And you didn't drag me from my bed either?" Jacobs asked. "In the spring of 1942, on a day about as bright as now? And you didn't kick me into a boxcar and bang the sliding door on my hand so that my finger got squashed? This finger? Isn't much left of it now, right?"

"Right," de Gier said.

Jacobs grinned. "Funny, trying to show something that isn't there. I amputated it myself, with a piece of broken glass, in the camp. It got too smelly and it throbbed all the time."

"In 1942 I was rather little," de Gier said. "Filling diapers, if I can believe my mother."

"I filled my pants when your colleagues arrested me."

De Gier put down his glass. "Amsterdam cops caught you?"

"That's correct," Jacobs said. "The SS was busy, so the local cops helped out. They didn't like Jews either. And those black slaves were sold by Amsterdam merchants. Their portraits are in the Rijksmuseum now, and one of them looks just like you. Same mustache and large innocent eyes. Fat lower lip. A trader with the West, his ships carried slaves there and came back with sugar, harvested by slaves. A most profitable merry-go-round. How do you think the splendid inner city of Amsterdam was financed?"

De Gier didn't answer.

"Never occurred to you where all that money came from?"

"My father was shot in Rotterdam," de Gier said. "He was coming back from his office and the underground army shot a German, so the other Germans arrested the first ten male citizens who happened to come along and put them against a wall."

"I know," Jacobs said. "I tend to simplify. The real thing is impossibly complicated. I sometimes think that it's people that are no good. Not this or that people, but all of us. Maybe we're a mistake and shouldn't be here at all."

"I still dislike Germans," de Gier said, "but there are occasions that I can help them out and I always do."

"And blacks?"

De Gier choked on his coffee. Jacobs patted his back. De Gier put his glass down again. "Blacks?"

"Blacks."

De Gier shrugged. "I think I rather like them. They look good to me. Smart color, snappy dressers. I think I'm glad they've come. A contrasting color improves the general picture."

"And all the crime?"

"Well?"

"You don't mind?"

"No crime," de Gier said, "no cops. I'm a cop. Besides, it's understandable, don't you think? They fly from one way of life to another, in a matter of hours. Bit of a change. Got to adjust. It'll probably take a few generations until their bad percentage equals ours. By that time there'll be something else. There's always something wrong."

Jacobs raised his hand. "Waiter? The same."

"Too much genever makes you drunk," de Gier said.

Jacobs raised his glass. "That's very true. Your health, sergeant."

De Gier drank more coffee. "Another question. You said Luku Obrian 'was not a good corpse.' Remember you said that?"

Jacobs stopped sipping. "I remember that too."

"You knew him?"

"Yes, since they put him in my care."

"Not when he was alive?"

"I'd seen Obrian," Jacobs said. "In the street. I live in the quarter too."

"Listen," de Gier said. "You and I have worked together before and your ideas have been helpful to me. Last year you looked after a certain Boronski."

Jacobs frowned. "Let me think. So many corpses. Boronski. Okay, I've got him, nice-looking but evil inside."

"His corpse bothered you," De Gier said. "That's what you were telling me at the time, and you had to protect yourself by manufacturing a shield, a transparent egg that you formed around your body. So that Boronski's spook couldn't annoy you."

Jacobs nodded. "I always do that when they try to get at me."

De Gier grinned. "A good trick. Use it myself sometimes, not with the dead but with the living. In a streetcar, for instance, or in the canteen."

Jacobs shook his head a few times. He sighed. "The alcohol is working. I need more genever now than I used to. Not that I get drunk all the time, but it does help once in a while. You mentioned Obrian. What exactly do you want to know?"

"Everything. Why was he killed? Know your corpse and you'll know your killer. But my trouble is that I never knew Obrian. I saw his corpse, but I'm not as sensitive as you are. I do know that he was a pimp and able to push people around, by hypnotic power probably. I saw his house, and his altar."

"Altar?" Jacobs asked.

De Gier's gesturing hands re-created the trestle table. "Loaded with the unusual. Bones. Christ in a straw skirt. Fluids in bottles, weird perfumes like you smell in the street market where the blacks buy their herbs. He had been burning incense, too."

"I read his form," Jacobs said. "Louis alias Luku Obrian. Luku was his nickname, and I know what the word means. I rent a room in a house where blacks live. I've been listening to their folklore. A lukuman knows tricks. Sometimes they can foretell the future."

De Gier rolled a cigarette. "Not Obrian. If he could have foreseen what was coming, he wouldn't have carried on the way he did. He kept bothering his competition until they bothered him."

"With a Schmeisser."

"Right."

"Good weapon," Jacobs said, accepting a fresh drink from the waiter. "A neutral weapon, too. The Germans created it, but it shot the SS too. I saw that after the liberation. It all depends whose finger is on the trigger. The blacks who live in the house where I stay are frightened of *wisi*, for that's their word for evil and they pray to *opo*, which is the opposite, but the power is the same. It all depends on how you use it. You know . . ."

Jacobs drank.

"What?" de Gier asked.

"Bah," Jacobs said. "Genever tastes great, but only for a while, or have they put me on another brand now?"

"*Wisi* and *opo*."

"Yes. The power being neutral in essence. I knew an SS soldier in Dachau who called his Schmeisser *mein Halt*. Meaning that he could stop anyone by pointing its ugly snout. When we took the weapon away, he was just as scared as anybody else. I call *my* Schmeisser my friend."

"You do?"

"Waiter?"

The waiter came. "One more," Jacobs said. "A single this time, and more coffee for my mate."

"Where is this Schmeisser of yours?"

"At home."

"And how did you get it?"

"Took it with me from Dachau. Belonged to the soldier I mentioned. We got it away from him, and while the others bashed his head in with bricks, I took the Schmeisser and I hid it in my gear. It neutralized my fear."

"Fear," de Gier said.

"Doesn't go away." Jacobs grabbed his glass. "Whenever I wake up at night, I think it's them, at the door. Then I reach for my friend."

"And you put your friend down again."

"I do. I used it as *tapu*, as a means to protect. *Tapu* is the means, *opo* the power behind the means."

"Say that again?" De Gier asked.

Jacobs' emaciated features had softened. His skullcap was stuck to his thin gray hair. He crossed his legs; sunlight shone in the nickel-plated bicycle clasps. "Black terms," Jacobs said. "Invoked by having Obrian's body in the morgue. Not a good man, that fellow you have delivered to me. An angry man who hisses his rage. If I'm not careful, the dead get into me and I think their thoughts. You have to learn how to deal with the *yorka*, but I learn slowly."

"Another black word?"

"Pitch black. The *yorka* is the spook, the soul, the spirit who has lost its body but still yearns for it."

De Gier memorized the words. *"Wisi,"* he mumbled. *"Tapu. Opo. Yorka."*

"They took the words with them," Jacobs said. "From the African west coast to the South American east coast, and now to here. They're strong words and sustain wandering minds. I have my own words. My people traveled too. Where haven't we been? Two thousand years in the desert, to Armenia, to Poland, to Danzig, to here, to Germany again, Amsterdam again, but always Jewish, one life after another, on and on, carrying our magic."

"I wonder if I have any," de Gier said.

"You do, but you don't need it as much as the minorities." Jacobs pointed at himself. "A magical Jew with a magical Schmeisser to shoot at the magical SS to prevent them taking me to hell." He got up.

"You're leaving?"

"I have to perform more ritual. Wet the spiritual wall with my essential fluid. Be right back."

Jacobs stumbled when he returned, holding on to chairs and guests. The waiter brought the bill. "I do believe your friend is somewhat tipsy, sir."

"Hardly surprising." De Gier paid. "I'll take him home."

Jacobs sang children's songs in the taxi, softly so as not to irritate the driver. *"Hop hop horseman,"* Jacobs sang. *"When you fall you cry."* His elbow touched de Gier's side. "Which is dumb, sergeant. To fall is fine, but we shouldn't be too noisy about it."

"That's absolutely correct," de Gier said. "Here we are, driver. You do live about here, don't you, Jacobs?"

Jacobs peered out of the car's window. "Let's see, now. Yes, I believe these houses are known to me. If this is where Straight-Tree-Ditch and Bent-Tree-Ditch meet, then I do live here."

Jacobs staggered away while de Gier put a note into the driver's hand. He got out. "Wait for me, I'll see you home."

Jacobs lay on his bed, in a room that, apart from the old-fashioned iron bed, contained no more than a wobbly table, a chair, and a cupboard. He covered an eye with his hand and tried to look at de Gier. "Coffee, sergeant? There's some powder in the cupboard. The kitchen is downstairs."

"No," de Gier said, "but I would like to have a look at that Schmeisser of yours."

"Just a minute." Jacobs managed to get off the bed and crawled about on the floor. He tried to pry up a board but his finger missed the crack. De Gier knelt next to him. "Let's see if I can do that." The board veered up.

"There it is," Jacobs said, and fell back on his bed.

De Gier picked up the weapon, yanked the clip out of its grip, and pulled the chamber back. A cartridge jumped free and bounced off the floor. "Careless, aren't you? This thing was ready to go off. Jacobs?"

Jacobs' mouth sagged as he snored softly. De Gier opened the cupboard and took out a towel. He wrapped the weapon in the cheerfully striped material.

"Hop hop horseman." Jacobs' eyes were still closed.

"That's clever," de Gier said. "Singing in your sleep. I don't think too many people can do that. Or are you awake now?"

"I'm not too sure," Jacobs said. "Could be dreaming, too. Good dream. Makes me sing."

"Listen to me," de Gier said. "I'm part of your good dream. I'm taking this thing with me. Possession of firearms is illegal. I know you work for the city and that you're official, but only the police are supposed to be armed. I'm going to surrender the Schmeisser, but I won't tell where I found it. Yes?"

"Into the ditch with a broken neck . . ."

"And I'll get your bicycle before someone lifts it."

"Then the birds will come and eat your wreck."

De Gier shook his head. "Aren't you a trifle morbid today?" He tiptoed out of the room. "Back to the living," the sergeant said when the front door closed behind him.

He returned twenty minutes later and rang the bell. A young black woman opened the door.

"Mr. Jacobs' bicycle," de Gier said. "Can I put it in the corridor?"

The woman stepped back so that he could maneuver more easily. "And where is Mr. Jacobs?"

"In bed. Didn't you hear him sing?"

"I only came home just now." The woman smiled. "Has it happened again?"

"Drunk," de Gier said. "Very. He does get drunk often, does he?"

"Not too often. He's always very nice when he's indulging. Such a lovable man, and he believes, too. That helps."

"I didn't know."

"That Mr. Jacobs believes?" the woman asked.

"No, ma'am. That believing helps."

"It does help me," the woman said. "I'm a believer myself. I believe in everything, but Mr. Jacobs limits himself. . . . Come with me." The woman guided him back into the street. "Turn around. What does this say?"

De Gier read the little plastic sign screwed into the doorpost: ELIAZAR JACOBS. He also read the text, clumsily lettered on a wooden strip, dangling from a single nail: *"He who believes in the Good."*

"You see?"

"I see," de Gier said.

11

"DO SIT DOWN," UNCLE WISI SAID. "NOW, WHAT CAN I offer a person of your enlightened status?" His hand dived between stacked bundles of dried leaves and returned with a stone jar. "A glass of whole bodied grain genever?"

"You will be joining me?" the commissaris asked.

Uncle Wisi lifted a piece of cloth and took two glass egg holders from a weathered board. "Most certainly. You won't be poisoned here, opo. Grain is health-giving but it's a sin to limit its use to the manufacture of sandwiches." The jar gurgled. "Here you are. Your most excellent health!"

The genever burned through the commissaris' chest while he tried to adjust to Uncle Wisi's surroundings. He was in the low living room of an antique artisan's dwelling, both long and narrow, under a plastered ceiling supported by sagging pine beams. The old colors—the yellowish white of the thick plaster and the crumbly dark red of the aged wood—framed a tropical exuberance. Bright-colored textiles had been pinned to posts and shelves, and collections of pots and jars filled all available space, between plants that bloomed and crept and hung everywhere, some reaching for the light, others content in dark corners. His host was talking, but what Uncle Wisi said hardly penetrated to the commissaris' brain. When he did listen in the end, he noticed the medicine man's perfect Dutch. This strange man, the commissaris thought, did manage to adjust well—or is it the other way around perhaps? Could it be that the ancient reliability of the house is serving a foreign influence? He got up and looked out of the window.

Uncle Wisi stood next to him. The commissaris raised his eyebrows at the obvious vigor of the exotic vegetation outside. "My private plantation," Uncle Wisi said. "Given to me, since it grew from seeds that I was allowed to gather in your botanical garden. Everything is always available, a noteworthy fact, and how easy it is to find, once you know what you're looking for. The world holds nothing back, all one needs is a correct formulation of any particular desire. I always thought that the idea that gods only live in the home country bears witness of stunted growth."

The commissaris searched his memory, until he saw an elementary schoolteacher whose thin cane glided over a linen map covering the blackboard. Its tip touched a red spot, Paramaribo, capital of Surinam. The droning voice stated that only the coastal region had been developed and that the hills and jungles of the far-away country were wild. Descendants of runaway slaves roamed the wilderness, far from foreign interference, obeying only their own chiefs. The Dutch, through necessity, acknowledged the chiefs' power and sent gifts once a year: silver medals for the captains and discarded officer uniforms to confirm their authority. In the old days the captains had to promise to surrender escaped slaves, but they didn't. They weren't idiots; even the schoolteacher thought so.

"Massa Gran-Gado has been always everywhere," Uncle

Wisi said, "but even so, we can't reach him because he's good enough to elude our efforts. Only his *wintis* live inside us, from the very first day, on the African coast, in South America, and in our present location. Another nip, opo?"

"No, thank you." The commissaris hid his egg holder under a convenient leaf. The mood invoked by Uncle Wisi's emanations reminded him of his early youth and he saw the child that he had once been hiding under a glass cupola, in an herbarium. He had fled the crowd milling about in the city's zoo, amusing itself by watching diseased animals: a thin lion with a festering skin, a camel burping bad-temperedly, squinting at his tormentors from infected eyes. The screaming toddlers chasing each other around a cage full of screeching parrots had become too much for him and he had ducked out of the throttling grip of educating parents. The herbarium was quiet, as quiet as Uncle Wisi's room, even when the old man held forth, for his voice was no more than the whispering of large leaves moved by a cool breeze.

Uncle Wisi corked the jar. He hid his hands in the sleeves of his gown and shuffled toward the commissaris. "I'll sit down next to you for a moment, opo, because I need to touch you. Liquor improves togetherness, but we might not need alcohol to open toward each other. Wait, I will return Bacchus to his shelf." The bottle disappeared behind the rag. "He's called differently by us. I had trouble, when I arrived, to learn the new names. New names for old helpers, differently arranged too. It takes time to find the simplicity again that is hidden in chaos, and if you lose your way in the many, you miss the one. Only the one matters, for it gave birth to all the others." He sat down next to the commissaris. "You ever lose the way, opo?"

"Often," the commissaris said. "The other evening again. My wife took me to her sister's birthday party. I talked too much and bored myself."

"One has to make a choice, every day again, many times a

day even." Uncle Wisi made the legs of his stool whine as he jerked his seat closer. "With the risk that we choose unwisely. I've done it many times too, sometimes out of foolishness and ignorance, but also on purpose, to see how far I could go down." He pointed at the rag hiding the genever jar. "The whole-bodied grain *winti* has shown me much, in a bar opposite my houseboat when I still lived on the Prince's Canal. Every morning I guzzled, and slowly the colors would glow again and my thoughts would boil so that I could hear my own wisdom, I could do even without the moon then, the collective eye of all the *gados*. The gods came straight down to me, and instead of listening to the palm trees, I heard water swish against my boat."

The commissaris made a desperate effort to push Uncle Wisi's whispering away. He tried to remember why he had come. The strange words danced around within his skull. *Wisi* would mean "magic," and not the most preferable type, because his host entertained connections with the criminal element of the quarter, or had he misunderstood Nellie's information? The red-light quarter had been smudged by the dark tints of pimps and muggers, and the dealers of the bad drugs, but its crime wasn't black by skin. Was he now attacked by a necromancer, a servant of imported evil gods? Were the *gados* bad? He himself, an incognito chief detective, had been recognized as *opo*. *Opo* would have to be the exact opposite of *wisi*. I must not allow the sharp sword of logic to be knocked out of my hands, the commissaris thought. All I'm doing here is gaining knowledge to aid my fight. The knowledge presents itself in the way it wants to, but the interpretation is mine. He glanced to the side and saw the old man's beaded cap move forward and backward and Uncle Wisi's sensitive hands caressing the room's warm air, afloat on the fluid breath of outlandish herbs.

But the environment is mine, the commissaris thought. This is Amsterdam, my own city, and the Dutch gods support me.

They can't be hidden behind colorful rags, and Wisi's magical plants don't harm them. Even that cat, staring at me with its wicked yellow eyes, was born in a local alley.

"You hurt," Uncle Wisi said, "and wish to be rid of your pain. I think you've come to the right place."

The commissaris wanted to lean back, but his stool offered no support and he almost fell off it. He tried again to collect his thoughts. Am I in pain? But I'm not. The room's temperature is too high. I only hurt when I'm cold or tired. Or afraid, he admitted, but fear hadn't bothered him in a long while.

A ticking became audible. Opete's sharp beak touched the glass of the door leading to the garden, the vulture's bald head silhouetted against the garden's moist greens. True, the commissaris thought, the bird is foreign, ready to wreak havoc in our placid souls. But then, he thought again, even Opete can be friendly if politely approached.

Uncle Wisi let the vulture in and rested his hand on the bird's head. Opete's eyelids sagged as he rubbed his beak against his owner's fingers. "There's a good Opete," Uncle Wisi said. "Isn't he good?" The bird flapped a wing. "Does he need more love? Or are the lice at him again? Need scratching, do you? All right, all right, hop along, now." He pushed the vulture out. "You see, opo? Even the demon of death needs to be reassured at times, even the *sukujan*, the stinkbird."

"I thought you called him streetbird?"

"The demon has many names." Uncle Wisi felt behind another rag, crudely painted with a human skull, a rose stuck in its grinning mouth. He extracted a small drum made out of baked clay tightly covered with skin. "I'll sing to you for a bit, to start the treatment."

Uncle Wisi's song filled the room. The drum throbbed. Perhaps I should surrender, the commissaris thought. If he really wants to cure me, I should give in. By resisting, I won't get anywhere, and even the wrong place should divulge interesting facts. He and I can't exchange much unless we find a common level where we're both at home. The enemy opens himself when he attacks. Let's see where he hides his weakness. But is he really hostile? Isn't he rather tricking me to fall into my own depth, where the true reasons are hidden?

Uncle Wisi no longer used words. His humming gave way to nasal clanging sounds, as if he were plonking the tight strings of a guitar. There were other, much deeper sounds too, originating in his throat and fiercely pushed out of flaring nostrils. The drumming had become louder and higher.

He's tearing the soul out of my body, the commissaris thought, and by my own consent. Hopefully, anyway; it won't do to calmly sit here being bewitched.

Uncle Wisi became busier. He stood between the commissaris and a cupboard containing hundreds of bottles, jumping on the shelves due to the vibrations caused by his stamping feet. The bottles held colorful beans and crushed leaves, in subtle shades of green. The music seemed to make them gleam. The commissaris began to shiver. He pushed the fear out. All nonsense, he thought. I'm done with that, and with sense too. There never was a sense, I knew that when I was small and forgot when I grew up, but lately I've gone back to the old truth. What can this man do to me, except play games? It's all a game, even if we fire a machine gun out of a burned-out sex shop, in an alley bathed in the cool light of early morning while a thrush chants. Nothing mattered then; it doesn't matter now either.

The chant broke off. "Yes?" Uncle Wisi asked.

"Yes," the commissaris said. "Go right ahead."

Uncle Wisi put the drum away and pulled his stool toward him with his foot. He adjusted his robe as he sat down. "Would you mind standing up, opo?"

The commissaris felt the dry hands touch his hips and thighs. Uncle Wisi mumbled. The charged atmosphere of the room, instigated by his recent goings-on, became even more noticeable.

The commissaris smiled. "Well? Doctor?"

"A soothing ointment," Uncle Wisi said. "It will help, but your pain is hard to reach. I'll try something more potent. Weereeweeree with salt extracts, and a bit of this and that. Say, now, does the sun get into your bathroom?"

The commissaris was amused by Uncle Wisi's familiar tone of voice, unexpected after the solemn introduction. "It does in the morning."

"Good, maybe you should bathe early. Let the sun shine on you first. It doesn't matter if it is tucked behind clouds, the light still penetrates. After that, you sprinkle the obeah in the tub, not too much, just so that the water gets a bit of color. Rub some into the sore spots too. Then soak away."

"Certainly, doctor."

"You've got a wife," Uncle Wisi said. "I could feel her presence. She'll have to be part of the cure."

"My tub isn't quite that large."

"She doesn't have to get into the water. Ask her to sit with you. She can talk if she likes. Maybe she wants to sprinkle you, a few drops on the sore spots."

"Very well," the commissaris said.

"I'll make up a good batch so that you don't have to come back all the time. You're a busy man. When I'm done, I'll give the bottle to Nellie."

"And the cost?"

Uncle Wisi rubbed his nose. "Pretty pricey, opo. I need three different kinds of weereeweeree; mangzasi, seeseebee, and smeery. My seeseebee is almost gone, but there's a new crop due in the garden."

"How much?"

"Leave the cash with Nellie. It isn't for me. I'll have to pass it on, to make sure that the obeah will work on you."

"How did it go?" Nellie asked when the commissaris walked into her kitchen.

"A most impressive performance," the commissaris said, "but I've forgotten what I went to ask him."

"Creepy, eh? I heard him sing. Did he frighten you?"

"A little," the commissaris said. "But that passed and we had fun afterward."

She stopped scraping carrots. "Fun? When he did it to me, I felt all hollow inside. That's not a fun feeling at all."

The commissaris raised a lid and sniffed. "Hollow is rather a good feeling, I would say. The emptier the better. What's this going to be? Stew?"

"When it's done it'll be ragout. I'm a gourmet cook, I don't make stews. And there'll be berries and cream for desert. Berries from the garden. Do you think you would like that?"

"I would," the commissaris said. "I should work, though. Get outside, snoop about."

Nellie's knife sliced into the carrots again. "That'll be later. The quarter only wakes at midnight, and you have been working, haven't you? I think you should take another nap."

12

"YOU'RE STANDING ON MY DUST PILE," CARDOZO SAID, pointing his broom. "I finally got it together, and now you'll track it all over the house again."

Grijpstra stepped aside. Cardozo dropped his broom and trotted to the kitchen. He was back immediately, kneeling at the adjutant's feet, sweeping dust into his pan.

"Mustn't exaggerate," Grijpstra said. "Clean is okay, but I don't want to face guilt at every step. Reminds me of home." He slapped a cupboard. "The paint is coming off, this place makes its own dirt. Never knew why people collect so much furniture. What else does it do but increase the mess? You should see my apartment now. I always thought that my rooms were too small, but now that all the rubbish has been taken out I suddenly live in a sea of space. Lots of light, too. Even the noise went away. We must have less, not more."

Cardozo studied the contents of his dustpan. "What happened to all your furniture?"

"It followed my wife and the kids."

"And where did they go?"

"To Arnhem."

"And will you be going there too?"

Grijpstra scratched his chin. "Now, what would I be doing in Arnhem?"

Cardozo stabbed his brush accusingly. "Take care of your wife and kids."

"Can't I do that on the weekends?"

"I don't follow," Cardozo said.

"I thought you were a detective. Can't you make your own deductions?" Grijpstra held up a finger. "My wife has a sister, about as fat as she is, and similarly addicted to TV serials. The sister had a husband, with money and without work. An interest collector, a fairly common phenomenon in the provinces. No kids, only that man who used to play snooker in the pub. A man with a red face, because he tried to follow politics. My age, and dead, all of a sudden, reading the paper on the toilet." Grijpstra looked at Cardozo triumphantly. "Now do you follow?"

"No," Cardozo said.

"Still not clear? It was Easter and the kids had their holidays. My wife took them to Arnhem. A huge house, on the edge of the forest. The kids had a good time. My sister-in-law had a good time too."

"A lonely woman?"

"Not when my wife is around, because she talks all day, and the kids rush in and out. A big mansion, with most of the rooms empty."

"So your wife moved in for keeps?"

Grijpstra lit a cigar and threw the match onto Cardozo's dustpan. "She did."

"And left you here in an empty apartment?"

Grijpstra sucked his cigar. He smiled. "Yes."

"You could ask for a transfer."

"I could."

"But you won't?"

"I don't think I would qualify. I'm not good enough, you see. I'm sure they commit very subtle murders in the provinces."

De Gier came in. "What's in the towel?" Grijpstra asked.

De Gier unfolded the towel carefully.

"You walked through my pile," Cardozo said. "Why don't you go away, the two of you, so that I can finish what I started."

Grijpstra grabbed Cardozo's collar and yanked him to his feet. "Look at this."

"Our murder weapon?" Cardozo asked.

"Just another Schmeisser," de Gier said. "Not the one we are looking for. An example, according to the handbook of automatic weaponry, of the improved model MP 40. The Germans manufactured at least a million of them before the war was over."

Cardozo picked the weapon up. "Loaded?"

"Not anymore."

"Pow-pow-pow." Cardozo shot enemies of the state. He replaced the weapon. "But if this isn't the one we need, we don't need it, right?"

"I thought you might be interested," de Gier said. "The weapon we're after is similar. Look at this gun and think. Maybe you'll have some useful associations. Besides, the previous owner of this thing isn't right in the head, and by taking it out of his slightly insane hands I'm helping to maintain order. I'm an all around policeman, not restricted to the particular case at hand."

"I wish you would be somewhat restricted," Grijpstra said. "Stop gadding about, sergeant. How come you had the time to hunt for illegal arms when you're assigned to the Obrian murder?"

De Gier rewrapped the machine pistol. Grijpstra pulled his sleeve. "Where did you get it?"

"You're my superior, so your reasoning should be superior too. Where was I when you left me?"

"You found it in the morgue?" Grijpstra asked.

"In the morgue keeper's private quarters."

"Explain."

Grijpstra listened.

"A coincidence," Cardozo said. "We happen to be looking for a Schmeisser and you happen to find one. Without even looking for it. I found something too. Can I tell him, adjutant?"

"What?" de Gier asked.

"A yellow pot with a metal handle."

De Gier sat down, rolled a cigarette, clipped the superfluous tobacco strands with his nails, and flicked his lighter. "I'm pleased, not only because you found a yellow pot with a metal handle but because you're actually telling me that you did."

"There was some spaghetti in the pot," Cardozo said, "and just a few drops of tomato sauce."

"Thank you again. For adding details."

"You're not really that stupid, are you?" Cardozo asked. "Isn't it true that earlier on today you were hit on the head with some hard object?"

De Gier jumped up.

"In my pile again," Cardozo said, "but I won't complain, because police training teaches endless patience."

De Gier tried to tear tobacco out of his mustache.

"The neighbor," Cardozo said, "A black woman who, due to circumstances beyond her control, has become addicted to alcohol."

"Tell him the rest of it," Grijpstra said, "before he tears off his lip."

Cardozo reported.

"Well done," de Gier said. "I had a question, and you, of all people, promptly provide me with the answer. Thank you, although your successful sleuthing won't get us anywhere. I'm hardly damaged, and the woman made a mistake. By arresting her, we won't achieve much. Therefore we won't bother her. But we will bother the suspect who poured lead into the Olofs-alley last night, because if we don't, he'll do it again and we won't have any pimps left in the city. No pimps, no whores, and no whores is not what the population wants. We must not forget that we serve the citizens."

"Could I make a suggestion?" Cardozo asked.

"That I refrain from philosophizing and do some work?"

"Yes, but the station here has a shooting range. Can't we take the Schmeisser and fire it there?"

"What for?"

"Fun?"

"Good idea," Sergeant Jurriaans said. "I've never fired an automatic weapon either. Let me get Adjutant Adèle, she's in charge of the shooting range."

Grijpstra, de Gier, and Cardozo faced the station's counter, Jurriaans defended it. He opened its little door while he telephoned. He put the phone down. "She's coming. Follow me."

"Adjutant Adèle can shoot first," de Gier said.

She watched while de Gier charged the clip. He pressed a button. "Here you are, set for rapid fire. Just touch the trigger and be careful the gun doesn't jump out of your hands."

The Schmeisser fired. Jurriaans peered through his binoculars. "Good, but a little too high."

"How many cartridges did I use?" asked Adjutant Adèle.

Jurriaans counted. "Six hits and there were thirty-two in the clip."

"Your turn," de Gier said to Cardozo.

"A little too far to the right," Jurriaans said. "Can I try now?" He gave his binoculars to Grijpstra.

"Too low," Grijpstra said, "but close together."

"Let's see how good you are."

Grijpstra also fired too low. He passed the weapon to de Gier. "Now for our very own champion."

"Perfect," Adjutant Adèle said. "All in the heart. Splendid show, sergeant, and with a weapon you're not familiar with."

"Sergeant de Gier is a bit of a show-off," Cardozo said. "He doesn't know about modesty being customary between colleagues. *We* aimed badly on purpose."

Adjutant Adèle smiled at de Gier. Her smile accentuated her beauty. De Gier noticed her attractive shape outlined by the well-tailored uniform, and suspected the presence of available but prohibited pleasure. She has a good mouth, de Gier thought, subtly curved under a delicate nose, and her eyes are moist and alluring also because they are partly hidden under lovely lashes.

"A joke," Cardozo said. "The sergeant is an excellent shot and I'm jealous." His apology raised no comments either. Cardozo shrugged and walked to the other end of the range, to dig in a sand-filled box.

"Coming?" Adjutant Adèle called. "I've got to lock the door."

Cardozo ran toward her. "What's going to happen to the weapon?"

"Take it to headquarters," Grijpstra said. "The arms sergeant can add it to his collection."

"And what do I tell him when he asks where it came from?"

Grijpstra looked at de Gier.

"Tell him I found it in the street," de Gier said, "after a little boy, who immediately ran away, pointed it out to me under a tree. Keep it as vague as you can. *Found*, that'll do. Headquarters won't care anyway, all they want to do is put it away."

"I don't know," Grijpstra said. "Why not tell him the truth? Jacobs is well-liked and won't be charged, everybody knows what happened to him during the war."

"I don't want a form on the public prosecutor's desk," de Gier said. "Found, I say."

"Found, it is." Grijpstra followed Jurriaans and de Gier to the counter.

"Your Adjutant Adèle is a most beautiful lady," de Gier said. "Married, I suppose?"

"Recently divorced," Jurriaans said, "but she's got a friend now, one of us, a black reserve sergeant, rather a special somebody. A sociologist on his own time and an assistant professor."

"A serious relationship?"

"He's got a wife, and our adjutant on the side."

"Why," Grijpstra asked, "is everything always so complicated? I don't approve. A man with his wife, and the kids belong to both, and all in the same house, that's what I like to see. The man goes to his work, the wife keeps the house, the kids go to school. General contentment during the weekends and holidays. If we could keep it that way, even our job would be a pleasure."

"You didn't really say all that?" de Gier asked.

Grijpstra grunted. "My case is rather different."

"Everybody's case is rather different," Jurriaans said. "My wife left too, but I don't have any kids. After years of joyful togetherness. I'm sure it was all my fault."

"She went to another?"

"She didn't say," Jurriaans said.

"Irresponsible behavior," Grijpstra said. "I'm against it all, of course, but I've been looking for a black policeman. The reserve is hardly professional because they can't become experienced if they only dabble at our job during their hours off, but something is better than nothing. Our corpse is black. A black colleague could maybe explain the situation a little."

"This man works from your station?" de Gier asked. "How good is he?"

"He's excellent," Jurriaans said. "Works here most evenings."

"A sociologist," Grijpstra said. "All long-haired nonsense, but if he is a professor, he might be intelligent."

"Very," Jurriaans said, "and he's got short hair. Been in the reserve for six years. They pass the same examinations as we do. I've been told that reserve cops are in a better position than we are—not stuck in a routine, better able to see what goes on."

"Name?" Grijpstra asked.

"John Varé."

"I'd like to meet him."

"You will." Jurriaans leaned against the counter. "You think the killer is black too?"

"We don't think much," de Gier said.

Grijpstra grinned. "We try not to think, but sometimes we can't help ourselves. I don't think the killer is black."

"I'm sure he isn't," Jurriaans said. "Obrian was admired by his race. The blacks here regret his death. In their eyes he was a demigod who could turn the white law inside out. Since Obrian staged that show on the bridge, where the most beautiful woman of the quarter went down on her knees for him and—"

"Quite," Grijpstra said. "We have been told. Let's keep it simple, shall we? The man was black and the man was killed. He had a black soul, and I can't look into it. Now, if you can find me this John Varé and he will guide us, we might see something. All I want to know is how Obrian provoked his own death."

"Varé'll be here," Jurriaans said. "Tonight probably, but tonight you two are otherwise engaged. I understand that you wish to visit Hotel Hadde to watch pimps, and for tomorrow night I'm planning a little raid on Lennie's brothel boat. Don't breathe a word about that yet, because it's my experience that our plans are public property a minute after they are conceived. I think I will only take Ketchup and Karate, who hate Lennie's guts for a variety of reasons, and if I need more force, I'll find it just before we leave."

"How about us?" Grijpstra asked. "De Gier and I could be clients and be inside the boat, make a little fuss maybe."

"Yes," de Gier said, "and you're outside and wonder what's going on, so you come inside too."

Jurriaans became pensive. "Could be trouble. Provoking is outside the law. Judges are known to disapprove."

"We go in anyway," de Gier said. "We keep quiet, but we take a friend and he doesn't."

"What sort of friend?"

"A colleague."

Jurriaans arranged a stack of forms on the counter. "If he's a cop, we're still in trouble."

"An outside cop."

"From where?"

"From across a border."

"Ah," Jurriaans said. "That's better. He won't be a cop here. You have anybody in mind?"

"Sublieutenant Röder," de Gier said. "Hamburg Municipal Police. He was clacking his heels here not so long ago. Profusely thanking us. Begging to be allowed to return the favor."

"Sounds better and better."

De Gier looked in his notebook. Jurriaans pushed the telephone to the sergeant. De Gier dialed. "What will this Röder do?" Jurriaans asked.

"Fight the bouncer," Grijpstra said. "Spill his drink. Use bad language. He'll do whatever one shouldn't do on that boat."

Jurriaans nodded. "They do have a bouncer. Ape by the name of Baf. Muscly gent, weighs a ton, used to be a professional boxer, but he's been hit on the head too much."

"I know Baf," Grijpstra said, "but he doesn't know me. Wasn't he a bouncer in a champagne bar once? Mashed a customer? Got three months?"

"The very man."

"I'm surprised Lennie hired him. I thought Lennie was smart."

"He is," Jurriaans said, "and Baf has a better temper now. So have Lennie's brothel customers. You forget that Lennie's place is a whorehouse. When the clients leave, they've had it all. Makes them quiet and polite. Champagne-bar clients only get champagne and a peck on the cheek. Makes them agitated. So they bounce the bouncer. Brothel customers tip the bouncer."

"Herr Röder?" de Gier asked.

Jurriaans and Grijpstra listened to their side of the conversation. De Gier put his hand over the phone. "He wants to know who pays."

"Really," Grijpstra said. "What sort of a favor is this? We invite him to misbehave in our great city's most exotic brothel and he expects us to foot the bill? What about the suspect we gave him the other day?"

De Gier waited.

"Why are you looking at me?" Grijpstra asked.

"You're in charge."

"Of wasting money?"

"No money, no Röder."

Grijpstra nodded. "We'll pay," de Gier said. "Herr Lieutenant. *Grüsz Gott.*"

"*Sub*lieutenant," Grijpstra said. "And why should he greet God?"

"A higher rank is a polite way of addressing somebody, and God won't mind, even if Röder does greet him."

Jurriaans fetched coffee and passed cups. "He may mind if Baf reverts to type and kills your Kraut, but if we've paid, maybe he won't. Provided he's the God of Justice."

"There are others?"

"I do believe so, adjutant."

"And John Varé? Will I get him or not?" Grijpstra asked.

"What do you want with Varé again?"

"Ethnic information," Grijpstra said. "What's a lukuman, for instance?"

"What do you think?"

"I think," Grijpstra said, "that a lukuman must be someone adept in the dark forces."

"Give me a break," Jurriaans said, "and Varé too. Of course a lukuman fights for the enemy. You don't suppose that an ordinary silly woods nigger would have been able to cause such havoc as our deceased prince of the quarter managed to bring about?"

De Gier replaced the phone. "Röder'll be here tomorrow afternoon."

Cardozo came to the counter, the rolled-up towel under his arm and a small carton in his hand. "I want coffee too."

"Later," Grijpstra said. "We're off."

Cardozo walked along with his superiors to the front door. "Why did Sergeant Jurriaans look so upset?"

"Because he's jealous," Grijpstra said. "He's hopelessly in love with adjutant Adèle but she already has a friend, who's black besides."

"I want to know everything," Cardozo said. "And without having to beg for information. If you want to make use of my intelligence and devotion, it won't do to keep valuable facts back."

"Don't pay any attention to Adjutant Grijpstra," de Gier said. "Jurriaans is jealous of me because I've just arranged to spend the night with Adjutant Adèle. What else would you like to know?"

"Does Adjutant Adèle really have a black friend?"

"Yes, a colleague."

"There are no black cops in Amsterdam, except three students who're much too young for such a full-blown woman."

"A reserve sergeant."

"More."

"More what?"

Cardozo jabbed at de Gier's stomach with his box. "More information."

"Watch it. That thing isn't loaded, I hope."

"You drive me crazy, sergeant. What about that black imitation cop?"

"John Varé," Grijpstra said. "Sociologist. Native of Surinam. Volunteer in the reserve. Assistant professor at the university here. Intimate with our Adjutant Adèle, occasionally, for he's also married."

"Thank you."

"And a little less rambam, please," Grijpstra said. "You're tiring me. I also found out what a lukuman is. A lukuman is a magician, flipped over to the wrong side."

"And dead," Cardozo said. "That's what the alcoholic lady said who attacked de Gier with her dinner. So now what? We already knew that Obrian wasn't your average victim, in view of that scene on the bridge. Remember? With that beautiful lady whore who gave Obrian a—"

"I don't want to hear anything more about it," Grijpstra said.

"But that's what it was. Oral sex, if you can't stand plain language. We're still not getting anywhere. I need real news, not information that merely confirms our serious suspicions."

"Good advice?" de Gier asked. "Can I give you some of that?"

"Yes, sergeant?"

"You're too eager. Don't push like that."

Cardozo looked hurt.

"And here are the car keys," de Gier said. "Take it easy, now."

"Our own little fierce ferret," Grijpstra said as the Volkswagen left the curb on squealing tires. "When he gets hyper like that, I always have to hold back. Needs his ears tweaked."

"Cardozo provokes," de Gier said. "An illegal activity in our line of work. Look who we have here."

Grijpstra nodded at the black cat that, gleaming tail neatly tucked around bottom and feet, was watching them from the sidewalk on the other side. Grijpstra craned his neck. De Gier grinned. "I did that too, but the vulture went home for his nap. Don't you have the impression that we are spied upon?"

They walked back to the station. "What would there have been in that little box Cardozo was carrying?" Grijpstra said. "The towel held the weapon. I hope he hasn't tried to pull the Schmeisser into parts and had a few leftovers."

Jurriaans waved at them from behind his counter. "A telephone call for you. Mr. Ober of headquarters. He's waiting for you in the police garage, something about a new Mercedes that has been confiscated at your request."

13

"COME IN," THE COMMISSARIS SAID.

Nellie showed him a bottle filled with a thick green fluid. "Your obeah. Uncle Wisi made it for you."

The commissaris studied the bottle. "Nice and fresh. What's the foam?"

"I shook it when I came up the stairs. You have to rub it into your skin, Uncle Wisi said, and then I'll have to pour a little into your bath."

"Would you put it on the night table?" He opened his wallet. "And could you give this to Uncle Wisi?"

"Isn't that rather a lot of money?"

"There are no free lunches," the commissaris said. "He did his best, I presume. And he said he would pass the money on."

"You're not being sarcastic, I hope," Nellie said. "Uncle Wisi is very honest. I'll have you know. He gives things away and treats people for free and all. But the rich have to pay, because they've got the dough. You can't shave a snake, Uncle Wisi always says."

"I wasn't putting him down," the commissaris said, and glanced at the bottle. "You really think that'll work? I don't want to get a rash. I can handle the pain somewhat, but a skin disease won't improve my condition."

"You really think that that neighbor of mine is a bit of a creep, don't you?"

The commissaris sat up on his bed. "You don't?"

"No," Nellie said. "At first maybe, but not when I got to know him. I was still in the business then, and I thought most men were creeps."

Nellie put the notes into her apron pocket. She looked at a chair. The commissaris got off the bed. "Would you like to sit down?"

She smiled. "You're always so polite. I'm only learning now again that gentlemen exist. You should have seen my customers. Those Japanese, for instance. They looked like proper gents when they came into the bar, but if I wasn't careful they would tear me apart. I prefer blacks myself, but they never stop, and I had to set an alarm clock. When it buzzed they went out."

"Not very romantic."

"Romantics," Nellie said. "I had those too. They wanted to flirt and so on; I put them on the buzzer too."

"You don't mind if I lie down again?"

"Shall I cover you up? I've got a nice plaid."

"No," the commissaris said. "Tell me, Nellie, what exactly was the connection between Uncle Wisi and Obrian—there must have been something between them. And how many animals does Uncle Wisi have now?"

"Two. Opete and Tigri. You met them both. They're nice."

"And if I tell you now that the vulture was flying above the Olofs-alley last night and that the cat was about in that street too?"

"Damn."

The commissaris turned his head. "What did you say?"

"I said, 'damn.' That must have been what Uncle Wisi was doing Sunday night. I wasn't sure then, but I think I am now."

The commissaris waited.

"You know," Nellie said, "when you were with Uncle Wisi this afternoon—after I left, I mean—he was singing for you, wasn't he?"

"Yes?"

"And drumming?"

"He made some pleasant music."

Nellie bowed toward him, her hands on her thighs. "He was making music Sunday night too. Not so pleasant. He was creaking and yelling and the drum sounded nasty too. I couldn't sleep, and when he finally stopped, I had the most awful dreams."

"About what, Nellie?"

"About him, of course. I was afraid of Uncle Wisi, for the first time ever."

"You think he was damning Obrian?"

"Yes."

"But weren't they friends?"

Nellie shook her head. "No, they weren't friends."

"But they did see each other. You told me yourself that Obrian used to visit Uncle Wisi."

Nellie got up and looked out of the window.

"I don't understand," the commissaris said.

She looked over her shoulder. "How can I explain it to you. Take Henk, for instance. He visits with you sometimes, doesn't he?"

"Sure."

"For no reason?"

"No, there's usually some purpose. We work together, so I sometimes ask my wife to invite him to dinner. We're friends."

"You're his boss," Nellie said.

The commissaris smiled. "These are modern times, Nellie. Nobody is a boss anymore. We all work together."

"But he's got to do as you tell him."

"Well . . ." the commissaris said. "In a way, perhaps."

"All the way. Now, suppose that Henk won't do as you say. All the time, I mean."

"That would rather interfere with our cooperation," the commissaris said. "But I don't think I would damn the good adjutant."

"I don't express myself too well, do I, now? But can't you follow me at all?"

"I can," the commissaris said. "Until what time did Uncle Wisi sing and drum last night?"

"Until daybreak."

"So he was still at it at twenty past three?"

"You don't think that Uncle Wisi fired that gun, do you? Uncle Wisi is no shooter."

"He's more like a curser," the commissaris said. "And the damnation certainly worked. All I need to know now is the name of the person who executed the curse so that I can close the case."

Nellie sat on his bed. "I don't know the name, but when Uncle Wisi really wants something, he'll make it happen."

"Whether people agree with him or not?" the commissaris asked. "That's kind of bad, Nellie. Not the proper thing at all. Just imagine if we all got into that. Like making puppets of suspects and sticking pins into them. Or collecting their cut-off nails or bits of hair to burn them—that's done too. Witchcraft, you know. A despicable activity."

She tried to smile. "You don't really believe magic works."

"I wouldn't be surprised if it did," the commissaris said. "And if Uncle Wisi really practices the evil crafts, we should have a serious talk with him."

"He doesn't," Nellie said. "You don't know him yet. I see how he helps people. He has time for everybody and he doesn't mind not being paid. He listens to what seems to be the trouble and he hands out medicine and he sings and he—"

"He sang for Obrian and look what happened."

Nellie pursed her lips.

"Well?" the commissaris asked.

"Obrian was bad. He had to go. How could it go on? He kept getting stronger and the station here couldn't hold him either. You've no idea what Obrian could do."

"Tell me what he did."

"There used to be a woman here who was called Madeleine . . ." Nellie said.

The commissaris listened.

"What do you think of that, eh? The cops were there, looking at the whole thing—*they* didn't know what to do either."

"Hmm."

"What would you have done?" Nellie asked.

"I think I would have looked too."

"And after that?"

"I would have worked on Obrian for a bit."

"And would you have caught him?"

The commissaris studied the end of his cigar. Nellie put an ashtray on the bed.

"Thank you. Yes, I think I would have caught him. He was a pimp and dealt in drugs. A criminal like that can be tripped up."

"Not Obrian," Nellie said. "Luku Obrian knew tricks. Whoever went after him tripped himself up."

The commissaris rubbed his leg.

"Would you mind taking your trousers off?"

"Would I mind *what*?"

Nellie had picked up the bottle. "Please take your trousers off." She slipped his suspenders off his shoulders. "Uncle Wisi said that you shouldn't wait too long. Now, where are the sore spots?"

The commissaris closed his eyes.

"Please?"

"No."

"Yes." She removed his shoes and pulled at his trousers. "I have seen men's legs before and you can keep on your underpants. I'll put my hands in from the side so that it doesn't get too private."

The commissaris groaned.

"Does it hurt?"

"It burns."

"Isn't that a nice feeling?" Nellie rubbed. "Is this the right spot?"

"A bit higher."

"Then the underpants will have to come off too." She poured more of the green liquid into her hand. It does burn a bit, doesn't it? Not too bad, though. Now turn over," Nellie said. "I have to do a complete job. Rheumatism is in the bones, they say. I suppose it'll have to soak right in. There you are. Now, how do you feel?"

The commissaris dressed. "Thank you. Now I'm sleepy again. I'm about ready for a rest home."

"You take a bit of a nap and I'll cook supper. Do you like steak and fried potatoes? With fresh peas from the garden."

"Sounds excellent." He walked to the door. "Do you mind if I use your telephone?"

"It's in my office."

"Dear?" the commissaris asked.

"Jan? Oh, I'm so pleased to hear your voice. Is everything all right?"

"Couldn't be better. I was very lucky. I'm in a pleasant little hotel and I'm doing some useful work too, but maybe you wouldn't think so if you saw what I was doing."

"What are you doing?"

"Napping mostly, dear. And there's a hammock in the garden, and flowers, decorative animals even. This is quite a pleasant place."

"Don't overdo it."

"I'll do my best."

"And where are you exactly?"

"Straight-Tree-Ditch, dear. I can't recall the number, but there's a sign outside, in several languages."

"And do they know who you are?"

"Only the owner, dear, a lady by the name of Nellie."

"Jan?"

"Yes?"

"Is it really a nice place?"

"Suitably decent, dear."

"And how long will you be?"

"Another day perhaps, or a little longer. I'm going to snoop about in the quarter tonight."

"Do be careful. Can I phone you?"

He read the number to her that was indicated on the phone.

"Good-bye, darling."

"Good-bye, dear."

The commissaris stumbled up the stairs, holding on to the

railings with both hands. His legs cramped and glowed. "A witch's brew, rubbish, why do I let myself in for stuff like that?" He slammed the door behind him and staggered toward the bed. He felt faint when he dropped down. He tried to get up again but his muscles seemed too soft and he flopped back. He tried to stay awake.

I'm rowing, the commissaris thought, on a canal. How many years have I worked in the city, and I always wanted to row, but this is the first time. He pulled on the oars and the dory pushed its slender nose through short waves that split on the bow and foamed past its sides. The commissaris looked up at the majestic trees and high silver houses, sharply outlined against a clear sky. This must be the bend of the Gentleman's Canal, he thought, an elegant power spot of the old city, and I'm not just rowing along, I'm in uniform and therefore engaged in the legal execution of my duty. I'm an admiral; there are golden bands on my sleeves and medals on my chest. I seem to be an important man, but that would be an illusion, of course, for I'm only an official and serve the people. Meanwhile I'm enjoying myself, which is fine, for we are allowed to take pleasure in our work.

The canal widened out and he could no longer see the quays. Dark gray clouds formed and sat on the horizon, and the commissaris leaned on his oars. The water around him swelled slowly without breaking. The surface was fouled with rotting leaves and slimy weeds. Another boat approached. A canoe, the commissaris thought, long and narrow and manned by savages, dreadful cannibals, listen to their yells. They aren't after me, I hope.

He noticed a sword at his side. He got up and pulled it from its scabbard.

The canoe glided past the dory. Obrian stood at the helm, his mouth open in a scream of fear. The beings that knelt in the boat paddled furiously. They rather look like turtles, the commissaris thought, but not of the pleasant type. Look at those hard little eyes and their open beaks filled with razor sharp teeth. And why are they yelling?

A smaller canoe flashed over the water, much faster than the first. Only one man stood in the little boat; a cat had clawed itself into the bow and a large ominous bird sat on the rudder. "Hello, Uncle Wisi," the commissaris shouted, and waved his sword. "Hello, Tigri, hello Opete."

Uncle Wisi touched his beaded cap but kept his eyes on the fleeing Obrian. The cat's hair bristled and her tail swished. Opete seemed angry too, and leaned forward, his sharp beak pointing straight ahead. The vulture had spread its wings and seemed ready to fly off.

The commissaris sheathed his sword and reached for his oars. The dory sped over the water. "Uncle Wisi," the commissaris called. "Let me do it. I'll grab the criminal."

"Too late," Uncle Wisi shouted. "Get him, Opete."

The vulture flew up and dived down. Obrian tried to defend himself while his paddlers jumped overboard and sank as they howled, pulled down by the weeds that grabbed them from all sides. Tigri jumped too and hung on to Obrian's back, tearing his flesh with her claws and biting him in the neck. Opete's beak hacked into Obrian's head.

Uncle Wisi watched. The commissaris watched too.

"I wish you hadn't done that," the commissaris said.

"Couldn't really leave it to you," Uncle Wisi said. "Maybe it's for your own good. We all have our responsibilities."

Obrian's skeleton disappeared into the greenish jelly. Tigri rubbed her head against Uncle Wisi's leg. Opete sat on his shoulder and cleaned his beak on a lifted wing.

"We may as well go back, opo," Uncle Wisi said. "Shall I pull you?"

"No, thanks," the commissaris said. "This is my own boat, and the water rather belongs to me too."

The commissaris woke up, grinning and sweating. He got up and went downstairs.

Nellie met him in the corridor. "I'm almost done." She pointed at a box that stood in the corridor. "A lady brought that for you."

"What's in it?"

"I'm not too sure," Nellie said, "but I think it's alive."

"What did the lady look like?"

"A very nice lady," Nellie said. "She had white hair. She came in a Citroën, but she had double-parked so she couldn't wait."

The commissaris lifted the lid off the box. The straw inside moved.

"Ugh," Nellie said. "It isn't a snake or something, is it?"

A small head peered over the top. "Old friend," the commissaris said. "Came to keep me company, did you? Now, isn't that thoughtful of you?"

"Is that turtle yours?"

"And the lady is my wife." The commissaris picked the reptile up. Its shell fitted his hand partly but the turtle's head and legs dangled. "See how tame he is?"

Nellie opened the door to the garden and the commissaris put the turtle down.

"He's so fast," Nellie said. "Look at him running at my lettuce."

"Whoa," the commissaris said.

"No, that's fine. He can eat as much as he likes. How are your legs?"

"Better."

"You see?"

Nellie went back to the kitchen and the commissaris sat in the garden. The turtle chomped on a leaf. "Some of your mates were in my dream, Turtle," the commissaris said softly.

The turtle looked up, lettuce hanging out of its mouth.

"The wrong type altogether."

The turtle ate.

"But all ended well."

Nellie came out, laid the table, and put down a bottle of wine and two stemmed glasses. "You can get the cork out."

He accepted the corkscrew. "Nellie?"

"Yes, Uncle Jan?"

"Opete is on the wall. He wouldn't harm my turtle, would he?"

"Never," Nellie said. She rubbed the turtle's shell. "You can come out now, that bird is a friend."

14

"THE POLICE GARAGE IS NOT EXACTLY NEXT DOOR," GRIJPSTRA said, "and Cardozo just left with our car."

"One moment," Jurriaans said. "Just one tiny moment." He breathed in deeply, leaned back and forward again. *"Ketchup!"*

Ketchup popped up and stood to attention.

"Take these colleagues to the police garage."

"Something good?" Ketchup asked. "Anything happening? Action at last?"

"A ride," Grijpstra said. "Nothing special. Sergeant de Gier took the time and trouble to stop a car this afternoon, and now there are extra complications. As if we don't have anything to do. One job at a time, I always say, blinkers on and straight ahead, then old age will come all by itself, but the sergeant begs to differ."

"Like me," Ketchup said. "I prefer to do everything at the same time. Karate, too. Making a mess, we call it, but we usually get to the end of everything nevertheless."

"You shouldn't talk when you're at attention," de Gier said.

Ketchup jumped up, came down with his legs apart and his hands on his back. "We're bad at protocol, because we serve with the uniformed branch. The detectives are higher, so they mind their manners, isn't that correct, sergeant?"

"Away at once," Jurriaans shouted. "Take the gentlemen and bring them back again, don't lose a moment."

Ketchup ran off and returned, driving a new Renault patrol car. Grijpstra and de Gier got in. The car's siren was wailing and its turning blue lights were reflected in passing bar windows. Grijpstra leaned toward Ketchup. "Easy, no need to panic, constable."

"Away at once," Ketchup shouted. "Not a moment to lose." The car screamed past the Prince Hendrik Quay, hardly braked for red traffic lights, veered away from the river again, turned sharply and raced into the Anna Frankstreet. Grijpstra cursed; de Gier grinned.

The garage doors slid up and the Renault shot into a large space lit by white neon tubes, a last complaint sighing from its siren. A white-haired gentleman in an impeccable suit jumped to the side.

"Good day, Mr. Ober," Grijpstra said.

"There was no need to rush, adjutant. Were the siren and chase lights being used under your orders?"

Ketchup marched up and saluted. "Mission completed, sir."

"I did not ask you anything, I'm talking to the adjutant."

"Yes, sir," Grijpstra said.

"Then I would appreciate a little less zeal on a future occasion."

"Yes, sir."

Ober waited.

"Sorry, sir."

"Yes, adjutant. Please follow me. There's the car that we caught, thanks to you. The suspects have been placed in custody. Good tip, adjutant."

De Gier coughed.

"It wasn't my idea, sir," Grijpstra said. "The sergeant spotted the suspect."

Ober never took his eyes off the adjutant's face. "I believe you two work as a couple and that you're the higher in rank?"

De Gier's elbow touched Grijpstra's side.

"Yes, sir," Grijpstra said.

"Right, adjutant."

Two mechanics reduced the remnants of the Mercedes into even smaller pieces. "I don't think we'll find any more," Ober said, "but we have enough to please the court. More than a pound of heroin in an aluminum tube dangling in the gas tank. Suspects deny any knowledge of the cargo of course, but they did tell us something already and the investigation is well under way. I wouldn't be surprised if further arrests will follow, and with a bit of luck we may even detain the Turks who smuggled the material in. Congratulations again, adjutant."

Ketchup whispered. "Who he?"

De Gier whispered back. "Chief Inspector Ober, Drug Brigade." The sergeant strolled off; Ketchup followed.

"Hello," a helmeted policeman standing next to a motorcycle said.

"Hello, Orang," Ketchup said. "Do you have a minute?"

De Gier walked on and admired neatly arranged heavy motorcycles being caressed by the screwdrivers of respectfully kneeling mechanics. Hairy bundles had been attached to some of the cycles' saddles. De Gier touched one. "What's that?"

"A scalp," a mechanic answered. "Whenever they arrest a Hell's Angel, they take a souvenir."

"Real hair?"

"Everything is real here."

"And that one over there? Real blood on it?"

"That one came from a Hell's Angel who harassed the officer."

"Whacked with a billy club?"

"Cracked the fellow's skull." The mechanic shrugged. "That'll teach them to fight our selected troopers. Who are you? A journalist?"

De Gier showed his card.

The mechanic returned it with two hands.

"And that?" de Gier asked. "Isn't that a kid's cart? Or was, rather?"

"The kid is dead," the mechanic said. "Hit by a drunk. The troopers got the drunk."

"This place is about as bad as the morgue." De Gier wiped his forehead with his handkerchief. He saw Ketchup, gesturing at the motor cop called Orang. The cop was listening attentively. The man was short and square and his long arms hung loosely, reaching beyond his knees. Under the edge of his orange helmet glittered deep-set black eyes above a beard that reached his cheekbones.

"That's Orang Utan," the mechanic said, "one of our worst, but the best rider in the city."

"Sergeant de Gier?"

De Gier walked toward the chief inspector. "Sir?"

"What made you stop the Mercedes?"

De Gier rubbed his chin. "Well, sir, something wasn't right, I thought. A black hoodlum in such an expensive car. Rather strange, I thought."

"We are supposed not to discriminate, sergeant. Would you have stopped the suspect if he'd been white?"

"Just a moment, now," Grijpstra said.

"Adjutant?"

"I don't agree, Mr. Ober. Last month we stopped a young man driving a new BMW convertible. The suspect was dressed in torn clothes and had long blond hair. It turned out that he had stolen the car. He was white."

"Not a nice young fellow," de Gier said. "Stayed in a

discarded houseboat where we found a female minor who prostituted herself for him."

"I see," the chief inspector said. "Would you two care for a good cigar?" Ober flicked his golden lighter.

The detectives thanked him.

"Society degenerates continuously," Ober said, sucking smoke out of his cheroot. "But we should be careful to maintain our morals. Take that bearded constable over there, for instance. Recently criticized because he wounded some teenage suspects."

"Suspected of what, sir?" Grijpstra asked.

"Cut him off and called him a nigger."

"But he isn't a nigger," de Gier said. "More like a gook, I would say, from one of our former colonies in the East, isn't he?"

"Sergeant!"

"Sir?"

"Orang Utan is from the island of Ambon," Grijpstra said. "The religion out there is martial. Very courageous, the Ambonese are supposed to be. And Orang was mentioned in the paper the other day. A little boy had gotten himself stuck between the automatic doors of a streetcar and was dragged along, held by his foot. Orang cut off the streetcar. The motorcycle was a total loss and Orang was injured, but the little boy was saved. Anything else we can do for you, sir?"

"No, adjutant."

Ketchup reversed the Renault and opened its passenger door. His hand slid to the dashboard. "No," Grijpstra said, pushing the constable's hand away from the siren's switch.

"You wouldn't be frightened of that martinet who swallowed a walking stick, adjutant?"

"Very frightened," Grijpstra said. "You behave, and we all stay out of trouble. Take your time, constable. Rinus?"

"Yes?" asked de Gier.

"Why didn't you tell Mr. Ober that you had seen the suspect exiting from a drug-infested house?"

De Gier stretched. "Does it matter? He's caught anyway. And the chief inspector irritated me a little."

Ketchup drove through red lights. Grijpstra touched his shoulder. "Don't."

"Sorry, adjutant. Matter of habit, I suppose. Look, there's Gustav, driving his Corvette." Ketchup waved.

The low sports car's driver looked away. "Never mind," Ketchup said. "We'll catch you tomorrow. Luku has been fried and you'll be stewed." He looked at de Gier. "I hear you'll go on patrol with us tomorrow."

"Yes," de Gier said, and got out. "Hello, Cardozo. What happened? Fall into something?"

"Fell into me," Cardozo said. "Tell me about the sun roof next time you give me your car. It won't close."

"Paint?" Grijpstra asked.

"The collected shit," Cardozo said, "of a complete squadron of until recently constipated seagulls. I saw it coming, but the roof was stuck."

"It's dripping out of your hair," Ketchup said. "Would you mind moving up a bit?"

Cardozo walked away.

"Not too even-tempered lately," de Gier said. "Now I've still not asked him what was in the little carton."

"It's just the right time to go and eat something," Grijpstra said, "and then to bed."

"And Hotel Hadde?"

"We'll get up again."

"Hotel Hadde?" Ketchup asked. "You better be careful."

"We're peaceful lads," Grijpstra said. "Befriending others wherever we go. Come along, sergeant."

"I'll have a bite," de Gier said. "But I don't need sleep. Will you be on duty later on, Ketchup?"

"Yes, sergeant."

"I'll go along."

"In uniform," Grijpstra said.

"No."

"Oh, yes. And then you'll change again and go to Hotel Hadde in your regular clothes."

De Gier turned away.

"Everybody seems a little short-tempered lately," Grijpstra said to Ketchup. "Rinus?"

De Gier turned back. "Now what?"

"Eat."

"Bah," de Gier said.

15

JURRIAANS GAZED AT DE GIER. "GOOD EVENING, GENERAL." He inclined his head. "So you are a real cop after all. Hard to believe. The uniform looks good on you."

"What did you believe before?"

"I thought," Jurriaans said, "that you had slipped in from some movie studio during the period that cops were still heroes. What can I do for you?"

"I'm reporting for duty."

Jurriaans bent over his clicking teletype. "Then you shouldn't be here. You should be in the south of the city. Riots again. Squatters who don't want to leave villas. We've got tanks helping us there, to crush the barricades."

De Gier read the message too. "Tanks indeed. Guns too?"

"They took the guns off, but one house is on fire and there are some wounded. And a dead Pekingese. Got crushed by an armored car. A lady's companion, with hair combed over its pop eyes. Nobody gets any respect anymore. Why don't you join the fray, before they get a Chihuahua?"

"I've got something else to do," de Gier said. "Dead pimp, remember? To patrol the area in order to acquaint myself with the local atmosphere."

"True," Jurriaans said. "Ketchup and Karate will be ready in a moment. You might help them with their report meanwhile. I didn't accept their previous attempt because the charge wasn't correctly stated. They're in their own room, at the end of the corridor."

De Gier found the room. The constables were huddled over a typewriter. He read the heading of their report: "Bicycle Without Rear Light." "You still bother with that?"

"Not really," Karate said, "but this bicycle belongs to a pimp. We've got to apply all available laws, so that the bad guys know we're still around."

De Gier read on. "Why was he on a bicycle? Something the matter with his Ferrari?"

Ketchup pushed the typewriter away and emptied a watering can into potted plants. "The suspect drives an antique Bentley, but we have a parking problem here and it's easier to collect his whores' earnings on a bicycle. Am I doing this right, Karate? The fern gets a lot and the little round leaves just a drop?"

"Other way around, I think." Karate typed on, poking at the keys with two fingers. "This is quite a complicated report, sergeant. The suspect's bicycle was equipped with a rear light but the generator hadn't been pushed against the tire because the suspect claimed the squeaking makes him nervous. Pimps are sensitive types, as you know. Makes it difficult for us. We were charging him with not having the light, while in fact it was there, but not working, and according to Sergeant Jurriaans we have to apply another article that states the charge more precisely but carries a lower fine."

"You're just irritating the citizen," de Gier said.

Karate arranged carbon paper between two sheets and started on the continuation of his report. "Not at all. When we're done with this, we'll think of something else to bother the suspect."

Ketchup picked up a plant and poured water from its pot into its neighbor. "And if we can't come up with something suitable, we'll just ring his bell to tell him that we haven't come to arrest him."

Adjutant Adèle came in. De Gier got up. She nodded. He sat down again.

"The plants are doing well, adjutant," Ketchup said. "I'll be giving them their vitamins tomorrow. The fern is trying to grow, it seems."

"You're drowning them again," Adjutant Adèle said. She read through the report. "My, haven't you been busy? And what was with the lady you've just dragged to the cells? Had she left her garbage can out after sundown?"

"The suspect was intoxicated," Ketchup said, "and talking to herself. She was also barefoot."

"Did you apply handcuffs?"

"She had driven her car into a tree, adjutant, and the car didn't have any license plates. And she pissed on the floor here."

"Bah," Karate said. "We were polite enough, and she had to wait a moment because the rest rooms were occupied. But she couldn't control herself and pissed straight into her pants. A silly suspect. I mean, you people also have muscles to close the opening, just like we have, haven't you?"

"That'll be enough," Adjutant Adèle said.

"And I was allowed to mop up the mess," Ketchup said, "because I had brought the lady in. It's always the street crew that has to do the work, and the inside staff sort of lolls about."

Adjutant Adèle left the room. De Gier watched her leave.

"Yes," Ketchup said.

"Yes what?" De Gier asked.

"The way you were watching the adjutant. I agree with you. Ladies are more sensuous, after all."

"The reserved approach wins in the end," Karate said.

"Madeleine could carry herself like that," Ketchup said. "She would never openly invite a man, but she did sit in a display window and if you had the money and looked decent you could get into her. Most of them smile and show a bit of flesh—that seems okay, but it turns you off after a while."

"Adjutant Adèle," de Gier said, "does not fit in the category on principle. Anyway, she has a friend."

"How did you manage to find that out so quickly?" Karate asked.

"A black Ph.D., Reserve Sergeant John Varé."

"Straight A's," Ketchup said. "But the Murder Brigade employs our best brains. You've also been told that Sergeant Varé is married?"

"He's being told now," Karate said. "By little blabbermouth himself."

A big man stumbled backward into the room and upset Karate's table. Karate was thrown against the wall. A second man, as big as the first, held on to the door post. He bled from his ear. Three constables wrestled themselves past him and pulled the first man to his feet.

The first man resisted. The second man attacked the first. The men punched each other and were punched by the constables.

"What's this?" shouted Ketchup and Karate.

The two men called each other names while they grappled. The constables pulled them apart. De Gier grabbed the first man and turned him toward a constable. Handcuffs clicked.

"That's one," de Gier said. "What happened to the other?"

The other lay on the floor. De Gier bent down and pulled

him to his feet. "Thank you, sergeant," one of the constables said. "Come along, men."

"But what seems to be the trouble?" de Gier asked.

"This one," the constable said, "the one with the swelling eye, is a youth of shame, and this one, with the bleeding mouth, is his customer. Mouth picked up Eye, in the Alley of the Crazy Nun. We saw the meeting from our patrol car but took no action since it's all right for two citizens to meet. When we saw them again, the meeting had become a fight, and when we made inquiries, we were told that Eye promised certain favors, and received a suitable payment in advance, but did not execute the favors properly, or so says Mouth."

"Fairies?" Karate said. "Such well-developed gentlemen?"

"My typewriter is broken," Ketchup said, "and my chair lost a leg. Would you mind stating that in your report?"

"I certainly will," the constable said. He turned to the prisoners. "Forward, march." He left the room.

"An efficient and also polite constable," de Gier said.

"A reserve cop," Karate said. "They don't know any better. Now all I have to do is get me another typewriter and another chair and type the report once more, because everybody wiped his footsies on the last version. And if there's still any time left, we might even go on patrol."

"I lost a button off my tunic," de Gier said. "Any needles and thread in this station?"

"Adjutant Adèle," Ketchup said. "I'll show you the way."

"Here's the needle," Adjutant Adèle said, "and here's the thread. You're on your own."

De Gier closed one eye.

"Very well. Now take it through your button and make a loop."

"Like this?"

"Right again. Now insert the needle into the material."

"Sergeant de Gier?" Ketchup asked. "You're wanted at the counter. Sergeant Jurriaans is asking for you."

De Gier followed Ketchup. "And the button?" asked Adjutant Adèle.

"Would you mind?"

"I'll oblige," Adjutant Adèle said. "But perhaps I shouldn't. If men could learn to take care of themselves and not to invade our space at inopportune times, there might be more balance and less conflict."

"The adjutant is an asshole," Ketchup said in the corridor.

"But lovely."

"A lovely asshole," Ketchup said.

"This gentleman," Sergeant Jurriaans said, "is a friend of our station and his name is Slanozzel. And this sergeant is also a friend of this station and his name is de Gier."

De Gier shook the offered slender sunburned hand and noted that Slanozzel had risen above the bourgeoisie, was no longer young, dressed expensively but well and carried a facial expression that could be defined as friendly, dignified, and experienced.

"Good evening," de Gier said.

"Mr. Slanozzel," Jurriaans said, "owned, up till half an hour ago, a wallet that contained his papers and a goodly sum of money. He visited with a local woman in the Saltstreet."

"Perhaps he will visit her again," de Gier said, "in my presence. I'll be right back. I left my tunic upstairs."

De Gier ran up the stairs. The adjutant was done. "Thank you," de Gier said. "Would you happen to know who Mr. Slanozzel may be?"

"Such a dear," Adjutant Adèle said. "Is he downstairs? I'll go and greet him."

"Not now, adjutant. There's a problem. What do you know about him?"

"A businessman residing on the island of Curaçao in the Caribbean. Owns factories on the South American mainland, in Colombia and Venezuela. Deals in junk metals and skins, tanned in Barranquilla. Wealthy, and a regular visitor to the quarter."

"Business?"

"Pleasure."

"Why does he copulate here and not where he lives?"

"He'll copulate there too," Adjutant Adèle said, "but he has sentimental ties with this city. He was born here but escaped just before the war broke out."

"Jewish?"

"Yes." Her nostrils flared. "So?"

De Gier showed his profile. "I have a Jewish grandmother. Do admire the gentle curve of my nose."

Slanozzel was still at the counter. De Gier saluted. "I'm all yours. Shall we go?"

"A peculiar feeling," Slanozzel said, strolling along with the sergeant. "To be without means all of a sudden. And without identification, which makes me a nonperson." He grinned. "Not a bad idea, don't you think? Nameless? Transparent? Like a statue made out of compressed air?"

"But you do want your papers back?"

"I do, sergeant. The liberty which the undefinable offers frightens me. I haven't seen you here before. Are you new to this station?"

"I work with the Murder Brigade."

"The Obrian case?"

"Yes, Mr. Slanozzel. You knew the victim?"

"We talked at times. A disgrace to his people, sergeant, and he could have been a gift. A most outstanding man. This is the Saltstreet, and there's the lady we want to speak to, on her way to her car."

De Gier ran after the woman and touched her shoulder. "Ma'am, I want a word with you. In your room. Lead the way."

The woman's hair had been dyed yellow. She had small eyes in a narrow face extenuated by a high forehead. Her skin seemed pulled too tightly over her skull.

"I didn't do anything." She unlocked the door. "And I don't know that man. Is he with you?"

"We'll talk inside."

The woman switched on a red lamp and closed the curtains. "Isn't this more cozy? What do you two want of me?"

"Can we sit down?"

A missing tooth showed in her smile. "You can lie down too. Two at a time? Quick or slow?"

"This man visited you about half an hour ago."

"Yes? I never remember faces."

"And Sergeant Jurriaans sends his regards. Don't make things too hard on yourself."

The woman sat on the edge of her chair and dug her nails into the material of her short skirt. "The client wasn't properly satisfied?"

"No complaints," Slanozzel said. "But you might return my wallet."

The woman looked at the floor.

"Been working here awhile?" De Gier asked.

"Just started, and in trouble already."

"Where are you from?"

"Rotterdam."

"So am I," De Gier said. "I was born on the Duke's Wall."

She tried another smile. "Me on the Resident's Alley."

"That's around the corner."

"Yes. But you've lost the accent."

"Been here too long."

She took cigarettes from her bag, hesitated, but extended the packet to the sergeant. "You smoke?"

"Please."

"And you?"

"No, thank you," Slanozzel said. "I'm fighting a cough."

She lit de Gier's cigarette. "That Jurriaans has a good reputation. The women here say so. He always helps, when there's trouble with the customers or with the sharks who rent us our rooms."

De Gier put out his hand. "The wallet, please?"

She studied a broken fingernail. "There'll be a charge?"

De Gier looked at Slanozzel.

Slanozzel adjusted the golden clasp of his silk tie. "If the wallet comes back, I'll forget I ever missed it."

"Ma'am?" de Gier asked.

The woman got up. "I threw it away."

De Gier got up too. "Over a wall?"

"Yes. You'll have to climb it."

De Gier returned with the woman. "Here you are, sir." He looked at the woman. "The money is in your bag?"

"Here you are," the woman said.

"I wish there was something I could do to show my gratitude," Slanozzel said back in the station.

"There's no need," Sergeant Jurriaans said. "Our services are funded by the taxpayers."

"I don't pay any tax, since officially I have no fixed abode. There are times that I'm proud of my clever evasions, but an occasion like this clouds my conscience."

"We all feel guilty," Jurriaans said. "To live with guilt strengthens character."

De Gier looked at his watch. "I'll have to go."

Slanozzel walked with the sergeant. "Are you doing well with the Obrian case?"

"We have some ideas, sir. Too vague for definition at this point."

"I have an ear for languages," Slanozzel said, "and I often go to Surinam. I can't say I'm fluent in their lingo, but I can understand most of what they say. I had a beer this afternoon in a bar frequented by blacks."

"You heard something?"

"Obrian's death was exhaustively discussed."

"Were any names mentioned?"

"Lennie?" Slanozzel asked. "Gustav? Two other pimps. I've met them both."

"You think they are capable of machine gunning Obrian?"

"Certainly," Slanozzel said, "but pimps are sneaky lads. A knife in the back, and the corpse slowly floating in a canal, a little more likely than a volley of automatic bullets within reach of a police station."

"What else did the blacks say?"

"They were discussing rules," Slanozzel said, "that Obrian would have broken—broken in two ways, an older man said."

"This is an unruly neighborhood, Mr. Slanozzel."

"Even chaos is subject to certain laws, sergeant. I'll turn left here. I think I'll have a nightcap on the Eastern Canal before I go to bed."

De Gier looked down. "Again?"

Slanozzel looked about his feet. "Did you see anything, sergeant?"

"Over there in the shadow," de Gier said. "A black cat. That's the umpteenth time we've met today, and she keeps staring at me."

De Gier squatted next to the cat. The cat pushed herself against the wall and crept along it. The sergeant put out a finger. The cat sniffed at its tip. "Hellish sprite," de Gier said lovingly. "Mean, aren't you? With your nasty yellow slit-eyes?"

The cat closed her eyes and rubbed her head against his hand.

"A real woman," Slanozzel said. "I take it you are good with women?"

"On rare occasions," de Gier said, "I am still successful." He pushed his hand under the cat's chest, lifted the animal, and made her turn over in his arm.

"I'll be off," Slanozzel said. "I'm glad I leave you in good company."

The cat purred and sighed. De Gier put her down again. Her long legs gave way so that she fell on her side. She meowed softly.

"Aren't quite done yet?"

The cat meowed louder.

"Some other time," de Gier said. "I have work to do, if you'll excuse me."

16

"RIGHT," GRIJPSTRA SAID, "THAT'S WHAT I LIKE TO SEE. A nonrestored gable leaning against another. This ruin is the goal of our search?"

"Hotel Hadde," de Gier said. "Dilapidated and dirty. A festering hole of the netherworld wherein evil leers nastily. But what is evil?"

Grijpstra scratched his bottom.

"You do that too?" de Gier asked.

"At times," Grijpstra said. "When I'm bothered by my own ignorance, as you are so often. How can I, a good man, be fascinated by evil?"

"You're a good man?"

Grijpstra's heavy head fell forward a little. "You think I'm bad?"

"Bad? No."

"You think I'm kind of colorless? Neither the one nor the other?"

"You're active on the good side," de Gier said, "which might have influenced your general character."

"And in my private life? What about the way in which I deal with others? With my superiors, equals, subordinates? My wife, children? Suspects?"

"We're on duty right now."

"Don't evade the well-meant question."

"Let's see," de Gier said. "I don't think you're bad. No. Not bad, I would say."

"So I must be good," Grijpstra said. "But I could be better, which isn't what we are getting into now. But I still liked that little tale you told me a minute ago, about the tanks rumbling through the south of the city. Great green machines of death, grinding the tarmac. The image is bad, however. Tanks are symbols of wicked power. A deluge of violence which I find fascinating."

"And the mashed Pekingese?"

"Another delightful picture. Horrifying of course, but almost subtly beautiful, I would dare to say."

"Yes," de Gier said. "Pulverized Pekingese. *Yecch.*"

"I shouldn't admit to my perverted taste. Where's Cardozo?"

"Wasn't he with you?"

Grijpstra looked at his watch. "He's supposed to meet us here. I do believe I made him angry again. He kept turning around me, and I sent him to the kitchen to wash dishes."

"Something torments him," De Gier said.

"Yes, and I didn't want to know what. That boy does talk too much. He's also too noisy, banging about in the kitchen. I shouted at him and he ran out of the house."

Grijpstra climbed the crumbling and moss-grown steps leading to the old house. "Pity you're not in uniform, sergeant. You look smart when you're officially dressed. I'll mention it to Propaganda, maybe they'll put you on a poster."

De Gier pushed the rickety door of the establishment.

"Belligerent but sympathetic? So how come I always feel like a fool when I'm in uniform?"

Grijpstra looked about suspiciously in the smoky room before pushing his way through clustered customers.

"Señores?" asked a morose hunchback. Grijpstra looked into the tired eyes under the bedraggled mustache. "Spanish?"

"Si señor, a sus órdenes."

"Cerveza, por favor."

"Y usted?" said the hunchback, addressing de Gier.

"Speak Spanish," Grijpstra said, "like I did just now. Spanish is easy and it'll make him feel better."

"Un wiski americano," said de Gier, *"pero un poco de calma con el hielo. El wiski de la marca Pavo Salvaje."*

"Como no, señor?"

"Don't overdo it," Grijpstra said.

"I thought you wanted me to speak Spanish," de Gier said. "Wasn't it you who sent me to the class Jurriaans taught? Languages are useful in our profession."

"You don't have to be fluent."

"Jurriaans is fluent."

"Jurriaans is a genius," Grijpstra said. "Besides, his wife is Spanish."

"Was," de Gier said.

"Because she left him? She must still be around somewhere. Hello, Cardozo, you're late."

Cardozo tried out a chair. He put it aside and took another. "Do you know there's war in the south of the city? Tanks versus squatters?"

"Ignore it," de Gier said. "We're working on pimps."

"Señor?" the waiter asked.

"Un martini," Cardozo said, *"con ginebra pura inglesa y un poquitiquitito de vermouth."*

"What is the pokeeteekeeteeto?" Grijpstra asked.

"The merest dash," Cardozo said. "You've got to say that or

they'll kill your drink by sugaring it and drowning the olive. Did you see Gustav?"

"I recognized him," de Gier said. "Man with the bangs. I saw him driving about earlier on in his spiffy sleigh, and now he's at the bar."

"Did you go out to watch the war?" Grijpstra asked. "How were the tanks doing?"

"Very well. Crunching the barricades. A sight for sore eyes. And our own helmeted robots bashing away."

"You like that, do you?"

"Not at all," Cardozo said. "Isn't Gustav an oily specimen? An expert at changing innocent country girls into mangy sluts. Feeds them on cut heroin. Who is the tropical squire sitting next to him?"

"A certain Slanozzel," de Gier said. "I've just found some of his money. He left it with a whore and Jurriaans made me recover the loot."

"So why is he ignoring you?" Grijpstra asked. "He saw you just now but he looked away again."

"So as not to interfere with my work."

"More," Cardozo said. De Gier explained.

"That Jurriaans," Grijpstra said, "is worth more than I gave him credit for. The man keeps amazing me. The ideal cop."

"Who lets things go?" de Gier asked. "That whore stole quite a package from Slanozzel, but I didn't even charge her. Maybe she'll do it again tomorrow."

"So why didn't you arrest her? You were the officer taking care of the incident."

"I didn't think an arrest would please Jurriaans," de Gier said. "I might have charged her if I'd been on my own, but I was trying to fit in with the local way of keeping order."

Grijpstra grunted.

"What would *you* have done, adjutant?" Cardozo asked.

"Please, Simon."

Cardozo chewed his olive. "Yes?"

Grijpstra scowled.

"Yes, adjutant?"

Grijpstra sighed. "Do I have to spell it out again? Why cause more trouble when we're trying to do away with trouble? Why fill up the jails? Whores are necessary, they absorb male aggression. Why close the gate?"

"The female gate," de Gier said. "I'll take you to the Municipal Museum when this case is done. There's an exhibit there that will clarify the adjutant's statement. An enormous statue of a naked woman, naked and with her legs apart. There's a door between her legs, which is always open. You can walk into her, out of your own misery. Don't you think that's nice?"

"I'll have to think about it," Cardozo said. "Hello."

"Hello," said the young man who had taken a seat between Grijpstra and Cardozo. He smiled at Grijpstra, nodding subserviently. A golden ornament dangled from his ear. "Hello, adjutant."

"Have we met?" Grijpstra asked. "I don't remember the arrest."

De Gier leaned forward and studied the young man's eyes, accentuated by mascara, and his mouth, painted beyond its true size. "Are you Karate's sister?"

"I'm Karate himself," Karate said. "But I'm known here, so I've changed myself."

"For shame," Grijpstra said. "I'll tell your chief."

Karate pouted. "Sergeant Jurriaans painted me up himself, and the wig came from his very own box of tricks. Have you seen Gustav? He who hunts elephants twice a year with a cannon?"

"We did," de Gier said. "He doesn't look happy."

Karate grinned."He'll be unhappier tomorrow."

"I say," Cardozo said, and was interrupted by the waiter, who smiled at Karate. *"Señorita?"*

"Tenga la bondad," Karate said. *"Un destornillador con más vodka que jugo de naranja."*

"By the way . . ." Cardozo said.

"He really hunts elephants?" Grijpstra asked. "Is that a pimpish pastime? I thought they flew small planes or played polo mostly."

"Elephants are more expensive," de Gier said.

"Can I say something?" Cardozo asked.

"There's Crazy Chris," Karate said, "working on a triple genever."

"I thought Crazy Chris drank methylated spirits," de Gier said.

"Not since social security," Karate said.

"I would rather think—" Cardozo shouted.

"Shsh," said Karate.

"—that we should discuss our procedure," whispered Cardozo. "We are engaged in looking for the killer of Luku Obrian, isn't that right?"

His audience stared.

"And we have decided, after much deliberation, that the murderer must be Gustav."

"There's no obligation," de Gier said.

"Because if Gustav fails us, we still have Lennie?"

"Right again," Karate said.

"And we choose to ignore that perhaps, maybe, somewhere on a far horizon, a possibility tends to exist that another suspect could be involved?"

"Do go on," Grijpstra said.

"Perhaps I went too far already," Cardozo said. "Maybe I'm being busy again, as I shouldn't, as I'm always told. I'm only an assistant in the brigade and not supposed to dabble in theories. I'm to ascertain facts only. But the facts do seem to raise a small question."

"Which is?" de Gier asked.

"You see Crazy Chris over there?"

"I do."

"Now, isn't he the same Crazy Chris who ventured to inform the staff of the local station that he saw no one flee from the burned-out corner building after Luku Obrian had been separated from his black soul?"

"Why black?" Grijpstra asked.

"Because that was the actual color, adjutant. Because the color matters in this case. And the suspect who Crazy Chris did see after all was of the same shade—clothes-wise, that is."

"Hold it," Karate said. "Crazy Chris isn't called crazy because he is sane. He will tell you whatever you like to hear. When he ran into our station, he hadn't seen a suspect. We rushed out at once. *We* means every cop available at that moment, which was about eight of us. We ran about everywhere and we alarmed the patrol cars. Everybody who happened to be in the neighborhood was questioned thoroughly."

"Including three roller-skating gentlemen?" de Gier asked.

"Tell me again about the suspect seen by Crazy Chris," Grijpstra said.

"Dressed in a black cape," Cardozo said. "Face hidden under a floppy black hat. Walked strangely because of oversized shoes."

"The phantom went where?" de Gier asked.

"Turned right after leaving the Olofs-alley, then followed the Seadike. Crazy Chris didn't follow the suspect because he isn't crazy enough to invite machine-gun fire."

"And why," asked Karate, "would Chris, who is crazy, I stress that fact to make sure that it will penetrate"—Karate tapped his wig—"hoohoo in the head, now why would Chris tell you a different story than he told us?"

"Crazy Chris belongs to the other side, not to our side," Cardozo said.

"Aren't you on our side?" de Gier asked. "Why would Crazy Chris tell you?"

"He's also Jewish, and so am I," said Cardozo.

"Don't look so angry," de Gier said. "We're all good friends, sharing a drink in this cozy establishment."

"Last question," Cardozo said. "Tomorrow we plan to catch Gustav. Right? Karate?"

"That's right."

"But now, respected colleague, do tell me how you can be so sure. Does Gustav misbehave so consistently that he can be arrested at any time we choose?"

"You forget," Karate said, "that the quarter is mine. I can feel the undercurrents so well that I can sometimes predict what will happen."

"How good of you," Grijpstra said, "that you allow us to be of some assistance."

"No," Karate said. "I didn't mean it that way. This is another type of district, different from the rest of the city. Just look out of the window please, adjutant. What do you see? Three whores showing themselves off under a street-light. That's strictly illegal, for the law says that prostitutes may not solicit within a hundred yards of the entrance to a bar. Now, look at the bar where we happen to be, and check your watch. After hours. They shouldn't be serving here, but they are. Do you know how many gambling joints you passed on your way here? And how many drug dealers and junkies? Does the law permit drugs to be sold? Is it legal for the addicted to inject themselves in public?"

His audience drank.

"It is not," Karate said.

"It is in-between," Grijpstra said. "Those who govern us know that not only we, but that they themselves are not what humanity pretends to be. They therefore allow the unpermitted under special circumstances and they do so at our own request, for this is a free country and we choose the executors of our own laws ourselves and whisper into their ears how we would like the rules to be applied."

"And Gustav?" asked Cardozo.

Grijpstra lit a cigar. "Gustav goes too far."

"In the Argentine . . ." said Cardozo.

"*Tabaco*," said the waiter, pointing at Grijpstra's cigar. Grijpstra looked at his cigar and raised his eyebrows. "*Que no*," said the waiter, and pointed at the ashtray.

"You're not supposed to smoke cigars in here," Karate said. "Maybe you should put it out."

"Why?" asked Grijpstra. "What could be wrong with this splendid cigar?" He pulled the tin out of his pocket and read the text printed on the inside of its lid. "*Empregando liga de legitimo fumo do Brasil, des melhores procedencias.*"

The waiter leaned on Grijpstra's shoulder. He put up a finger and waved it in front of the adjutant's face. "*Aqui no. La señora no lo permite.*"

"The waiter only speaks Spanish," Karate said, "and what you were reading was Portugese. He doesn't understand Portuguese."

"*Que no, que no, que no,*" the waiter shouted in Grijpstra's ear.

"The poor fellow is having a fit," de Gier said. "There's enough going on already. Why don't you put out that cigar?"

Grijpstra screwed his cigar into the ashtray.

"Thank you," Karate said.

Grijpstra pointed at Karate's cigarette. "What are you

complaining about? That's pretty strong tobacco you're burning there."

"It's cigars Mrs. Hadde objects to," Karate said. "And if you hadn't done as you were told, we would have been out on our ear. In which case my wig would have come off and I would have been shown up as an idiot again."

"And who would have thrown us out?" Cardozo asked. "The hunchbacked dwarf?"

"Mr. Hadde."

Grijpstra peered through the smoke in the room. "All I see is a painted skeleton with frayed rope ends on her moldy skull.'

"That's Mrs. Hadde," Karate said. "Mr. Hadde is resting."

"So how can he throw out customers while he rests?"

"Mr. Hadde is quite gifted."

"Are they making trouble at the bar?" Grijpstra asked. "Hey, watch where you're going."

A bald man whose leather suit was decorated with chains crashed into their table, pushed by surging combatants and tripped up by the leg of a little old drunk dressed in an outmoded worn coat and whose head, hidden under a wide-brimmed felt hat, rested on his chest. A small metal flag, consisting of a red-white-and-blue tin plate attached to rusted wire, fell on the floor. The intruder stumbled back. Grijpstra bent down and picked up the flag, pressing it back into shape with his thumb. "Shouldn't trample the flag, you know."

"Want to be bashed?" the man asked.

De Gier raised his lanky body. "We are terribly sorry, sir, that you crashed into our table. It won't happen again."

The intruder shook shaky fists.

Cardozo was getting up too. Karate pushed him back and smiled. "Flower power," he said to the man. "Love. Ban the bomb. Let's surrender to communism. Kill the Americans."

The intruder patted Karate's wig. "That's my boy." He staggered back to the bar.

"The pimps are a bit nervous," Karate said. "The prince of the quarter is no more, and they're trying not to die with him. Identification with the victim."

The order around the bar decreased further. Karate indicated the yelling mob. "Why don't you all watch Mrs. Hadde now. Can you see her?"

"She's growing," Grijpstra said.

"She's climbing steps so that she can reach the little doors behind the bar. She knocks on the doors, see?"

"They must hide a built-in bedstead," de Gier said.

"And a built-in baboon," said Cardozo.

"In pajamas," Grijpstra said, "striped flannels. You don't see that type of pajamas much these days."

"That's no baboon," de Gier said, "that's a gorilla. Hairy all over. A gorilla with a cudgel in his fetid fists."

"That's Mr. Hadde," Karate said.

Mr. Hadde veered down and up again, with one hand on the counter. He hopped over the bar. Mrs. Hadde pointed at customers. Mr. Hadde raised his stick.

"He isn't going to kill them, is he?" Grijpstra asked.

"No," Karate said. "They haven't paid yet."

The clients put notes into Mrs. Hadde's hand. It was quiet in the room and the silence became eerier. The clients had frozen in uncomfortable attitudes. The waiter leaned against the bar, chewing a match.

"Out," Mr. Hadde said softly.

The clients selected by the raised cudgel tiptoed to the door.

"Hop," whispered Mr. Hadde.

The pimps sneaked faster. The door banged behind them. Mr. Hadde scaled the bar again, extended an arm to the edge of the bedstead, swung himself inside, and closed the doors behind him.

A clock without hands hung under the bedstead. Mrs. Hadde's bony hand ticked against its cracked glass. She shrieked, "Time to leave."

"See you tomorrow," Karate said.

"I'm going to bed," Cardozo said. "I've thought much today and understood little. I'm very tired."

"I would rather go for a walk," Grijpstra said. "Care to join me, sergeant?"

"I'd rather turn in too," de Gier said. "Can I walk with you, Simon, or are you still upset?"

"I'm not upset," Cardozo said to the sergeant walking next to him. "I'm mixed up." He caressed de Gier's arm. "Tell me all is in order Rinus."

De Gier admired ducks bobbing sleepily on the canal.

"Rinus?"

"All is *not* in order," de Gier said.

17

Grijpstra strolled steadily along. The alcohol that hides under merry beer foam had washed his fatigue away but the mental no-man's-land that it had cleared provided little room for detached rumination. Amazing, Grijpstra thought, this is my best time, the streetlights are off and the sun not yet on and the city is at rest.

He walked on, trying in vain to free himself from the memory of the hellish cave, but he kept seeing the skeleton behind the counter, and Mr. Hadde swinging his club. He also saw Karate; showing his female aspect, glancing at his superiors from amorous painted eyes, provoking them with pursed blood-red lips. The adjutant concentrated on the canal's hardly moving surface, reflecting wide elms, their freshly leaved branches calmly extended toward sedate silver gables. He looked at gulls, gliding down to the barely wrinkled water, and once afloat, changing into daintily arranged feather bundles.

Grijpstra tripped over a root and rearranged his balance by

wildly waving his arms. His wheeling arms disturbed a rat eating from a torn garbage bag. The adjutant grabbed a car mirror that gave way under his weight. The rat stayed where he was, tearing at chicken bones.

"Away," Grijpstra said, but the rat didn't move his naked pink legs. The rat was of a good size but nevertheless considerably smaller than the cat approaching him from the rear, flattened in the shadow of a wrecked handcart. The cat, a fighting tom, wide-chested and with a square head on which its torn and crusted ears lay low, crept on.

The cat jumped, the rat yelled, Grijpstra shouted. He tried to kick the living tangle, but the cat dragged its prey out of reach. The rat died as it squeaked. The cat turned the rat over and studied its soft belly.

Grijpstra leaned against a parked car hood and felt the mirror that his grip had loosened. The car was new. The adjutant scribbled on his visiting card: "Excuse. Please mail the bill, which will be paid promptly." He mumbled while he inserted the card behind a windshield wiper. "Tanks in the south of the city. Cat kills rat." Firmly decided now to ignore all further violence, he turned to determine the cause of the tearing sound. The cat had activated the next stage of its program and operated on the rat, neatly, with a single sharp nail stuck into the throat of its fellow animal, which it yanked toward itself. Grijpstra saw blood spurting from the slit.

It shouldn't be, the adjutant thought. But that's the way it is, he also thought. It cannot always be denied that violence takes place.

Here I am, a peaceful man who should be enjoying the mystery of daybreak, the mystic moment when darkness turns into light, when creation renews itself under the endless splendor of heaven's pale-blue cupola. I partake in the position of God Himself, when He set the wheel into motion, and I should be able to affirm that all is well, which I can't because it is not.

He lifted his foot to kick the aggressor and send him back to his dish heaped with hygienically manufactured pet food, but the cat hissed furiously. In order not to waste his movement, the adjutant kicked a carton standing next to the garbage bag.

The cat ate.

"Enough," howled Grijpstra. The cat snarled and swished the tip of its misshapen tail through the dust.

The adjutant hissed too, bent down, and showed the cat his fist. The cat ran away.

Grijpstra removed the lid of the carton and pushed in the rat's remnants, using the side of his shoe. He put the lid back, took the box under his arm, and walked on to the Newmarket, where he got into a waiting cab. The driver started his engine and turned his head. "Everything to your satisfaction tonight, sir?"

Grijpstra gave his private address. The driver hooked a thumb at the box on the rear seat. "What's in it?"

"A useful souvenir."

The cab sped along the Rokin. The driver's eyes showed in the rear mirror. "Not too fast for you, sir?"

"What?" Grijpstra asked. "No."

"It's all right to race at night," the driver said. "No traffic anyway. I mentioned the box just now because I was supposed to. Regulations, right?"

Grijpstra grunted.

"It's the police, you see," the driver said. "It seems that bad people transport parts of corpses at night, and the police want to know, so we tell them via our radio."

"You do?" Grijpstra asked. "Isn't that dangerous?"

"After the client has left the cab," the driver said. "Here you are."

"Wait for me," Grijpstra said. "I have to get something and will be back at once."

"Where do you want to go?"

"Back to the quarter."

"Sir does have energy," the driver said.

Grijpstra got out. He fetched a fishnet from his closet and walked down the stairs again. He heard the cab drive away. The box stood on the sidewalk. He was picking it up when a squad car turned the corner. Two constables jumped out.

"What's in the box?" One constable squatted; the other reached for his gun.

"If you don't touch anything," Grijpstra said, "you can have a little look."

"Flesh," the constable said, "and blood."

"Disgusting, isn't it?"

The other constable touched Grijpstra's net. "What do you want with that?"

"Three guesses," Grijpstra said.

The cop holding the gun spoke compassionately. "Now, sir, just turn around and hold your hands over your head." He felt the adjutant's pockets. "What's under your armpit?"

"My pistol," Grijpstra told the wall. "And there's a wallet in my inside pocket. You'll find my police card in the wallet. Don't touch the pistol or you'll tear my jacket."

The constable read the card. "Henk Grijpstra is the name, and adjutant the rank." He replaced the wallet.

"Sorry, adjutant. May I ask what you are up to tonight?"

Grijpstra dropped his arms and turned around. "You may ask. And because you've bothered me, you may take me to the Newmarket."

The patrol car stopped next to the waiting cab. Grijpstra walked away, box under one arm and fishnet under the other. The cabdriver left his car and walked over to the cruiser. "That's the man I was radioing about. You're releasing him again?"

"Yes," said the constable behind the wheel.

"But there was a bleeding mess in that box, didn't you look?"

"A dead rat, dissected."

"And he takes that to whores. He's just been to the whores. I picked him up there. What does he want with the net?"

"I don't believe I know," said the cop.

The driver watched Grijpstra's diminishing shape. "Pleasant-looking gent, too, but what he's doing should be forbidden. I get others of his type. A few days ago I had one, carrying an inflatable doll, also in a box. About the same time as now. My fare inflated the doll in my cab. You know the type of doll I mean? Like they sell in sex stores?"

"Yes?" asked the constable.

"And where did he want to go?" asked the other.

"To the southern park. Naughty, in a way. But this fellow is worse. The doll wasn't bleeding. Now, why is he coming back?"

"Driver?" Grijpstra asked.

The driver shrank back against the squad car.

"What's with you?" Grijpstra asked. "Have you forgotten that I didn't pay you?"

"That's fine, sir," the driver said. "Never mind. Go away."

"What are you doing?" Cardozo asked.

Grijpstra swept his net.

"Are you catching something?" Cardozo got out of his bed. "Can I help?"

"No," Grijpstra said.

"Going fishing, are you?"

"No," Grijpstra said.

Cardozo followed Grijpstra. "What's in the attic?"

"I don't care much. I'm going to the roof."

"What's in the box?"

"Hold the trapdoor," Grijpstra said. He turned the box over. "That was a rat, which I'm putting out to catch a vulture, see? With the net. From this staircase, while hiding under the trapdoor. Step aside now, because I have to get into position, to be ready when the vulture comes down."

"There are no vultures in Amsterdam, adjutant."

Grijpstra and Cardozo sat next to each other.

"We've been here for half an hour now," said Cardozo, "and it's close to five o'clock. Aren't you tired?"

"I'm not. There are no vultures in Amsterdam? So what's that flapping about?"

The vulture lowered itself carefully, shuffled around the rat's parts, and hacked its beak into the meat. "Aha," Grijpstra said. Cardozo pushed the trapdoor up. The net came down over the bird. "Got you!" Grijpstra shouted.

The adjutant stepped onto the roof, flattened the carton and pushed it under the net. "Give me a hand, Simon. Make sure the carton doesn't slip away."

"And if the vulture rips the net?"

"Then you grab his head."

"What's all this fuss?" de Gier called from the trapdoor. "I can't sleep when you stamp on the roof."

"We caught a vulture, sergeant."

De Gier looked at the bird caught in the net. "So you did. A bit smaller than I thought. What's the next step?"

"To the kitchen?" Grijpstra asked. "Put him in the garbage can? Sit on the lid?"

Cardozo sat on the lid. "What's a vulture doing in Amsterdam, adjutant?"

"I don't know," Grijpstra said. "But I want to find out. That's why I caught him. He flew over the Olofs-alley last night."

"You saw him too?" Cardozo asked de Gier.

"Yes."

"Why didn't you tell me?"

De Gier listened to the scratching of claws within the garbage can. "I prefer to keep my insanity to myself."

"Would the commissaris have seen the vulture?"

"Yes," de Gier said. "Very likely he did. Maybe that's why he took off for the healing baths."

"Peculiar," Cardozo said. "A black vulture flying above a black corpse."

"I know what species that bird belongs to," Grijpstra said. "We've got some in the zoo. They're from Surinam, but according to the legend on the cage, other South American countries have them too. Protected eaters of carrion, keep the roads clean."

The vulture squeaked. "Poor thing," Cardozo said. "Shouldn't he eat? He never got a chance to get at the dead rat. There's some salami in the refrigerator."

De Gier closed the kitchen door. "Let him out, let's see what he does."

The vulture hopped out of the can and shuffled about on the floor.

"He's tame," Grijpstra said. Cardozo cut slices off the salami and put them on the linoleum. The bird, bowing politely, hopped toward the food.

"A house vulture," Grijpstra said. "Knows how to behave himself. He belongs to somebody."

The vulture picked at Cardozo's trousers. Cardozo jumped back. "Ouch."

Grijpstra squatted. "He never harmed you, just pushed a little. Would the nice bird care for another helping?"

"But what fool would own a vulture?" de Gier asked. "Why don't we let the bird go and watch where he goes?"

"I can't fly," Grijpstra said, "and I don't want to walk about with a vulture on a leash. If that cabdriver sees me, he'll lose his mind. First a box full of dead rat and now . . . No."

"Rat?" de Gier asked.

"I tried to save a nice rat from a nice pussy, but the pussy killed the rat anyway, and as I was in need of carrion to catch a vulture, it all turned out well in the end."

The vulture jumped on the sink and looked out of the window. "He's not really bad looking." Cardozo said. "Eh? Vulture?"

The bird flapped its wings and looked around.

"Wildlife is protected," Cardozo said. "And rightfully so. This vulture should be free. Can we let him go, adjutant?"

Grijpstra felt in his pocket and put the little metal flag taken from Hotel Hadde on the table. He looked at the bird's legs.

"You want to mark him?" Cardozo said. "So that he can be differentiated from other vultures? I don't think there are too many vultures about."

Grijpstra folded the metal flag around the tough yellow skin and squeezed it closed while he stroked the bird with his other hand. The vulture squeaked softly. "Nice bird. Cardozo?"

"Adjutant?"

"Pick our pet up. We'll take him back to the roof."

Cardozo threw the bird into the air. The vulture fluttered away, came back and landed next to Grijpstra.

"Wants more salami," de Gier said. "Come on. Hop. You're free. Fly away." The bird hopped about undecidedly. The sergeant picked it up again. "One, two . . . *three*."

"He does fly high," Cardozo said. "I can hardly see him now."

"I can't see him at all," Grijpstra said. "You? Rinus?"

"Just about," de Gier said. "No, I've lost him too."

"I see him," Cardozo said. "He's circling, over there, this side of the Montelbaan's Tower, a little to the right. Now he's going down."

"Let's see," Grijpstra said. "What street is that? Old Waal? No, that would be more to the left."

"Straight-Tree-Ditch," de Gier said. "That's where he must

have landed. Well-known area. Doesn't that Nellie of yours live there?"

"Yes," Cardozo said. "Your girlfriend, adjutant."

Grijpstra observed Cardozo pensively.

"She is your girlfriend, right?" asked Cardozo. "That lady who used to run her own private bar and now owns a small hotel?"

"Hmm," Grijpstra said.

"Listen," de Gier said. "I've got to hunt pimps today, and Cardozo should have another sniff at the immediate area. Why don't you have a good time with Nellie? Have breakfast at your leisure and then maybe ask her if there might be a vulture living in the neighborhood."

"Yes," Cardozo said. "A vulture is a rare sight, or would he only be about in the very early morning? If he keeps early hours, your girlfriend might not know him."

"Breakfast," Grijpstra said. "And what about you two?"

"We'll all be right," de Gier said.

"Can I go with you?" Cardozo asked.

"No. You can go to bed. You're tired and you talk too much."

"Now what did I say wrong?" Cardozo asked when the adjutant was shaving in the bathroom. "She *is* his girlfriend, isn't she?"

"The wise hide their knowledge," de Gier said. "That overeagerness of yours, you've got to get rid of it. We've discussed that before. First one collects facts, then one ponders and considers, and then one may express a tentative opinion in a modest and hesitating manner."

"But aren't we among ourselves?" Cardozo asked.

"Also among ourselves," de Gier said.

18

KARATE SAT BEHIND HIS DESK AND GAZED INTO A MIRROR resting against a file carton. He had made up his eyes and unscrewed a lipstick to touch up his mouth. His modish jacket hung over the back of his chair, caressed by the long hairs of his neatly combed wig, and his silk shirt opened on a hairy chest sporting a gold locket displaying a full-length picture of a lady resembling the queen. The lady was nude.

De Gier coughed. Karate looked up. "Morning, sergeant."

De Gier's tall body filled the open door of the small office. The buttons on his tunic gleamed, his gun belt shone, the creases of his blue-banded dark trousers were knife-sharp and parallel, his shoes sparkled, his cap stuck neatly between his chest and forearm. He stooped and studied the locket. "Quite a stately woman, isn't she?"

"Morning, sergeant," Ketchup said. Ketchup's hair and been slicked up and sprayed with green and purple paint. His leather jacket was covered with tin advertising pins, his embroidered purple jeans were stuck in yellow plastic boots.

"Party today?" de Gier asked. "Your chief has a birthday?"

Karate jumped up and poured coffee into paper mugs. "No, sergeant, these are our hunting clothes. Aren't we going to grab Gustav? You'll have to get out of uniform too, and we'd like to borrow your car. Ours is marked as a squad car."

De Gier looked at clotted milk powder floating in his cup. "Sneaking up on the poor fellow? Three against one?"

"Two," Ketchup said. "We tossed a coin, and I lost. I'll take a bicycle and spot him from between the cars parked in front of his house. You and Karate'll be in your car, around the corner. As soon as Gustav leaves, I'll pass the news."

"Then what? Trail the suspect until he commits a traffic offense? Kick him in the shins and arrest him when he defends himself on a charge of harassing us? What sort of policemen are you two?"

"Never," Karate said. "Whatever made you think all that? We have proper plans."

"A surprise," Ketchup said. "Aren't you temporarily attached to our patrol? We know what we're doing and you only have to tag along. It'll be a change for you and maybe we can help you some other time."

De Gier drove the Volkswagen. Ketchup listened on his walkie-talkie.

"Hello?" asked the walkie-talkie.

"Here," said Karate.

"Gustav is getting into a blue Peugeot 203, I can't read the number plate from here. Not a new car, and a dent on the rear fender. Driving along Old Waal, direction Bent Waal."

"Good," grunted a deep voice.

"Who is that?" asked de Gier. "Who else is on that radio?"

"Going," Karate said.

"Good luck," said the walkie-talkie.

"Who was talking just now?" asked de Gier while the Volkswagen nosed around the corner.

"You see the Peugeot?"

De Gier increased speed. "Isn't Gustav driving a new Corvette?"

"Gustav has lots of cars," Karate said. "He drives a different one every day. Watch it, sergeant, that van is trying to slip between us." He spoke into the walkie-talkie. "Peugeot nearing Prince Hendrik Quay."

"I see him," the deep voice said. "He's in my mirror."

"Are you answering me or not?" de Gier asked. "Whose voice is that?"

"Orang Utan's, sergeant. He is riding ahead of us, on the East Dock Quay."

The Volkswagen followed the blue Peugeot along a curve. De Gier saw the white motorcycle ahead, ridden by the easily recognizable silhouette of the Ambonese motor cop. Orang Utan's almost square upper body made a ninety-degree angle with his rear mudguard. De Gier put his foot down to stay ahead of the pushy van. The Peugeot was driving faster too.

"Gustav saw Orang," Karate said. "Gustav smells blood. Did you see him sit up?"

"And now?"

"Just follow, sergeant. We're going to see something. Orang Utan is the best motor cop on the force."

The police Guzzi rode slowly, on the extreme right of the tarmac, almost touching the curb. Central Station came into view. A flight of pigeons slid down from one of the station's towers and landed on a barge in the river. The Peugeot braked and turned sharply to the right, making contact with Orang Utan's rear wheel. De Gier cursed. Karate cheered. The Volkswagen pulled to the left to stay away from the Peugeot. A bus klaxoned and cyclists rang their bells. The Peugeot shot forward. The police cycle roared onto the sidewalk, heeling over sharply. De Gier also drove onto the sidewalk. Orang Utan's gloved hand grabbed the brake on the cycle's handlebar. Orang Utan tried to readjust his machine's balance by leaning over to the left. The motorcyclist did straighten up and would have gotten back to the road if he hadn't had to change direction again to avoid a fat lady holding up her shopping bag to ward off disaster. Orang Utan applied both his brakes, but his machine rode on.

The cycle flew, seemingly aimed at a ship moored along the quay, but hit the water instead. De Gier wanted to get out of the car. "No," yelled Karate. "Get Gustav. I'll take care of this." He banged the door behind him. De Gier reversed around the screaming woman. The Volkswagen thumped off the sidewalk. The Peugeot was still visible, waiting between buses and trucks at Central Station's traffic lights. De Gier kept his hand on his klaxon while the car pushed its way through cyclists. He pulled the microphone toward him. "Headquarters, car three-fourteen."

"Car three-fourteen," said the soft well-articulated voice of a female radio constable.

"Colleague in trouble," de Gier said. "A motor cop, known as Orang Utan. De Ruyterquay, Central Station. Colleague has been willfully pushed into the river by a blue Peugeot, which I'm following now. West Dock Quay, heading west."

"That is understood."

"I'm driving an unmarked white Volkswagen, detective branch, Sergeant de Gier." He let the microphone dangle on its cord. The Volkswagen was behind the Peugeot. Gustav looked into his rear mirror. De Gier drew his pistol and waved it to the right. The Peugeot increased speed. De Gier kept following the small blue car, his hand on the klaxon, cursing at Gustav's tanned crown, contrasting with a fringe of floppy thin curls bleached by a southern and expensive sun.

Gustav drove through an orange light, de Gier followed through red. Hunter and prey reached the western throughway and their speedometers veered to illegal numbers. The little engines whirred, the minute shock absorbers creaked.

What happened just now, de Gier thought as his knuckles whitened on the steering wheel, was both a mean and out-and-out attempt at murder of a uniformed policeman. Or was it mere manslaughter if we assume Gustav's ignorance of a possible meeting with Orang Utan? Murder involves some premeditation. How premeditated was Gustav's attempt?

A fresh set of traffic lights approached rapidly. Both drivers snarled as they ignored the forbidding colors. The Peugeot's brake lights came on as the car heeled over. An ugly little cloud burst from its exhaust as the car spurted to the right. The Volkswagen skidded but found its direction again, snorting and burbling through a short tunnel.

Wonderful, de Gier thought, hitting his accelerator and brake by turns. This is just what I like doing. I no longer have to be concerned about measuring my activity; no bothering with proportions now, no thought for the civilians I endanger while they go about their lawful business. I revenge an assault on the state itself, and my violence is justified. The sergeant sneered while the raging compacts kept changing directions, negotiating the twisting turns of alleys. He laughed while cyclists flattened against fences, cars against lampposts, pedestrians against walls. Relentless pursuit, de Gier thought, pursuit of the perverted fiend, to be run down and terminated in cold blood, to be squashed and spattered, but I do have to get hold of him first.

Gustav's car was elusive. It kept appearing and fading. The alleys twisted back into themselves and the small cars met head-on, but the Peugeot reversed, turned, smashed the doors of a workshop, and appeared again, hurrying away, its tires squealing. The Volkswagen lost time, waiting for a woman gathering her toddler and exploded grocery bags. The Peugeot lost time too, further along the street, for a delivery boy hit it with a milk bottle that broke on its hood and spattered its contents against the windshield. Gustav switched on his wipers, but he had braked and provided the boy with an opportunity to shove his bicycle into the car's path. The cycle crumpled under the Peugeot, raising its broken spokes so that they could penetrate the pursuing Volkswagen's tires. An old woman screamed in despair as she watched her umbrella-javelin miss the demonic vehicles. A sporting lady, de Gier thought. I've seen her before, scratching my fenders with that same umbrella. I keep hitting the same streets. A bald man, running for a doorway, seemed familiar too. The sergeant honked his horn at a menacing truck, growling slowly out of a side street, aiming for the diminishing space between Peugeot and Volkswagen. The driver shook his fist. Gustav was being threatened too, by huddled pedestrians, advancing slowly, holding on to each other for strength. He aimed his car at them, revving his engine. Once again there was a blur of red brick walls, spaced by gaping holes and scraggly trees, but the alley was a dead end terminating in a high fence partly obscured by stacked gray garbage bags.

The Peugeot dug into the flimsy mass and emerged flying a streamer of used sanitary napkins from its aerial before bumping posts and tearing boards. It bounced free, into a muddy field. Its wheels screamed before grabbing hold on clustered weeds. The car slithered about, missing the Volkswagen several times. Behind the field the river surface glistened, but de Gier couldn't see the sparkling water, for assorted rubbish covered his windshield. The sergeant cursed, got out, and listened to the last air hissing from his tires. He was out of luck now. Gustav would get away; the Peugeot was racing back to the broken fence.

Gustav couldn't see either. His wipers were smearing a

greenish fluid on his windshield. The Peugeot hit a stack of moldy insulation material. Gustav jumped out and ran toward the river. De Gier ran too. Gustav stumbled and fell. De Gier wanted to jump on top of Gustav but stumbled himself, rolled over on his shoulder, and got back on his feet. Gustav crawled out of reach. "Hold it." De Gier shouted. "Or be shot."

The sergeant fired, aiming the ever-ready modern Walther pistol at a shrub, which he hit, for the Walther, according to the instruction sheet, will hit any target at less than two hundred meters' distance. The bang of a cartridge filled with high-powered explosives should have stopped the fugitive, but Gustav never heard the crack; a freighter plowing the river noisily while hooting its powerful horn erased all other sounds.

Gustav was up, jogging frantically, and de Gier knelt, took aim carefully, and squeezed the trigger gently. Now, he thought, another thousandth of an inch, and *wham*. No wham; the trigger clicked back into its original position. The sergeant's nail ticked against the trigger's guard. Why? de Gier thought while he got up. Why wound the bastard? I know who he is. I'll catch him some other time. He's not attacking me; on the contrary, he's running away. He's running nowhere; there's only the field, and the river beyond. A bit of sport; let's honor the rules. He reholstered his gun.

Gustav fell and disappeared.

De Gier looked down the decline of the dike. "Gustav?"

Gustav rolled on. His falling body hit an iron rod stuck between cobblestones. Splendid fellow, the sergeant thought; your identity and address are known, you can be arrested later, but I want to do it right now.

Gustav bounced off the rod and hit a rock farther below. De Gier followed slowly, holding on to cracks between the stones. He grabbed Gustav by the collar and yanked carefully.

It took ten minutes of pulling and slithering, hoisting and finding the right leverage before Gustav was back on the field, lying on his back, between yellow flowers on high stems swaying in the breeze. De Gier knelt next to his prisoner.

"Asshole," said de Gier.

"Pain," said Gustav.

"Pain where?"

"My leg. I broke it on that rod."

De Gier stuck his finger in a tear of Gustav's trousers and ripped. He looked at a bloody bone sticking through pale pimply skin.

"You won't run away, now," de Gier asked, "while I get back to my car and order the care you don't deserve?"

Gustav whimpered. The sergeant patted Gustav's shoulder. "Do you know that I'm sorry for you? I must be crazy." He got up and walked to the Volkswagen. The car's engine was still running and its engaged gear made it shuffle forward in a wide circle, dragging on its flat tires. De Gier turned the key and pressed the microphone's button.

"Headquarters? Car three-fourteen."

"Car three-fourteen," said the soft female voice.

"An ambulance, please," said de Gier. "Somewhere beyond the end of Woodman's Alley, on a field with yellow wildflowers. And colleagues, lots of them, for my car is done for and I should have a mob after me soon; we may have caused some accidents."

"The suspect?"

"Wounded."

"Are you all right?"

De Gier sighed.

"Three-fourteen?"

"Right here," the sergeant said. "I think that I'll leave you now and throw up for a few minutes."

"My name is Marike," the gentle voice said. "Telephone me when you have time. Over and out."

19

CARDOZO DRAGGED HIMSELF UP THE POLICE-STATION STAIRS. The door flew open and hit him. Cardozo's arms swung up protectively and embraced the constable who came running out of the door. "Easy now," said Cardozo.

"Hurrah," shouted the constable.

"That happy?" asked Cardozo.

"Yes, sir," the constable said. "What can we do for you today? Have you been mugged? Did anyone sell you cowshit instead of hashish? Do you want to know where the healthy whores live? Are you drunk and do you want to be driven home? State your request. We'll take care of everything."

"It's me," said Cardozo.

The constable stepped out of Cardozo's embrace. "Ah, so it is. I didn't recognize you. How good to see you again."

"I want coffee," said Cardozo, "and cake."

"Be my guest, Simon, for today is a great day once again."

"I thought you were going somewhere," Cardozo said in the canteen. "You were running out of the station, remember?"

"I wanted to spread the good news. Here's your coffee. Here's your cake."

"Another superpimp has been shot?"

"Arrested," the constable said, "and wounded. Caught by your Sergeant de Gier, our hero. Hurrah."

"And why?"

"Haha," said the constable. He whispered, "You want to know why? Because that superpimp, our perverted fiend Gustav himself, attacked a colleague without the slightest provocation. Could it be better?"

"Tell me everything exactly."

The constable supplied details. "Well?"

"I see," Cardozo said.

"Well? Well? Well?"

"Would Sergeant Jurriaans happen to be in the station?" asked Cardozo.

"Upstairs. In his private office."

"Thanks for the coffee and cake." Cardozo got up.

"Do you have a minute, sergeant?" asked Cardozo.

Jurriaans indicated a chair.

Cardozo sat down. "Congratulations."

"You've heard the latest news?"

"Yes," Cardozo said. "And I heard more. May I tell you about it? And could I ask you a question afterward?"

"Anything you like." Jurriaans picked up the phone. "Coffee perhaps? Some cake?"

"No, thank you, sergeant." Cardozo took the offered cigarette. "I just visited the arms room at headquarters and was told by the sergeant that the bullets I handed in yesterday, that originated from the Schmeisser we were firing here on the shooting range, are identical to the bullets which were taken from Obrian's corpse."

Jurriaans nodded. "All Schmeissers take nine-millimeter bullets."

"No," Cardozo said. "Some scratches. Indentations, I think the sergeant said. My bullets and the killer's bullets came from the same weapon."

"Amazing."

"Isn't it?" Carodozo lit his cigarette. "Now, would you perhaps know how we managed to locate a Schmeisser when we happened to be looking for one?"

Jurriaans smiled helpfully.

"And never paid attention to the coincidence? Never wondered whether the Schmeisser we found was the Schmeisser we wanted?"

Jurriaans closed his eyes. "Absolutely amazing."

"You think it's just amazing?"

Jurriaans opened his eyes. "You wouldn't want to wait until your Sergeant de Gier returns?"

"No, I would not." Cardozo said. "And Sergeant de Gier isn't mine."

Jurriaans spread his hands on the blotter that lay in the exact center of his desk. He pushed his hands toward each other with some force. The soft green paper rose and cracked on the folds. "Right. Well. Where did the weapon come from? Hadn't Sergeant de Gier found it in the street?"

"No," said Cardozo. "That's what I told the arms room, but I was asked to lie on the sergeant's behalf."

"Now I know," Jurriaans said. "The Schmeisser had been found in a room occupied by Mr. Jacobs, *our* Mr. Jacobs, chief of the morgue. Didn't de Gier say that Jacobs wasn't right in the head and that society had to be defended against the madness that forced our Jacobs to keep an automatic gun in his room?"

"True," Cardozo said. "But can't we ask now whether society should also be protected against Sergeant de Gier's insanity? Can we really live quietly if the sergeant is allowed to create situations in which this fellow has to ride his motorcycle into the river and that fellow breaks his leg? Must we put up with a mind that is so deranged that it forces its owner to race his car through dense traffic, forces innocent civilians to climb lampposts and trees, old ladies to walk through store windows, insurance companies to pay out a fortune to cover dents?"

"Don't carry on," Jurriaans said. "Who cares about insurance companies except themselves? No one was wounded except Gustav, and Gustav is a perverted fiend and his leg has meanwhile been set."

Cardozo took a pencil from a mug placed on Jurriaans' desk.

Jurriaans took the other pencil from the mug and pointed it at Cardozo's chest. "Sergeant de Gier is an experienced detective who has proved himself so often that we know he'll make the right decisions. He came, he looked, he won."

"Ha," Cardozo said.

"You don't believe me?"

"I believe that Sergeant de Gier was set up, saw nonsense, and lost."

"You're burrowing," Jurriaans said. "Just like a mole. Blindly. Without considering either personalities or facts."

Cardozo broke his pencil, studied the halves, and threw them into the wastepaper basket. Jurriaans gave him the other pencil. "And that's wrong, for both personalities and facts have to be taken into account. You're a mole, Cardozo, and you know what moles do. They mess up lawns and get dirt in their mouths."

Cardozo broke the second pencil. "Sergeant?"

"Let's hear it."

"Do you think Jacobs shot Obrian?"

"I do not," Jurriaans said. "Jacobs only shoots the Gestapo, and the Gestapo hasn't been near him for years. If evil doesn't wear a German uniform, Jacobs won't shoot. I know as much because I've often listened to Jacobs. You know where he lives?"

"I know him personally," Cardozo said. "He lives at the end of the Straight-Tree-Ditch." He threw the halves of the second pencil into the wastebasket. Jurriaans opened a drawer and gave him a third pencil.

"You know the house," Jurriaans said. "Jacobs lives in a room. There are more people staying there, including some young women who work for Gustav. They display themselves in the windows around here but they live in that house. Gustav visits those women at home. He knows Jacobs. He knows Jacobs owns a Schmeisser. He knows that Jacobs often gets drunk and passes out on his bed. Gustav borrows Jacobs' Schmeisser."

"Did Gustav say so?"

"Maybe he did," Jurriaans said. "All I know so far is that de Gier arrested Gustav. I doubt whether Gustav will ever confess to the Obrian murder, but we do have him for attempted manslaughter of Orang Utan. The charge will stick. What does it matter if other charges won't?"

Cardozo got up.

"Where are you going?"

"To Jacobs' house," Cardozo said. "He isn't at the morgue, so he's probably at home."

"But why? Jacobs knows nothing."

"I'll go anyway, to make quite sure."

The pencil creaked in Cardozo's hands.

"You're still burrowing," Jurriaans said.

The pencil creaked again. "A superior brand," Jurriaans said. "The wood is stronger."

The pencil broke. "Sergeant?" asked Cardozo.

"Yes, colleague?"

"It can't be."

"What can't be, colleague?"

"It can't be," Cardozo said, "that de Gier was following Gustav when Gustav assaulted Orang Utan."

A large fly landed on the ruin of Jurriaans' blotter. Jurriaans' flat hand smashed the fly. "You saw that, colleague?"

"You killed a fly."

"Exactly. That fly has been irritating me for an hour and I was hunting him for an hour too but he managed to escape me. I kept my eye on him, however. Patience and luck, the ideas are interchangeable."

"Really, sergeant."

Jurriaans smiled hopefully.

"Good-bye sergeant," Cardozo said, and pulled the door closed behind him.

20

Adjutant Grijpstra sighed contentedly from a cane chair behind a table covered with a red-and-white-checked cloth. He had taken off his jacket and loosened his tie.

"Aren't you my sweet duck," Nellie said, "and haven't we been petting marvelously. Why don't you come more often? Isn't it cozier here than in that stuffy apartment of yours, on that moldy little canal? Just look at the way you're sitting there, all happy and relaxed. Nothing to worry about and everything coming up at just the right time. What would you like now? Some medium-rare steak on toast? Yes? With a gherkin on the side?"

"No," Grijpstra said, "because I have to go."

"Do you want to go?"

The adjutant folded his hands on his belly and rubbed his shoulders against the chair's back.

"You don't want to go at all."

"I've got to work," Grijpstra said. "I now know that the

vulture belongs to your neighbor and that your neighbor isn't home. To merely wait means wasting time. I've got to rush about the neighborhood and gather more information."

Nellie bent over him and kissed his bald crown. "Gather information from me. I probably know more than you need to know."

"Shouldn't you be working?" Grijpstra asked.

"Do I talk too much?" Nellie asked. "Would you like a nice nap? Shall I get the hammock? Or would you rather have coffee first?" She ran into the kitchen.

Nice and quiet here, Grijpstra thought. A good idea to have a yard. Protected within your own world. A yard to think in. Quietly. Logically, of course. Everything in the right place. Where was I, now? Let's start at the beginning. Without the slightest rush, very carefully, paying attention to every detail. Connect causes and events. I close my eyes and concentrate. Like this. I won't overconcentrate, I just hold on to the thread. Obrian. Obrian who? Obrian what?

What do I care about Obrian? Grijpstra thought. He saw a street in old Amsterdam, with sidewalks behind which closed doors protected the privacy of patrician homes. A dignified quietness pervaded the street and was enjoyed by Grijpstra, who had dressed in his best blue three-piece suit, had just visited the barber and polished his shoes. He was a patrician himself, and the street was his. Two ladies came along—he knew them but he didn't have to acknowledge the acquaintanceship. The ladies walked slowly by. He studied them from the front, the side, and the rear. They were aware, in spite of their sedately lowered eyes, that he was paying them his fullest attention, but they didn't react, not because they were angry with their suitor or because they shouldn't know he was there, but rather because they wanted to be admired completely, in pure detachment, and also because any activity on his part would have been despicable. He only had to know that they were there, a condition Grijpstra silently agreed to. The ladies wore hats, woven from straw, and red-and-white-checked streamers hung over their naked shoulders and backs. Their skirts had been cut from the same material and were really pieces of cloth loosely wound around their hips and tucked in. Whether they wore shoes, Grijpstra didn't know, because the skirts dragged on the sidewalk. One bare-bosomed lady was Nellie, the other Adjutant Adèle.

They must be wearing shoes, Grijpstra thought, their heels click on the cobblestones, but the sounds were made by the coffee cups Nellie placed on the table.

"What kept you so long?"

Nellie said, "I couldn't help it. Uncle Jan wanted to take a bath, and the one faucet sticks and I had to find a hammer to hit it with."

Grijpstra stirred his coffee.

"Uncle Jan is a guest," Nellie said. "An old man who sometimes stays here. He's from Utrecht. . . . Hello, Tigri," Nellie said to a cat that appeared from the bushes. Grijpstra put out a hand. The cat approached and pushed herself against his fingers.

"The cat belongs to your neighbor too?"

"Yes," Nellie said. "Isn't she beautiful? So delicate on her high legs. She sometimes visits me at night, when I'm alone in bed. Then she'll come through the window." Nellie grinned. "She always crawls into my arm, puts her paws around my neck, and purrs into my ear, and sometimes she turns over and wants me to knead her belly."

Grijpstra picked the animal up. "You like men too?" Tigri put out a leg and touched the adjutant's nose with her paw.

"Oh," Nellie said. "Just look at that. You really have a way with animals. She never cares for strangers at all."

"This Tigri," Grijpstra said, while he shook the cat softly, "is a witness, for she was in the Olofs-alley yesterday morning, and the vulture that I'm looking for flew over the roofs of the same street."

"Yes?"

Grijpstra's voice shot up. "You don't think that's strange?"

"Not at all," Nellie said. "They have to be somewhere, don't they? The vulture flies about in the early hours, when everything's still quiet, and Tigri is an animal of the night. They were curious, I suppose, and wanted to know what was going on in the alley."

Grijpstra put the cat down and got up.

"Stay a little longer."

"To work," Grijpstra told himself.

She pushed him back into his chair. "And what if I had murdered Obrian? Would you stay with me then?"

"You?"

"Me. I'm quite a good shot. I detested Obrian. I just nipped out of my bed, bang bang bang, and nipped back again. Why couldn't it have been me?"

"You're not a good shot."

"I am, and I've told you so before. Don't you remember the Germans who left their stuff at my father's farm at the end of the war? And how my brother found their gear many years later? And how we were shooting crows?"

"You did tell me," Grijpstra said. "Weren't you using a rifle then?"

"A machine pistol, a nasty black short barreled thing, with bullets that you had to push into a holder, and the holder had to be pressed into it from underneath."

"Didn't your father call the local constable to have all the weapons confiscated?"

"Some detective you are. Couldn't I have lied? About that constable and all?"

Grijpstra shook his head.

She smiled and held his hand. "You really think I wouldn't lie to you?"

"You shouldn't lie to me. I'm your friend."

She pushed her chair against his. "You're my lover."

"Okay," Grijpstra said. "Let's assume you did lie. You own a Schmeisser. But to have and to shoot are not the same thing. You're a sweet woman. You couldn't kill anybody." Grijpstra caressed her hair. "Why should you? You've got me, haven't you? I'll always help you out. The slightest trouble, and I come marching in."

"And you shoot Obrian?"

Grijpstra withdrew his arm. "Didn't I protect you, even against Obrian?"

"Not really."

Grijpstra turned his head. She looked away. "Obrian was after me, Henk, he was sucking me in. I was getting very nervous. I knew what he wanted of me." She laughed.

Grijpstra stared at her.

She looked up and pushed his face away. "Don't look like that."

"I don't understand," Grijpstra said. "We're discussing murder. What's so funny all of a sudden?"

"Something I thought of. Shall I tell you?"

"Please."

"Maybe this'll help to make you understand women better. Remember the heat wave last month? I had to go out, to wash my clothes, and on the way I bought some bananas. It was a hundred degrees in the laundry and I sat there waiting, and next to me a man in shorts waited. There was nothing to do except watch the clothes go around, so he kept pushing his stool closer to mine, and when my machine was finally done I looked up at that man and he was getting all excited. Know what I mean?"

"I don't want to know," Grijpstra said.

"Don't be silly, now. He was all stiff and I could see it because I was practically on the floor. It annoyed me because I wasn't there for anything else but my laundry and I didn't need his attention. So I went to the manager to complain, but the manager wanted to understand precisely what I was complaining about."

"You don't really have to tell me all that."

"No, wait, it'll get worse. That manager pretended he didn't know what I was talking about, and he had shorts on too—crazy, hardly anybody wears shorts these days, but they both did. I got tired of repeating myself and I knew that he wasn't going to do anything anyway and my laundry was still in the machine, so I knelt down again and looked up, and the manager had sat down too, and he had gotten all excited as well."

"Please," Grijpstra said. "What sort of tale is this? Why didn't you just leave?"

"That's the point. I should have, you see, but I was getting so nervous and I had those bananas, and suddenly I was eating them, one after another, just to have something to do."

"Nellie . . ." Grijpstra pleaded.

"You think that's crazy, to eat bananas with those two next to you?"

"Bah," Grijpstra said.

"I'm sorry," Nellie said. "I didn't mean to upset you. You don't like that much, do you, now? But it's nothing out of the way, you know. All women do it to their men. I would do it to you too if I thought you would enjoy it."

Grijpstra stared at the tiles between his chair and the table. He breathed heavily. Nellie stroked his hand. "Are you unwell?"

Grijpstra scraped his throat. "That's what Obrian wanted of you?"

"Yes, but I wouldn't have given way to him."

"That's why you shot him?"

"I didn't shoot him," Nellie said. "I was only teasing you. I can take care of myself, especially since I got to know you. A crazy black can't make me go against my own likes. But with Madeleine it was different, she was alone so she had to give in, and hang herself later."

Grijpstra's head rested on her shoulder. She put her arm around his neck. "Poor Henk, he works so hard, and all I do to help is tell him dirty stories."

"So who shot the bastard?" Grijpstra asked. "What sort of a case is this anyway? What am I doing in it? The commissaris would have solved it long ago, there are indications enough, but all I can come up with is a vulture, and vultures don't fire machine guns. This has to do with witchcraft or with religion or something. You should have seen Obrian's altar. Jesus Christ in a straw skirt and a naked woman rubbing herself against a bottle of tomato ketchup and skulls and crazy drums. In a room with rags hanging from the walls. He probably prayed in there. What am I to make of that?"

"Poor Henk."

"Even the Dutch Reformed Church gave me the willies," Grijpstra said, "and that's kid's stuff compared to this. Chanting psalms and the blood we had to drink at Easter, and the bones they made me gnaw. Sure, it was only wine and bread, but the reverend said we were eating a corpse. I fainted, and I never went back."

"I know," Nellie said. "That happened to me too. I was a Catholic, of course, but *I* couldn't stand the incense, and once the prayer wouldn't stop and I looked up and Christ was on the wall. He was made of plaster, but it looked real enough to me, and there was blood running down his leg. I pissed in my pants that time."

"Yes," Grijpstra said.

"And the dreams," Nellie said. "When I was still in the faith,

I dreamed almost every night. Churches that were on fire, but the basements were still working and I had to go in, and there were altars downstairs too, with live pricks on them, bent a bit forward and leering at me with their one eye."

"No," Grijpstra said.

"True enough. But I didn't mind, I think, because then I knew that God is dirty too and that all that holiness and sin and so on is a lot of baloney." She kissed Grijpstra's neck. "I dreamed last night, too."

"No bananas," Grijpstra said. "And no eyes."

"No, it was something else. I was in a church again, and there was a statue, of a devil or demon or something, but not really a bad one. He had a biggie and I had to kneel—"

"Please, Nellie."

"No, no, just kneel, and pray. If I prayed well, fruit fell into my hands, delicious apples, but if I forgot what I was praying about, the apples hit my head and hurt me."

"Apples," Grijpstra said.

"There's nothing wrong with apples, is there? Granny Smiths they were, but I did think it was strange, for where did the apples come from? Well, from the rear, of course."

"Of the demon?"

"Yes. I didn't believe that God was really rewarding or punishing me, so I sneaked away and found out what was happening behind the statue, and just as I thought, there were a lot of little priests there, throwing the apples into the devil's ass. It was all a show, you see, to bamboozle the stupid."

"Good dream," Grijpstra said.

Nellie held up a hand. "I think I heard something. Uncle Wisi must have come home. Do you want to see him now?"

21

"UNCLE WISI," NELLIE SAID. "THIS IS THE MAN I'M ALWAYS telling you about. He wants to meet your vulture."

"Good day," Uncle Wisi said, and pushed his beaded cap to the back of his head so he could scratch his ear. "It's warm outside, even for me. Opete? A visitor."

The vulture hopped from under a branch loaded down with flowers.

"My wicked pet," Uncle Wisi said. "Now, what do you have on your leg, Opete?" He knelt down and felt the bird's sinewy ankle. "Here. The tricolor of the fatherland?"

The vulture squeaked.

"The flag looks well on you, Opete." Uncle Wisi rubbed his finger along Opete's beak. "They caught and decorated you, and you accepted the distinction. Are you getting weak in your old age?"

"Crazy," Nellie said. "Who would want to catch Opete? But they let him go again, so they must have meant well." She held up her arm, and the vulture flapped its wings and jumped so that he could settle on her wrist. She stroked the head that bowed to her chest.

"I'm a policeman," Grijpstra said.

"I know," Uncle Wisi said. "Nellie told me. You're quite an authority, eh, official? This visit has to do with the death of my compatriot?"

"Luku Obrian, sir."

"Uncle," Uncle Wisi said. "That's what I am now, uncle to all and everybody, regardless of race or religion. Come in, official. Nellie tells me that you're good on drums."

Nellie followed them, with Opete in uncertain balance on her arm. "Ouch." She pushed the vulture softly away. "If he bends his knees, his talons get into my skin." Opete flew to a cupboard.

"An official on drums," Uncle Wisi said. "That does make me feel at home."

"Henk's really quite good," Nellie said. "He plays in his office, on a set that Lost and Found gave him."

"Nothing special," Grijpstra said. "I used to play in the school band and I've picked it up again now. To bang away every now and then kills time pleasantly."

"And his partner plays flute," Nellie said. "He's a real artist, too. They play that old-fashioned kind of music, chorals and sonatas, and all the other policemen come to listen."

Uncle Wisi pushed a stool toward his guest. Grijpstra looked at he multitude of objects in the small low room. "I have to get back," Nellie said. "Uncle Jan'll want his dinner soon. I'll be waiting for you, Henk, when you're done."

"Yes," Grijpstra said.

"Yes, who?"

"Yes, dear Nellie."

"Let's have it, official," Uncle Wisi said, "or do you only want to talk to my vulture?"

Opete squeaked from his perch.

"I only wanted to know who owned the bird."

"The bird is mine," Uncle Wisi said solemnly.

Grijpstra talked quickly. "The vulture was in the alley. Olofs-alley. Near the corpse. Obrian's corpse. The vulture is yours. So is the cat. The cat Tigri. Also in the alley."

"But was *I* in the alley, official?"

"Were you?"

Uncle Wisi stepped sideways. "I." He stepped back. "Was." He jumped a foot off the floor. "Not there. . . . Because," Uncle Wisi said, "I was here."

"So you didn't kill Obrian?"

Uncle Wisi removed his cap, stuck his fingers into his crisp gray hair, and put his headgear back. "That's to say, official. Yes and no."

Grijpstra leaned back but the stool offered no support and he waved his arms desperately, just managing not to fall off. "Yes or no, Uncle Wisi?"

Uncle Wisi sat down too. "You know, official, that's what makes it tricky. Out methods differ. I do not say that yours aren't valid, because they clearly serve many purposes. If it isn't this, it must be that—one can argue that way mathematically, and if you're handy as well, you have manufactured a rocket before you know what you've done. That method of yours works well, but mine is different. Yes and no, I say. Yes *or* no, you say. And neither of us is wrong."

Grijpstra flapped his handkerchief. "Did you shoot?" He blew his nose. "Or did you not?" He wiped the sweat off his forehead.

"No." Uncle Wisi laughed. "A machine gun does not belong to my collection of tools."

That man is very old, Grijpstra thought, and he still has all his teeth, and not too many wrinkles, but I don't like his eyes, they're too sharp.

"Although I did own a gun once," Uncle Wisi said. "In the West. I used to fire it, too, during services for the dead. It was my magic rifle."

"Not a real rifle?"

Uncle Wisi nodded. "Very real. Used to belong to you people, and with you everything is real, right? An ancient muzzle-loader, used at the time of importation of slaves; you fellows shot with bullets, but I used only powder, to make noise, to help the *yorka* on his way. You've got to do that at times, you know, because the spirit is frightened and wants to stay, and you help him along, in your function as magician."

"You were the magician?"

"I *am* the magician," Uncle Wisi said.

"Wah," Grijpstra said. He pointed at the table. "You've got one too."

"What are you indicating?"

"That Christ, in the skirt."

"I've got more," Uncle Wisi said, and held up a framed portrait. "This is the great Indian who rules the jungle where his followers allowed our free men to settle. We took the great Indian too. And Jesus of course, for you people told us he was the son of Massa Gran-Gado and supposed to love us. Why shouldn't we believe you? And this we have as well." He showed a jar of genever. "A glass, official?"

"I'm on duty," Grijpstra said.

"So am I," Uncle Wisi said. He poured and passed Grijpstra an egg holder filled to its rim. "Your health, official."

"Your health, Uncle Wisi."

Uncle Wisi sat down and looked at Grijpstra through his glass, with one much enlarged eye.

"To magic," Grijpstra said. "Is yours white or black?"

"I'm black," Uncle Wisi said, and held his hand next to Grijpstra's. "See? All my grandparents were niggers."

"That's not what I mean."

"Oh," Uncle Wisi said. "You mean the color of my art? That *used* to be black." He sang, *"Powers beyond, powers below, the dark death, sure but slow."*

Grijpstra couldn't remember ever having drunk such strong genever. All tension had been burned out of his body and he felt slightly paralyzed. "The slow death, Uncle Wisi?" To his surprise, he recognized his own voice that sounded kindly inquisitive and quite clear.

"But the power works both ways," Uncle Wisi said. "Like the boomerang the black brothers of Australia use." He smiled at his guest. "The people became frightened of me, official, like they have fear of you. People don't appreciate powers in others. And the other wisimen got together and arranged their altars and sang and danced. They set off fireworks and asked the *gados* who lived under their mulberry trees to hunt me, and I needed all my time and strength to defend myself." Uncle Wisi grinned slyly. "But I had gold, for a good wisi-man doesn't take mere money, and the world is wide. I went a-journeying to the land of the queen." He touched his cap respectfully. "She's the great holy spirit-woman who doesn't only protect you but us too. Her photograph hung in my cabin. I prayed to her, and advised her of my arrival, and she received me well." Uncle Wisi grabbed his egg holder, drank, and smacked his lips. "A good woman, and I became good too, for I had been bad already, and a man has to move along, don't you agree?"

"You still are?" Grijpstra asked. "Good, I mean?"

Uncle Wisi looked at the floor.

"Yes?"

The keen eyes filled with light and stared at Grijpstra. "No," Uncle Wisi said. "That's all too simple. Isn't good as stupid as bad? I haven't been good for a long time now." His voice softened. "But it took some doing, to be done with definitions, or to soar out of them; it can be put that way too, although that doesn't sound modest. We have to stay simple or the trap may close again."

Grijpstra's nose wrinkled. "Whatever you say."

"You don't understand?"

"No."

"Not difficult at all," Uncle Wisi said. "Or rather, nothing at all, but it took me a while before I could see that, but I had more time, of course. I'm somewhat older than you are. Another sip?"

"No," Grijpstra said. "Thank you. I should be on my way. So you don't know who did away with Obrian either? Who shot him, I mean?"

Uncle Wisi lifted a hand. "Just a moment, official. We could pursue this matter together."

"How, Uncle Wisi?"

"Yes." Uncle Wisi lifted his stool and put it down closer to Grijpstra. He sat down again and arranged his robe. "Listen here, official. As I said, you've your method and I have mine. Yours doesn't work now because you've got to find someone who saw what happened, and there doesn't seem to be anybody, except the one who fired the gun, and he doesn't want to show up, true or not?"

"True, Uncle Wisi."

"Well, let's try it my way, then. You're a bit of a drummer, aren't you?"

"Magic?" Grijpstra asked.

"Magic frightens you?"

"Yes," Grijpstra said. "No. I know nothing about magic."

"But I do. It's easy, official. I burn some dry herbs to make a good smell, and you play a drum, and so do I, and we are in the alley, you and I, making time turn back, and then we see what happened."

"We go to the alley?"

"We stay right here," Uncle Wisi said. "But keep your cool,

or my method won't work either. And we sing," he said. "You sure you don't want a little more genever?"

"Just a little, perhaps."

Uncle Wisi poured. "To the *yorka.*"

"The what?"

"The spirit of the deceased, Obrian's in this case—he'll have to be around too."

Grijpstra nodded morosely.

"One drum for you," Uncle Wisi said, "another for me. You think you can handle this type of drum?"

Grijpstra made his knuckles glide along the tight skin. "Yes, feels okay, Uncle Wisi."

"A moment," Uncle Wisi said while he mixed ground herbs in an earthenware dish. He poured genever on the mixture and lit a match. A flame shot from the dish, and sharp smoke crinkled up. Uncle Wisi took hold of his drum. "Right. Ready?"

Grijpstra lifted his hand.

Incoherent improvisation. Grijpstra thought. We'll never get anywhere this way. That old man drinks too much.

But it wasn't quite like that, Grijpstra had to admit. Dry bones and hollow sockets, the adjutant thought, Uncle Wisi is shaking a skeleton.

"Eee," Uncle Wisi sang. *"Eeehee, EEhee."*

Grijpstra looked up. The stench of the smoldering herbs, the green haze of plants all around him, the subtle colors of grains and seeds in the jars arranged on shelves, seemed to indicate a melody that Uncle Wisi was already playing, and a rhythm that the adjutant drew from his own drum. *Wham, turrick, wham-turRICK* rattled Grijpstra's stubby fingers. This may seem primitive, the adjutant thought, but in reality it's impossibly complicated, the formula is somewhere between the softest scratching and loudest thumping and it's the whole rigmarole de Gier is always searching for when he tootles his flute, and even finds at odd moments, but now I don't have to help him along, since Uncle Wisi has it dead center and I can follow without paying attention. *Turrim, turrám.*

Most pleasant. Good music. But I could do without the ghosts. There's Obrian, marionette Obrian. Uncle Wisi pulls the strings, and Obrian jumps and dances to our tune.

The corpse regains its life.

Grijpstra played energetically. Uncle Wisi took care of the solos but the adjutant expressed introductions and afterthoughts, always in the right intervals and never losing a beat. He was enjoying himself. Uncle Wisi sang nicely too, using open vowels mostly, interspersed with short foreign words, to command the corpse.

Corpses don't put me off, Grijpstra thought. I saw so many. This stuff works well. We are in the Olofs-alley and daybreak hasn't come yet and Obrian strolls along over there and will be shot in a moment. Obrian pretends he doesn't know what will happen to him, he acts the scene out, a most helpful fellow. In a minute he will explain exactly why he had to be murdered—if only he won't use his own language, because then I won't understand what he's saying.

But now, Grijpstra thought, fervently hitting his drum, how did we get on this little bridge? We're losing track. It isn't dark anymore either, the sun shines. That woman is on her knees and edges forward. She's begging Obrian with her smile, and he gives his consent, and her mouth, her mouth . . .

The drum fell out of Grijpstra's hands. Spittle dribbled down his chin. His body swayed and crashed to the floor.

"Pity," Uncle Wisi said.

"Where am I?" Grijpstra asked.

"With your very own Nellie." She stroked his cheek. You're quite heavy, you know. Uncle Wisi and I nearly broke our backs when we lifted you into the hammock. Did you sleep well?"

"I'm thirsty." Grijpstra whispered.

She brought a glass of water. The taste was bitter.

"What did you put into the glass?"

"Obeah, made by Uncle Wisi, to make you feel better."

"Am I ill?"

"No," Nellie said. "But you did faint just now. Now you're okay again."

"Pity," Grijpstra said.

She kissed him. "Aren't you a funny fellow? And the two of you were drumming so well. I could hear it from here. But then it suddenly stopped and Uncle Wisi came to fetch me. I didn't worry at all. With Uncle Wisi you are safe." She pushed the hammock. Grijpstra swung slowly.

"Uncle Wisi is a thingamajig," Grijpstra said.

Nellie laughed.

Grijpstra head dropped to the side, and he stared at her mournfully.

"The land," Nellie said dreamily, "of the thingamajigs. When I was little, I once stayed with my grandma, and the sky was so blue that day, no clouds at all, everything seemed empty, and I asked my grandma what could be behind the sky. For everything does go on forever, but everything comes to an end too, and I didn't understand that, for if the sky comes to an end, there must be something behind it."

Grijpstra looked up. The sky was blue and empty. "Behind the sky?"

"Yes, and my grandma said that beyond what we know is the land of the thingamajigs."

Grijpstra groaned.

"Poor Henk."

He wriggled until he was on his side. "You're my dearest, Nellie."

"And you're mine, Henk."

Grijpstra waved his hand. "What's there? Between your lettuce?"

"Where, Henk?"

"That's a turtle," Grijpstra said accusingly.

"The turtle belongs to Uncle Wisi."

"A well-known model," Grijpstra said.

She held on to his hand. "You know, Henk, maybe you're right. I do believe Uncle Wisi is a thingamajig."

"You have too many uncles," Grijpstra said, "and you know too many thingamajigs."

She dropped his hand. "Poor Uncle Jan, he's still in his bath, and I promised him coffee."

"Then you better give him his coffee," Grijpstra said.

Grijpstra looked out of the hammock. He tried to remember what the woman who had been creeping toward Obrian had looked like. The color of her hair? Red, like Nellie's?

I should be able to remember, Grijpstra thought.

22

CARDOZO LOOKED AT ELIAZAR JACOB'S NAME SIGN AND read the text underneath: *"He who believes in the Good."* He noticed that he was trembling. "I'm not well," he said aloud. "Probably have the flu." He didn't have the flu, as he knew, he didn't even have a cold. He read the text again, without surprise, for this wasn't the first time he had visited Jacobs at home. I also know him from the synagogue, Cardozo thought; we're brothers in the faith. In the faith of what? In the good of what? In the good that created Dachau? In Him who created all possibilities when He set the whole thing off? In the benevolence of Him who did not bother to create all details—you can only blame Him for the origin, Cardozo added, I'm not stupid, after all—and allowed the terrible results to be created by that which He created himself? Does it make any difference? Or does Eliazar Jacobs believe in the good that permitted him to survive disaster, in the ultimate cruelty of survival to remember? What do I know about it anyway? Cardozo thought, I only arrived later, and the evil has moved since then, to Argentina and other out of the way countries. As I'm here, and not in Argentina, I can persist in believing in the good; all I have to do is to ignore what evil is doing further along, and all Eliazar has to do is to forget. Am I burrowing again? Cardozo thought.

He rang the bell. The house remained quiet. He tried again and pushed his ear against the door. The bell worked.

The good of a Schmeisser, Cardozo thought—what might that be? The perfect functioning of the weapon?

The door opened and Cardozo nearly fell into the corridor. A slender black woman looked at him kindly. "Yes?"

"Good afternoon, miss," Cardozo said shakily. "Is Mr. Jacobs in?"

"Eliazar is on holiday."

"A pity," Cardozo said. He rubbed his cheeks. My teeth are going to chatter, Cardozo thought, but this is not the right moment. He handed her his card. "I'm a policeman, miss, and I have to talk to Eliazar urgently."

The woman looked at Cardozo's crumpled corduroy jacket, strengthened by leather patches on the elbows, one of which was dangling from a thread. "You are a constable?"

"A detective, miss. But I'm also a friend of Eliazar's, and it is important that I see him."

"Eliazar is on leave," the woman said, "and will be away for at least two weeks. He went to Jerusalem, to cry at the Wailing Wall. He goes there often."

Cardozo's lower lip trembled. She returned his identification. He took a deep breath, to be used in further communication, but his words slipped away and he swallowed instead. He smiled his good-bye.

Cardozo sat on a bench at the waterside, staring at the Straight-Tree-Ditch's rippling surface. His mind functioned somewhat again and he tried to arrange facts into a theory. The weapon, the time, the place, the victim, the motivation. His hand slapped his thigh as the facts moved about, shakily, like Eliazar's head approaching and receding, without touching the wall's surface. Cardozo knew what the Wailing Wall in Jerusalem looked like, from a photograph in a magazine that he had cut out and hung above his bed. He visualized the gray-green stones, square or rectangular, and the solemn black-suited worshipers, their heavy hairy heads covered by wide dark hats, bowing to the wall, crying at the wall, wailing in devotion. Wailing in general, not so much about their private pains—Jacobs wouldn't do that either.

Cardozo no longer trembled. I'm glad I'm crying myself now, he thought, for it removes tension, but the tears also wash my facts away, and the theory I hung them in. It would be better to stop crying perhaps, because it doesn't look good. I'm not in Jerusalem here.

The sobs continued, seeming to form themselves at the lowest point of his spine and pulsate slowly upward. To restrain himself seemed useless. It would be better to let the suffering, or whatever his affliction could be, release itself. Maybe the crying would clean him up, inside, for on the outside he was getting rather soppy. He no longer wiped the tears away and helped the sobs along by nodding diligently.

The music he was hearing fitted in well and he only understood that the sounds took place beyond his own confinement when the ensemble glided past his bench. The musicians manned a good-sized rowboat, moved by the efforts of two young ladies. An upright piano rested on boards placed across the boat's sides; a saxophone player stood in the bow and the drummer in the stern. The music was sad, but underneath its lament rose cheerful undertones as if, finally, reality was about to be properly represented and lies would no longer be necessary. The girls rowed slowly and the boat inched ahead. While the saxophone filled empty caves with voluminous clouds of sounds, the drum thumped softly and helped the piano to supply outlines, with a single discord here and there, placed in the center of space, deliberately overlooked by the saxophone.

Although the boat moved slowly, it did float on, and Cardozo got up and walked with the music, placing his feet carefully, until he reached the next bridge and climbed up on it. He bent over the railing, first on one side and then on the other, so that the boat was swallowed up and rebuilt slowly again. Under the bridge the music sounded even more wistful, first accentuated by the drummer's representation of straight grief, then by the saxophone's version of a whispered complaint.

Cardozo shuffled on, watched the boat moor and the musicians clamber ashore. The three young men wore turtle-necked blue jerseys and faded jeans, the girls old-fashioned cotton dresses with flower patterns. The girls landed too, unscrewed a thermos, and unpacked sandwiches from a hamper. Cardozo stood, his head oddly askew, as if he were still listening.

"You're still listening?" the piano player asked.

"Why are you crying?" the drummer asked.

If I tell them, Cardozo thought, that I'm crying because of Eliazar Jacobs, who's taking the suffering of the world upon himself in Jerusalem, eight hours a day, for he is a disciplined man who feels comfortable in a daily routine, then my explanation would probably be quite plausible.

He looked at the girls, because their faces were softer. "I'm no longer crying."

"That's good," the saxophone player said. "Would you like a ham sandwich, or do you prefer sliced chicken livers?"

The hamper contained an apple. "Could I have the apple?" Cardozo asked. "Why are you making music?"

The piano player clarified their motivation later, after the used napkins had been replaced in the hamper, for there was no hurry and Cardozo had taken his time peeling the apple and chewing it well.

"So you are a society," Cardozo said.

"Yes," the piano player said. "The Secret Society Without a Name. We perform unusual acts, so that we may consider the creation from new angles, but we only do that from time to time, so as not to get used to the unusual, because then we would be back where we started. Whatever we do has to be done as perfectly as possible, and to keep thinking of new possibilities is too difficult, and unnecessary besides. This week is exercise week. We're on holiday anyway, so no time is lost."

"You work?"

"We study."

"What?" asked Cardozo.

"Mathematics," the drummer said. "Medicine," said the girls. "Psychology," said the saxophone player.

"And you?"

"Police Academy," the piano player said.

Cardozo took the apple's peel and threw it over his shoulder. He looked around to see what had become of its shape. "A flattened circle," the drummer said. "No, a zero, probably the best shape anyone can throw, for everything fits into nothing."

"Today you made music," Cardozo said. "Just what I happened to need. Thank you. What did you do yesterday?"

"Yesterday we were roller-skating," the saxophone player said. "From midnight to five A.M. We were dressed up in our best suits and carried briefcases. We stayed within the limits of the inner city, along the canals mostly, the experience was quite beautiful, but what it did for us is still unclear. We might discover it later, or never."

"You did not," Cardozo asked, "happen to see a Negro being shot to death?"

"We did," the drummer said. "In the Olofs-alley. We didn't

see the actual shooting, but we heard it, and the victim was black, according to the newspaper."

"And you did not, by chance, see somebody leave a burned-out building, corner Seadike and Olofs-alley?"

"We saw her," the piano player said. "A woman. Tall. Black hat, black skirt. Large shoes. A cape half-covering the skirt. She crossed the street and followed the Seadike. We almost skated into her."

"What time?" asked Cardozo.

"Three o'clock," the saxophone player said. "The carillon in the Saint Nicholas church was playing."

"We weren't skating," the girls said. "Because we aren't really members yet. We're still on trial."

"What do you do?" the drummer asked.

"I'm a police detective," Cardozo said, "and if you don't mind, I would like to write down your names."

"We'll have to be witnesses?" asked the piano player.

"Probably not," Cardozo said.

"You were crying about that dead black man?" the drummer asked when Cardozo started his good-byes.

"I cried about everything, I think," Cardozo said, "but the worst is over. Does your society have many members?"

"Thirteen," said the piano player, "and the members who graduate from the university have to leave. After that, daily work will be the exercise, or whatever one happens to be doing at the moment."

"You're already working," the saxophone player said.

"And you're after certain results?" Cardozo asked.

"One has to stay away from that," the drummer said, "for aim-setting defeats the purpose of the whole thing."

"I didn't pity you when you were crying," the one girl said. "That would have been degrading."

The other girl kissed him.

"Thank you," Cardozo said.

23

TUESDAY NIGHT AND ALMOST DARK. ON THE SECOND FLOOR of the police station in the quarter a meeting was in progress, in a solemn high-ceilinged room, under gold-framed portraits of ancient Civic Guard officers wearing steel armor over silk shirts and holding sharp swords in their blue-veined hands, indicating their readiness to guard the peace.

That the actual authorities were ready too was proved by Grijpstra, who embraced himself with his right arm so that the little finger of his hand could rest on his pistol butt, outlined in the material of his jacket. Jurriaans' arm hung down. The palm of his hand touched his gun, hidden under his tunic. All present were armed, including Adjutant Adèle, whose old-fashioned pistol, with the shortened barrel—the ladies' model—was visible. She leaned back, so as to be able to gaze better at Reserve Sergeant Varé, and the movement made her holster slide down her belt until it hung free from her skirt.

Varé sat in between de Gier and Ketchup, opposite Adjutant

Adèle, and contrasted with the others, not so much because of his color but rather because of his relaxed attitude.

Karate grinned at Varé, and the reserve sergeant grinned back. I'm just sitting here, thought Varé. You're just sitting there, thought Karate. Karate was pleased that at least one member of this task force was not quite taken in by current events. One should never overdo anything, Karate thought, even though it could be important that they would arrest, a little later along in the foggy night, the redoubtable Lennie, the third and last revolting head of the scaly monster that had such a terrible grip on the quarter. Lennie, Karate told himself, is the devil, to be caught and removed by us—to be buried in a hole dug by a bulldozer, to be kicked out of an airplane, or to be pulverized, for instance by means of fireworks shoved into his body's openings and lit all at once. But, Karate was thinking secretly, it's also good to know that all this frantic activity does not quite take over, for we are citizens of Amsterdam after all, and shouldn't forget that everything will be fine in the end and that too much concern is both irritating and fatiguing.

Varé was indeed keeping his distance, because he had been scientifically schooled and was used to observing quietly and also because he had just dined well and sat easily and enjoyed the cigar which Grijpstra had just given him, and because de Gier was telling an interesting tale.

Jurriaans interrupted de Gier, "So Gustav does not confess to the Obrian murder?"

"No."

"Naturally," Jurriaans said, "considering that Gustav's leg had just been set and he was still drugged. A suspect filled with morphine feels safe, between clean sheets, with nurses at his beck and call. He can afford to smile at us."

"Gustav was sorry," de Gier said.

"That he pushed Orang Utan into the river?"

"That he hadn't shot Obrian with a Schmeisser. Gustav

would just have loved to kill Obrian, but someone else was too quick. So he's sorry now."

"You did give him the full treatment, didn't you?" Grijpstra asked worriedly. "Maybe you should have called me. It's easier when there are two of us."

"I couldn't find you," de Gier said. "And I am able to work by myself sometimes. Gustav knows how weak his position is. His assault on Orang Utan was witnessed by Karate and he'll never break our charges, so he has lost his freedom; there's no doubt in his mind about that. Possession is power, but he no longer owns anything because the tax detectives have gone through his house and come up with proof of undeclared income, by finding German notes, Swiss bonds, and even bars of gold."

"Drugs?" Grijpstra asked.

"Mr. Ober is content. An ounce of heroin, and Gustav's women are telling us about his connections."

"But is Gustav aware of his hopeless situation?" Jurriaans asked. "Suspects tend to be optimistic sometimes, especially when they have listened to lying lawyers."

"Don't lawyers want money?" de Gier asked. "Does Gustav have any left? The tax department is fining him more than they've found."

"Okay," Jurriaans said, "but you say he won't admit to the Obrian killing. What if we push a little? Couldn't we get that too?"

"I hardly think so."

"Why not?"

De Gier smiled winningly.

"Well?" Grijpstra asked.

"I'm sorry," de Gier said, "but I'm quite sure that Gustav is innocent."

"Gustav is a hunter," Ketchup said. "He shoots elephants with a cannon. Why shouldn't he shoot a competitor with a machine pistol?"

De Gier smiled apologetically. "Gustav is a coward."

"A coward?" Karate pointed at the ceiling. "An elephant is that high." He held his fingers along his mouth. "And has big teeth. If all that comes thundering from the bush . . ."

"And your cannon is aimed straight at the poor thing's chest." De Gier asked, "You're in a jeep with an experienced driver at the wheel. The jeep is already in reverse. The safari leader is right behind you and points another cannon. You know that all hunters always return safely to camp. Where the champagne waits in the ice bucket."

"Hunting is hunting."

De Gier smiled unwillingly. "And where was Obrian's hunter positioned? In a burned-out ruin within shouting distance of a police station. He fired and had to leave the very same second, slithering down a rickety staircase. And he was alone."

"Could I interrupt for a moment?" Varé asked.

"Please," Adjutant Adèle said. "You say something too, John."

"I'm a sociologist," Varé said excusingly, "and occasionally peruse the literature of my discipline. I happened to come across an article on pimps the other day. Pimps live on the proceeds of female lasciviousness, and women have been known as the weaker sex. The hypothesis this article tried to prove was that pimps are not courageous."

"Did it succeed somewhat?" Jurriaans asked.

I'm getting in a foul mood, Grijpstra thought, due to the blackness of Varé and my own racism. Unpleasant but true. I'm surprised because I've obviously always thought that Negroes are stupid by definition. I still see blacks as liberated slaves who should not climb higher than the level of a mailman or a bus driver, but this gentlemen is a scholar, and I, a white man, am neither one nor the other.

"Factual material," Varé was saying, "can be easily misinterpreted, but I would venture to state that the study provided sufficient proofs, based on well-executed tests, to assume that pimps, in general, are cowards."

"So it wasn't Gustav," Adjutant Adèle said. "So what? We still have Lennie. And Lennie is due next."

Varé addressed Jurriaans. "You feel sure that Obrian has been done away with by the competition?"

"Isn't that logical?" Jurriaans asked. "Personally, I believe out theory will hold. We know that the murder has been executed in a sneaky manner, by a mean little man."

"By a mean little *woman*?" Cardozo asked. "Dressed in a cape and a floppy hat?"

"That's what Crazy Chris told you," Grijpstra said. "What was it again? Tall? Black clothes? Slippery gait? Moving along the Seadike, direction Damrak?"

"*Crazy* Chris," de Gier said. "Drunken Chris. We saw him in Hotel Hadde. An old toothless bum, blue-skinned from the methylated spirits that he guzzled before socialism."

"Tramps with dissolved brains," Grijpstra said, "are known to hallucinate. Our report says that the shooting took place at three twenty A.M. Perhaps drunken bums don't have their clearest moments at that time."

"Sergeant de Gier?" Cardozo asked.

"Yes, Constable First Class Cardozo?"

"Do you remember what else you saw that morning? On your way to the Olofs-alley?"

De Gier thought.

"Roller-skaters?" Cardozo asked. "Gentlemen on little wheels? Three-piece-suited? Carrying briefcases?"

"So I said. But were they there? Not only bums hallucinate. Grijpstra never saw them?"

"I never turned around," Grijpstra said. "It would have been near the National Monument on the Dam. You were speeding again, and I was looking ahead to see what sort of accident we were about to have."

"I found those roller-skaters," Cardozo said. "They claimed that they heard shooting at three A.M. and that they saw our suspect leave the corner house. They described her as a woman. Their testimony agrees with that of Crazy Chris."

"Tell me more about the phantoms," Jurriaans said. "The witnesses who saw something happen twenty minutes before it actually took place. Three future-gazing roller-skating gentlemen."

Cardozo reported.

"The Secret Society Without a Name?" Ketchup asked. "Roller-skates on Monday, becomes a floating orchestra on Tuesday, what would they be doing on Wednesday? Masturbating in the window of a department store?"

"Interesting," Varé said. "The technique is known, of course. You see it today in Gestalt and E.S.T. and even in Zen. The mystic from Armenia, Guru Gurdjieff, imported it from Tibet. The idea is that you force yourself to execute an almost impossible task under unlikely circumstances. A technique aimed at increasing consciousness. But nothing is new under the sun. In Africa, for instance, the young tribal members are initiated in that way into the secrets of the jungle, and in Surinam the witch doctors have kept the method alive. Material I have been working on lately. Voodoo as practiced by the city blacks, a subject that hasn't been investigated properly."

"Mr. Varé," Grijpstra asked, "what are witch doctors called in your country?"

"My country is the Netherlands," Varé said. "My passport is Dutch, but privately I try not to be bothered by nationality. Freedom provides more space to work in."

"But what are they called," Grijpstra asked, "these witch doctors in Surinam?"

Varé loosened his lips from his cigar. "Let's see, now, they come in various types. The so-called good ones are obeah men and their opponents are known as wisi-men. But good and bad are haphazard terms. When we analyze we always try to reserve room for nuances."

"Goddamnmystupidsoulforeverafter," Grijpstra said.

"I beg your pardon?"

"Excuse me," Grijpstra said. "I had to curse for a moment. You do know the terms, obviously. Obrian's first name was Luku. What does Luku mean?"

"Well," Varé said, "there are several variations. Lukumen in general are psychically gifted. Some can predict the future, and the gift is often coupled to hypnotic power. Lukumen are always talented, but only the wisimen know how to manipulate the force. One could say that a wisiman starts off as a luku, but how the talent is used is up to a number of factors."

"Brr," Adjutant Adèle said, "there's a draft here."

"Shall I close the window?" Cardozo asked.

"No, because then it'll get too smoky."

"So the luku becomes an apprentice of the wisiman?" Grijpstra asked.

"Yes," Varé said. "Wisimen need disciples and attract the lukus. The luku may not even want to be influenced by the wisi, for he'll have to surrender himself to a possible *keenu*, the curse that always accompanies training and becomes effective when the luku breaks the taboo the wisi will include in his treatment. You see, the luku has his gift, his talent, and the wisi will do everything to develop that power in his disciple, but certain rules will need to be adhered to. Each development is fraught with taboos—with conditions, one might say."

"Yes yes yes," Grijpstra said.

Jurriaans looked up. "Thank you, Varé, but there's still work to do, and we should be about ready to leave now. De Gier, did Herr Sublieutenant Röder contact us today?"

"I spoke to him this afternoon," de Gier said. "He was due to arrive at Amsterdam airport tonight and didn't want to be met since he knows his way about here. He's staying in the

American Hotel and will report here at midnight." He checked his watch. "It's ten after twelve now. He's probably waiting downstairs."

"Just a minute," Grijpstra said. "How is the attack on Lennie planned?"

Jurriaans walked to the rear wall of the room and pulled down a map. "Here is the Catburgh Canal, where Lennie's luxury brothel floats. You and de Gier will be going there in a minute and pretend to be partying clients. Röder will go there too. He has the main part in our charade; he's got to provoke trouble, while you and your sergeant should stay to one side."

"Isn't that boat rather exclusive?" de Gier asked. "We might not even be admitted."

"You have an introduction. Slanozzel will take you in. He should be waiting in his Maserati now, on the Newmarket."

"Slanozzel is acquainted with Lennie?"

"He goes there often."

"Poor fellow," Grijpstra said. "He won't be so welcome after tonight. Isn't the man taking unnecessary risks? Imagine if we cause distress?"

"You *will* cause distress," Jurriaans said, "but Slanozzel claims that he owes us, and it isn't charitable to refuse all gifts."

"Why don't we just march in?" Cardozo asked. "Rush the joint, pistol in hand? If we pull that ship apart, we're bound to find everything we're looking for, provided the contraband is kept aboard."

De Gier sat on the table. "Simon, my boy . . ."

"Wrong again?" Cardozo asked.

"Right," Jurriaans said. "And clever, but what you suggest is not appropriate under the circumstances. Raids are out of fashion in the quarter. Why, I wouldn't know with any degree of certainty, but raids always take us into empty space. We have changed our tactics. We sneak rather than crash."

"With nothing to support us on the outside?"

"I'll be on the other side of the window," Jurriaans said, "and glass breaks easily. Look at the boat's position. The Catburgh Canal is the vertical line in the T and the horizontal is the Dike's Canal. If Lennie decides to run for it, he'll escape across the water and there'll be a boat of the Water Police here and my boat will be there."

"The Water Police have been advised?"

"They will be, at the last moment. When they arrive, I'll already be in position, with Karate and Ketchup at the oars."

"And where will I be?" Cardozo asked.

"And I?" asked Adjutant Adèle.

"Can't I join the party?" asked Varé.

Jurriaans looked at the reserve sergeant. "You? After eleven P.M.?"

Varé produced a folded sheet from the breast pocket of his tunic and passed it to Jurriaans. "My dispensation, sergeant. Since I joined officer training, the special regulations applicable to the reserve no longer apply to me."

Jurriaans returned the paper. "Be our guest, but my boat is full."

"I'll provide another boat," Cardozo said. "If I'm allowed to join."

"You'll have to be in uniform so that you won't be shot by accident. Is there enough time for all that?"

"I live on the New Emperor's Canal," Cardozo said, "and I keep my uniform there and my brother has a boat, a fourteen foot dory with an outboard. Where do I meet you?"

"Under the bridge at the Marine's Quay."

"And I?" asked Adjutant Adèle. "Which is my patrol?"

"Adèle," Jurriaans said, "you serve with the bureau staff."

'I do?'

"And you're a woman."

"Listen to me," Adjutant Adèle said. "I'm a qualified policewoman and I have passed all my swimming tests. I shoot about as well as you do. I've been practicing judo for years. My rank is higher than yours. Either I go or I'll be phoning the chief constable within the next minute."

"Maybe he wants to come too," Karate said. "I've been told he's rather an adventurous type."

Someone knocked on the door. "Yes," Jurriaans said.

A female constable came in. "There's a Kraut gentleman downstairs who has been banging on the counter."

"I'm coming."

"And Mr. Slanozzel phoned. He says he's getting a little bored."

"Yes," Jurriaans said. "Did everybody understand everything?"

"Did you?" de Gier asked Grijpstra.

"No," Grijpstra said.

De Gier glided his flat hand over Grijpstra's bushy hair.

"I never understand anything," Grijpstra said, "but it does seem to me that we're being sucked into another soppy mess."

"Yes."

"Don't grin like that."

"Am I grinning?" de Gier asked. "Maybe I like this sort of thing. I hope that there'll be a hellish glow about that ship and that the ducks on Catburgh will be skeletons that will light up whitishly, floating on slimy green water. The women should all be nude, and poisonous yellow flames will flash from our phallic weapons. The music is Wagner, and it'll be quiet at times, and then you will hear, if you really listen, Johann Sebastian's harpsichord. And the clanging of chains dragged over sharp rocks."

"If it's quiet, there'll be nothing to hear," Adjutant Adèle said, "and if you don't mind, I'll keep my clothes on."

"You're not at home in the sergeant's fantasies," Grijpstra said.

"Not yet." De Gier's encouraging remark was accompanied

by a show of his perfect white teeth, a slight bow from his narrow waist, an increase of the width of his ample shoulders, a sultry glistening in the tender brown of his large eyes, a display of short but wavy curls, a possible caress of his hands that approached the adjutant's body.

"Out of my way," Adjutant Adèle said. She marched past the sergeant.

"I don't think she cares for you," Grijpstra said.

De Gier agreed. "But she's a lovely woman nevertheless. That dark hair, framing a dainty face, and those green catlike eyes with the deep gaze. She's exotic, don't you think?"

"Like Opete," Grijpstra said. He got no answer, and looked aside. De Gier was replaced by Varé.

"Opete?" Varé asked. "I thought you knew nothing about voodoo."

"All I know is that a vulture is called Opete."

"Opete," Varé said, watching Adjutant Adèle marching through the door. "The term signifies a special power and it is said that it often possesses vultures. Opete is the flight of the wisiman, the power that lives in his wings so that he may be free of the earth and watch from the sky."

"And Tigri?" Grijpstra asked. "What does that word signify?"

"The wisiman's claw. When it touches, it won't let go." Varé sighed. "That's rather unpleasant for the victim, but the victim's position is about as bad when the wisiman *does* let go."

24

"THIS UNIFORM MAKES ME LOOK SILLY," CARDOZO TOLD THE mirror, "and it also makes me look smaller." He left the room and met his brother in the corridor. "Admiral," Cardozo's brother said, "what do you want my boat for? I've just revarnished it. You're going to scratch my dory."

"Can I have it or not?" Cardozo asked.

"Not."

"Then I hereby confiscate your boat."

His brother put his hands on Cardozo's shoulders. "Would you like to be beaten up, Simon?"

"Assault on an officer is a serious offense."

"I admit," Cardozo's brother said, "to having returned my party card to the Communists, but the gesture does not mean that I subscribe to current conditions. I'm still against everything."

"Let me go."

"No."

Mrs. Cardozo stumbled up the stairs.

"Mother," Cardozo said. "He won't let go of me and I've got to work and I need his boat. On behalf of the state. Tell him to give me the key."

"Give the key to Simon, Samuel," Cardozo's mother said, "and I want you two to stop squabbling, your father has a headache."

"I have to make a telephone call," Cardozo said.

"You'll have to speak softly."

Cardozo tiptoed into the living room and picked up the phone. "Shsh," his father said. "Yes, Dad," Cardozo said. "I will dial gently."

"Who are you phoning?" his mother asked.

"The commissaris."

"Isn't the commissaris on leave?"

"Yes?" the commissaris' wife asked.

"This is Cardozo, ma'am. I'm sorry to have to bother you at this time of the night."

"Yes," Cardozo's father said. "You're bothering everybody. I can't sleep and I've got a headache and that's why I'm sitting here. You've just woken up your mother with your stamping and yelling."

"He woke me up too," Samuel said, "and I have to go to work tomorrow. He's going to wreck my boat. Tell him I don't have to give him the key of the outboard."

"My husband isn't here," the commissaris' wife said.

"I know, ma'am, he's in Austria, but I have to speak with him urgently. Things aren't going right here."

"That's correct," Cardozo's father said. "Why don't you all leave this room? I was here all by myself, not harming anyone, and it's one o'clock in the morning. This is like the Central Station, and I have a headache."

"Perhaps I can find him," the commissaris' wife said. "Would you like to leave a message?"

"Something is very wrong here," Cardozo said.

"Would you care for an aspirin?" Cardozo's mother asked his father.

"I would care for some silence," Cardozo's father said. "I'm retired. I have a right to peace and quiet."

"There are still some payments due on my boat," Samuel said.

"But things never go quite right, do they?" the commissaris' wife asked.

"Why don't you go to bed?" Cardozo's mother asked his father.

"Because you'll snore and wake me up."

"He wants to *confiscate* my boat," Samuel said. "I think the country is at war again."

"Perhaps your husband should come back," Cardozo said.

"Water squatters," Samuel said. "That's who they'll be after now. First they brought in tanks, and now there'll be warships. It's all the same to me, but I don't quite see why I have to lose my boat."

"I'll tell him," the commissaris' wife said.

Cardozo replaced the phone. He put out his hand.

"Give Simon the key, Samuel," Cardozo's mother said.

25

A SLICK SOUNDLESS CAR GLIDED ALONG THE POLISHED cobblestones of the Catburgh Quay, edging its slender nose through the fog, drawing stripes of light under the large orange bowls radiated by street lanterns into the moist air. Slanozzel switched the engine off by lightly touching a button with his long suntanned fingers.

"Here you are, gentlemen."

"That's all it is?" de Gier asked. "A villa on a tub?"

"A brothel," Slanozzel said. "Three stories filled with pricey pleasure, with what used to be forbidden, because nowadays anything goes. I think we had more fun in Victorian times."

De Gier lowered his window. Music screeched out of the houseboat. "Violent violins," de Gier said. "Hardly what I had expected. And a singing lady, vocalizing vulgarity. How can anyone get anything up when they pour that sort of slop down your ears?"

"It won't be too difficult," Slanozzel said. "The ladies are helpful, and a drop of alcohol stimulates."

Grijpstra grunted in the back of the car. "You're spoiled, your generation has trouble enjoying anything."

De Gier turned around. "Do I hear pity?"

"Yes," Grijpstra said. "But you were born too late. There were better times when you weren't around yet."

"What do you know? You ever visit brothels in the remote past?"

Grijpstra smiled. "My pleasures were always simple. An evening in the quarter wasn't as costly then as now. You could have a square meal at the Chinese for a few guilders and spend another ten on hard drinking later in some speakeasy where American Negroes howled through trumpets and where they had some wild women on the floor, bouncing their boobs." Grijpstra nodded. "Even flashing their tongues."

"Did you flash back?"

"I was at the bar," Grijpstra said kindly. "There was nothing I had to do, except think my thoughts."

"I remember the very place you must have in mind," Slanozzel said. "On the Seadike it was. No sniffing or shooting, you're right, the joy was simple, but I already had too much money in those days and I'd be carousing again later in the night. I would prefer to remember even further back—walking about with just a little money, hard-earned too, roaming along the canals to admire cleavages, choosing continuously but never quite coming to a decision, until you finally had to make up your mind, satisfy greedy lust, always too early."

"Exactly," Grijpstra said, "and then it was all shot, but the final moment might still be worth the trouble, for you didn't just have the woman of your choice, but a conglomerate of everything you had seen that night."

"What has changed?" de Gier asked. "I embrace Marike and think of Adjutant Adèle."

"Have you done that already?" Grijpstra asked.

"I should be soon," de Gier said. "I might even do it the other way around."

"Are you talking about positions now," Slanozzel asked, "or persons?"

"The other way around seems hard to realize to me," Grijpstra said.

"A floating house," de Gier said. "A bad imitation of a suburban villa, constructed out of hardboard sprayed with plastic paint. Would this be a temple dedicated to lechery? With dead potted plants on the balcony? It's a good thing the whole thing is shrouded in fog."

Shreds of clouds floated low above oily waves breaking slowly against the canal walls. Grijpstra had rolled his window down too and listened to the lazy swish lapping at the weed covered stones. Gulls sailed past, perched on a dark log and surrounded by bobbing offal. A taxi pierced the haze and eased toward the gangway. A man whose legs were wiped out by the fog floated aboard.

"Röder," Grijpstra said. "I didn't know he was a comedian." He put up the collar of his jacket so as to be more anonymous.

Slanozzel laughed. "Policemen have to be actors."

"Only detectives," Grijpstra said. "The uniformed branch doesn't need to act. All they do is stare grimly from under their cap visors, even if they're bareheaded."

"That Röder may be helping us out now," de Gier whispered, "but he's still a fascist. The last time we had the pleasure of meeting Röder, he wanted a few words with our suspect in private. When we saw the poor slob again, his face glowed like a bulb in a whore's room and Röder was taking off his gloves."

"The suspect was a German too," Grijpstra said. He began a sigh. "Even so." He finished the sigh. "And now we use one fiend to catch another. The means foul up the goal."

"You're upset?" Slanozzel asked. "Don't be upset. Heroin justifies a dubious approach. I rather think that Lennie should be caught improperly."

Grijpstra's teeth showed in the car's dark interior. "You're a moral man. Mr. Slanozzel? I hope you don't mind my asking. I often doubt whether I have morals. But do you have any?"

Slanozzel's carefully sculptured profile became visible, featuring a thick eyebrow, tufted at the end, and the gleam of a dark eye above the subtly curved nose. "I don't know. I would prefer not to have any morals, not to believe in anything. Such a lack would ease my life, but so far I haven't succeeded." Slanozzel smiled politely. "In business I'm trustworthy, but I wonder whether that noble trait is caused by high principles. It could also be that I keep my word because I know reliability improves profits in the long run."

"Drug dealing is beyond your scope?"

Slanozzel's other eye stared at Grijpstra too. "Drug dealing isn't business. In business both parties profit and the consumer benefits by the use of the product. I don't sell weapons either, since guns tend to kill the client." Slanozzel's raised hands supported his question. "Can I sell anything to a corpse?"

"You sell scrap metal," de Gier said, "and leather, or so I was told."

"Your informant is right."

"Aren't arms sometimes manufactured out of scrap metal and whips out of leather?"

"Certainly," Slanozzel said. "I also sell chemicals, and chemicals are often poison. Explosives are made out of chemicals too. Perhaps you know where decent business begins and ends?"

De Gier bowed his head. "I was merely curious."

"Your help is appreciated," Grijpstra said, touching Slanozzel's shoulder.

"Why am I helping you?" Slanozzel asked. "Because this city is mine too? I cannot always fathom my motivation."

De Gier opened his door and swept his arm invitingly so that Slanozzel could walk to the houseboat first. The gangway was narrow and blocked by the doorman. Baf lifted his cap. "Mr. Slanozzel! We missed you!" He pressed himself against the railing.

"These are my friends, Baf."

"Who are therefore our friends. Do come in, gentlemen. We aren't busy yet and you can choose your ladies. The assortment is even more varied than usual."

The doorman's chest, bulging in a black T-shirt, resembled half a fifty-gallon drum and his head a ball screwed tightly on a solid neck. His hair had been millimetered and his small eyes peered out of deep sockets set in blubbery fat. He edged along with his guests until they had reached the relatively spacious rosewood-paneled corridor. The corridor led to a large low room where easy chairs and couches surrounded a round bar. "Mr. Slanozzel," the barman said, "we have been looking forward to your visit."

"Evening, Henri," Slanozzel said. "I brought you two guests, who are also mine."

"Welcome," Henri said, and took Slanozzel's credit card, which he pushed into his machine. He tore the slip free and unscrewed a thin fountain pen. "Three times, the usual rate. Please sign, sir, at your leisure."

Henri was a tall man dressed in a white tight-fitting suit garnished with small golden epaulets. Ex-captain of a tourist cruiser, de Gier thought. Too much champagne one night, Grijpstra thought, and the pride of the fleet hit an iceberg. The passengers drowned after the captain left the vessel first.

"You were a sailor?" de Gier asked.

Henri's restored teeth gleamed. "It still shows?"

"Tell my guests about the rules," Slanozzel said.

Henri giggled. "There aren't any. Once admission has been paid, as it has in your case, the drinks are on me and the ladies will bestow their favors freely."

Grijpstra grabbed the credit-card slip that Henri was about to drop in a drawer. He produced his spectacle case, took out his half-glasses, cleaned them with his handkerchief, and placed them carefully on the tip of his nose. He studied the amount that Henri had written down. He pushed the slip away and shook his head.

"Something wrong, sir?"

"Not at all. But the slips you are using are too small, the last zero could hardly be squeezed in."

Henri frowned. "I will pass your suggestion to the management." He waved at the bottles lined up behind him, sorted by color. "What will it be?"

Henri poured steadily, in spite of the slight movement of the ship. Ice tinkled and silver stirring rods pricked between the cubes. Damask napkins slid across the walnut counter. Crystal dishes appeared, filled with nuts, hot pastries, and toast covered with slices of raw fish.

Grijpstra drank and counted girls. He had reached ten when he had to start counting again. They moved about, coming and going, through side doors and up and down a staircase. He also counted the guests and totaled eight. One was himself, and three others were known to him. An older fat little gent could be the conductor of a famous orchestra and his mate might be an oil sheik hiding behind sunglasses, and two young men, overdressed and much the worse for early wear would be labor brokers, renting illegal aliens to the highest-bidding building contractor or bribing government representatives to obtain valuable contracts directly. The girls were whores—that conclusion had to be correct—but they would be special whores, in view of the size of the amount Slanozzel had underwritten.

But why, Grijpstra thought, are these whores not more beautiful than they are? Is Lennie's taste limited or is this the best there is? What I see here, displayed on leather couches and Louis the Later armchairs, these women decked out in finery or nothing at all, are no more attractive than what can be sampled in a dentist's waiting-room magazine.

De Gier thought along a similar line. The sergeant had compared the brothel's interior with that of the Royal Palace. Supposing, the sergeant argued, that the Royal Palace represents the best of the country and Lennie's premises the worst, then we must admit that evil is no better than good.

"Evening, Lennie," said Slanozzel to a man who had come in.

That man is no more than a man, Grijpstra thought. And yet he is a superpimp. He emanates nothing out of the ordinary. His clothes are sold in most department stores. He has a face like a thousand others, and I can meet him ten times in the Leyden Street and never notice him. Lennie resembles John Doe but is the incarnation of Beelzebub himself, and this boat is only part of his pernicious activity. Our files claim that he handles the ninety percent of all drugs that we can never find and that his tentacles reach to the highest and mightiest levels. He has done it all and will do it again tomorrow and very likely is doing it right now. There he stands and shakes Slanozzel's hand.

"Dear guests," Lennie said when he had greeted Grijpstra and de Gier. "I am grateful that you're willing to amuse yourselves here. Another round, Henri. Let us raise our glasses to the trouble that does not exist."

"*Prosit*, Lennie," said Slanozzel.

De Gier smiled over his glass. A man like that should be squeezed, de Gier thought, so that we can do away with half our administration. But how to catch the slimy toad? That girl over there, with the nude left buttock and the nude right breast, is a minor, but if I dare to state that fact, she will immediately turn twenty-one, with a battery of lawyers supporting the falsified figure. If we find drugs here, we will be told that they somehow blew aboard, and if we point at the roulette, it will change into the royal game of geese and the money on the table just happened to be there.

"Bruha!"

"Did anyone perhaps say something?" Lennie asked.

Henri dived under the bar and popped up in the middle of the room. Baf rolled out of the corridor. In the rear of the room some disorder was evident. "I think I'll take a peep," Lennie said, and ran off.

He came back. "A grumpy customer." He smiled reassuringly. "A German gentleman who claims that his soul squeaks because of the violins. Henri will change the cassette. The tape will be thrown overboard. The customer is king, and I don't particularly care for violins myself."

The violins flew out of a window and were replaced by an electronic piano accompanied by double bass. Jungle voices sang about the Buhuhu and the Beeheehee instigating a serious relationship that proved to be subject to tensions. How all was well in the end was told by drumbeats and a muted trumpet solo. Grijpstra listened. De Gier listened too. Both liked what they heard. They hunched their shoulders and half-closed their eyes and only noticed the ladies presenting themselves to Slanozzel, when the suite came to an end.

"My name is Eugénie," said a black woman dressed in white, from her crown to her ankles, for she also wore a veil. "Charlene," said a girl who wore nothing but high heels and shoestraps. "Virginia," said a bulbous blond whose fluffed hair bobbed and whose heaven-blue eyes shone. She was dressed plainly, in a dress printed with a pattern of copulating butterflies. "I'm called that because I'm a virgin and overdue to be raped, so it better be tonight. Who would like to ravage me thoroughly, in such a rough and painful manner that I might not be there afterward to applaud the outrage?"

"You can choose or have us in turns, just as you like," the girls suggested.

"The gentlemen are ready?" Lennie asked.

"It's still early," Slanozzel said.

Lennie clapped his hands. "Away with you. Climb the stage. Deflower Virginia, who is under orders to be passive. Be as impish and cynical, after a suitable introduction, as your lecherous minds will allow for. Rip her dress, but take your time, for the guests aren't in a hurry. Possess her as far as you can and let the spotlights shine."

Well, de Gier thought, maybe something will happen after all. Let us try to follow Lennie's flight of imagination. Lennie isn't as average as he looks—he can't be or he would never have sunk so deeply.

Henri pressed buttons hidden behind the bar that extinguished the red lamps that were scattered throughout the room. Baf zipped curtains aside and disclosed a raised stage. The music changed again—a sensitive hand plucked the strings of a lute. Virginia, grabbed by Baf and put down tenderly again, tripped to a rococo cast-iron garden table and sat down primly on a matching chair, but her skirt moved up and her shoes were tight so that she had to bend down and adjust their straps, and then her neck itched, an insect buzzed in between her legs and had to be removed, she also had to climb on her chair to pick a grape, the grape had to be eaten, sweetly pressed between her lips, lusciously squeezed by her tongue. The pantomime took a while, but the public was fascinated and unhappy when Virginia rang a little bell to call the maid.

The maid was Charlene, wearing a servant's outfit. She belonged to the servile type that is so often mistreated in pornographic magazines. She arranged cups and saucers, but not properly, so that madame had to scold her and beat her even. Virginia turned Charlene upside down on her lap and hit her smartly on the bare buns. Charlene cried but dried her tears, for a visitor arrived. The visitor was Eugénie in a modest costume. Eugénie sat down and was served with tea and bonbons. Conversation, most polite. Compliments to and fro. About clothes, jewelry, quality of skin. The ladies got up, pirouetted around each other, felt each other's parts admiringly. Eugénie went too far. The audience understood that the visitor, herself female, was perhaps overly fond of women, but poor Virginia didn't seem to catch on. She giggled and tittered while submitting to further lewd approaches. The lutist was no longer plucking his strings; on the contrary, the minstrel yanked and banged, degenerating rapidly into a rock guitarist quite incapable of controlling his lower lusts. Servant Charlene was also manhandling her employer, and Virginia finally understood that she was attacked by both the denizens of Sodom and Gomorrah, and yelled for help, but Eugénie's hand smashed the desperate request.

Virginia howled. She had been pushed backward on the table, after Charlene had swept the tea things away and stamped on their debris. Virginia sobbed when Eugénie, tearing and ripping, split her dress and discarded the rags. Virginia groaned when Charlene, her trusted handmaiden, pulled her up by the hair, stripping her of her underwear at the same time.

"Bruha!"

Whether Herr Sublieutenant Röder of the Hamburg Municipal Police came to save Virginia or whether he, not being confined within his own frontiers, wanted to air the subconscious part of his soul, wasn't clear to the stunned but interested audience.

"Baf!" shouted Lennie.

Baf came, grunting. He didn't come gracefully, he fell, his foot lifted by Grijpstra's leg, and hurt his chin on the edge of the stage. "Alas," shouted de Gier, and veered across the bar, grabbing hold of Henri. "Help," yelled de Gier in Henri's ear, but Henri couldn't be of much assistance because de Gier held on to him. Too tightly probably, for panic doesn't know its own strength. De Gier's hysterically shaking head bumped against Henri's chin. Henri became unwell. De Gier, surprised by Henri's detached silence, let go. "Do you want to lie down?" de Gier asked. Henri lay down.

Baf pushed himself onto the stage but slipped back because Grijpstra pulled his leg. "Save that poor woman!" shouted Grijpstra.

Lennie fought with the two young labor brokers, who wanted to help too and mistakenly thought that Lennie was detaining them. De Gier threw bottles. One hit one of the young men in the head. The young man, in defense, hit Lennie on the nose. The barman was up again, but de Gier's elbow hit him accidentally once more in the chin. Henri sighed and held on to a shelf that gave way. More bottles fell and were caught by de Gier. De Gier aimed better now, hitting spotlights that exploded. There was a sharp smell of burning.

Some light penetrated from the quayside through tulle curtains and Röder's misdeeds on the stage were all too visible. Even skeptics knew at that moment that there could be no more thought of good intentions. The unfortunate Virginia was indeed being raped.

The smell of burning became sharper.

"Police!" shouted Slanozzel.

"Charge!" shouted Jurriaans.

Sergeant Jurriaans came in through the door, Karate and Ketchup through the windows. Broken glass clattered on the hardwood floor and was crushed by a furiously striding Baf, now definitely removed from the stage by Röder. Röder's shoe had hit Baf in the face, and because Baf was rubbing blood into his eyes, his sight was impaired.

The labor brokers fought on dauntlessly, only attacking women, who were losing their clothes as they bounced back and forth.

"Light!" shouted Karate.

De Gier pressed Henri's buttons.

"Fire extinguishers!" Ketchup shouted.

De Gier handed them out.

The fire consisted of some sparks in a far corner, but the fire extinguishers contained many gallons of foam. Röder was finally restrained. He was done with Virginia and working on Eugénie, herself on the table now, and sideways on Charlene, who begged for mercy until she had to close her mouth, hit by a stream of bubbly liquid.

De Gier saw the conductor and the sheik escape and sprayed them as they crawled around the bar but let them go, out of pity and lack of interest, but Lennie was leaving too. Lennie stepped out of a window. De Gier was quick, but not quick enough. The labor brokers threw him a woman who scratched. Jurriaans was faster. Jurriaans saw how Lennie dropped into a powerboat. Jurriaans stepped out of the window too, but the powerboat was leaving. De Gier heard the splash and dived out of the window.

The powerboat reversed. Jurriaans and de Gier swam out of its wake. The powerboat jumped forward, raising its bow and leaving white waves that rushed at its pursuers.

"At last," Adjutant Adèle said, peering from the bow of Cardozo's brother's dory. "Something is coming at us. Catch it, colleagues."

Cardozo pulled the starting rope of his outboard engine. The engine burped and stalled. Cardozo rewound the rope.

"Let me try," Reserve Sergeant Varé said, and stumbled to the rear of the dory. Varé's position was port. Cardozo, yanking his string, moved to port as well. Adjutant Adèle, still observing the powerboat approaching rapidly, leaned to port too. The dory capsized.

Patrolboat M-3 of the Amsterdam Municipal Police started up its twin engines while its crew of six water constables manned their battle stations. Lennie saw the approaching danger, increased speed, and turned his wheel sharply. The powerboat shot off at a tangent and hit Cardozo's brother's dory.

Cardozo swam. He saw Lennie's head.

"I can't swim," Lennie said.

"I'll save you," Cardozo said. "Turn over on your back and go limp."

Lennie obeyed. Cardozo swam around him. Lennie turned over again, leered, seized Cardozo's throat with both hands, and squeezed.

Lennie didn't see Varé, but Varé saw Lennie. Varé grabbed his left wrist with his right hand, made two fists, and made them come down with force on Lennie's head. Lennie released Cardozo.

"You okay?" Varé asked Cordozo.

Lennie popped up again.

"You're under arrest," said Varé. "Keep quiet or I'll drown you. Swim to the shore. You have a right to a telephone call, and if you can't afford to hire a lawyer, the state will hire one for you."

"Why don't you accompany the suspect," Adjutant Adèle said. "Then I can save Cardozo. Turn over on your back, Cardozo, and stop bulging your eyes."

"Hello?" the water constables shouted. "Anyone in the water?"

The water constables saved everybody.

"That fellow," Jurriaans said, "needs handcuffs."

"Hey," shouted de Gier.

"No," said Jurriaans. "The other fellow. This fellow is a splendid chap."

"Sorry," the water constable said. "But it's hard to see anything in this fog."

"And take us to the Catburgh Quay," Jurriaans said. "That's about all you can do for us. Thanks for the assistance."

"Our pleasure," said the water constables.

"Now what shall we do?" Karate asked Ketchup. "The fire has been taken care of."

Karate looked about him. Slanozzel rested on a couch and smoked a cigar. Baf still bled, leaning against the stage, and against Henri, who bled too.

"Those two won't be going anywhere," Ketchup said. "You know what? We start the interrogations." He grabbed Charlene. "You come with me." Karate grabbed Eugénie.

"Where do you want me?" Charlene asked.

Ketchup indicated a door. "Into there, on the double."

"And now?" Charlene asked, opening herself on the bed. "Do you want to enjoy your break? Why don't you go ahead?"

"No," Ketchup said. "You tell me where the heroin is kept. We'll find it anyway, but it'll take time, and in a minute they'll all be back and get in my way."

"I don't know what you're talking about, darling," said Charlene, and extended her arms. "Come along and let's get this over with."

"Dearest," Ketchup said, "cooperate a little, will you? Lennie has been caught. You'll have to look for another job. Try being more helpful for a change."

Charlene opened herself further. "Just for a moment? Do make an effort, dear."

"I wouldn't mind," Ketchup said, "but I'm working right now. Tell me where Lennie keeps his junk."

Charlene sat up and crossed both her legs and her arms. "Spoilsport. The heroin is in the safe, and the safe is in Lennie's office."

The door flew open. "What's going on here?" asked Sergeant Jurriaans, dripping on the expensive rug. "Since when do we segregate ourselves while dallying with unclad women?"

"Join us," Charlene said, and picked up a pink telephone. "Shall I call another girl for you?"

"It's in the safe," Ketchup said. "And the safe is in the office."

Jurriaans pulled Ketchup back into the room. "In the what?"

"In the safe, sergeant. They don't even bother to hide heroin anymore."

Karate looked out of half-opened door. "The witness here says that it's in the safe."

"I'll get the key," Jurriaans said.

Adjutant Adèle stood in the gangway. "I've called the station and they're sending a van, and blankets in case we catch cold." She wrung out her hair. "Bah, I've got dirty water everywhere."

Lennie stood behind Adjutant Adèle and in front of Varé, who guarded the suspect.

Jurriaans put out his hand. "Key of the safe."

"In the right pocket of my jacket," Lennie said. "I've got handcuffs on."

Jurriaans looked at the key. "You really keep it in your safe?"

"Where else?" said Lennie. "Isn't a safe safe? Do you know what heroin costs today . . . sergeant?"

"Yes?"

"Don't touch it, sergeant. There's a notebook in that safe too, with the names of those above you. They won't go after me if you mess with my junk, but they'll go after you."

Jurriaans put his finger on Lennie's nose and pressed.

"Ouch," said Lennie.

"You talk too much," Jurriaans said. "We're going to stew you."

26

"ARE YOU TELEPHONING FROM AUSTRIA?" ASKED SERGEANT Jurriaans.

"No," the commissaris said, "from my garden."

Jurriaans frowned, took the phone from his ear, and looked at it suspiciously. He pressed it against his ear again. "Are you inquiring about the Obrian case?"

"I will be," the commissaris said, "but not now. How about tonight, at six sharp in your station, and if you would, see to it that all colleagues who have worked on the case are present."

"Sir," Jurriaans said in confirmation.

"And, Jurriaans?"

"Sir?"

"Don't tell them that I'll be there."

It was evening, the weather sultry, and the windows of the room were open. The commissaris sat by himself and smiled at the framed Civic Guard officers. The officers looked grim but not altogether unsympathetic because the little old man was their successor and carried their prestige; they forgave him his lack of plumed hat and sword.

The invited entered. "Welcome," the commissaris said. He got up. "Good evening, Adjutant Adèle." He sat down again. "Hello, Sergeant Jurriaans . . . Hello, Grijpstra . . . Hello, de Gier . . . Hello, Cardozo." He got up again. "I don't believe we have met."

Varé introduced himself. The commissaris shook Varé's hand. "Delighted to make your acquaintance, sergeant. I've heard your name mentioned. The chief of this station appreciates your contribution, and so do we at Headquarters."

Varé and the commissaris smiled at each other. The commissaris waved at a chair. "Do sit down, sergeant. And here we have the valiants who bring up the rear. Hello, Ketchup . . . Hello, Karate."

The subordinates scraped their chairs. The commissaris leaned back in his chair, folded his hands on his waistcoat, and curved his eyebrows.

The colleagues mumbled.

"Well?" the commissaris asked.

The colleagues kept quiet.

"I'm here," the commissaris said, "because I was sent for. Something, I was told, appears to be wrong. What's wrong?"

De Gier admired his face mirrored in the waxed table's surface. He spoke to his reflection. "Weren't you supposed to be in Bad Gastein?"

"I am here," the commissaris said, "because one of you telephoned my wife, and my wife telephoned me."

"Who?" asked Grijpstra.

"Me," said Cardozo.

"You?" asked de Gier.

"Why?" asked Grijpstra.

"Because," Cardozo said, "I thought that something was

wrong. I had hoped that I would be able to speak with the commissaris in private."

"There's nothing like teamwork," Sergeant Jurriaans said.

Cardozo looked straight ahead.

The commissaris coughed. He also touched his nose. He took his spectacles off and blew on his glasses. "When I left," he said softly, "I left orders that Obrian's murderer be apprehended. There were two suspects, Gustav and Lennie. I passed by Headquarters this afternoon and read all reports. Both Gustav and Lennie have been arrested." He pulled a handkerchief from his breast pocket and polished his glasses.

"Can I smoke?" Grijpstra asked.

"No," said Adjutant Adèle.

"Can *I* smoke?" asked the commissaris.

"Certainly, sir."

"Could Grijpstra smoke with me?"

"Certainly, sir."

The commissaris and Grijpstra bit the ends of their cigars and struck matches. They puffed smoke into the direction of a window.

"So what's wrong?" the commissaris asked. "I would say that the preliminary investigation has been closed, for your reports do not mention the possibility of finding new facts." He refolded his hands and talked around his cigar. "But what seems strange is that you accuse neither Gustav nor Lennie of Obrian's death, although just about every other charge has been crammed into the forms. Who would care to explain?"

"Sir," said de Gier. "The suspects have not been charged with the Obrian murder because of lack of proof, their fervent denials, and the possible validity of a theory."

"What theory?"

De Gier mumbled.

"We're here anyway," the commissaris said, "and theories

can be quite interesting. Tell me of your thoughts, sergeant, I can do with some entertainment."

"Coffee?" asked Jurriaans, and put his hand on a telephone. "Delicious cake?"

"If you please," said the commissaris.

The coffee came, as did the cake. Everybody busied himself with the tearing of sugar packets and the passing of the milk jug. There was diligent stirring.

"Gustav," de Gier said, "was apprehended first and I've listened to his comments. My impression is that Gustav didn't kill Obrian, but he did attempt manslaughter on Orang Utan and he's definitely a deranged and dangerous criminal. He should go to jail for a long time because of what he did—and would still do if he weren't incarcerated."

"Not a nice man?" the commissaris asked.

'No, sir. I think," de Gier said, "that Gustav had to be imprisoned. In order to realize that intention, the quarter's police station had come up with serious suspicions. Because there didn't happen to be any at the moment, they had to be fabricated. They were fabricated by manipulation."

"Who manipulated whom?"

De Gier looked at Karate.

"Me?" Karate said. "Why me? What can I, a simple constable manipulated by higher forces, manipulate?" He frowned sadly. "Me, caught in the banality of anonymous existence, me, a mere minion . . ."

De Gier looked at Ketchup.

Ketchup blew his nose.

De Gier waited.

Ketchup put his handkerchief away. His small face grinned morosely. "Could I, my colleague's colleague, cause the tiniest deviation in the path of destiny?"

"Miserable modesty," de Gier said, "is a weapon I'm learning to handle too, but let me theorize further. Orang Utan is a brother with a violent reputation. He has been reprimanded several times. His last offense was an assault on rebels riding Harleys. They called him a nigger, but he is an Ambonese."

"Who are brown," said Varé.

"And Obrian was black. I mention the color"—de Gier kneaded his chin—"but color hardly fits in my theory. What does fit is that Orang Utan detested Gustav. He persecuted Gustav. Gustav usually drove a Corvette. The morning that he attacked Orang Utan he drove a Peugeot. I have found out why Gustav wasn't driving the Corvette. That car had been towed away by the police but couldn't be found on the parking lot where the police trucks customarily deposit their catches."

"Why had the Corvette been towed away?"

"Because of double parking, sir. The ticket had been issued by Orang Utan. According to my information, Orang Utan made a habit of sticking tickets on the Corvette and then radioed the tow trucks so that they could impound the car."

"A feud between Gustav and Orang Utan," the commissaris said. "Very good. The two men knew each other? There had been arguments?"

"Yes, sir."

"And on this occasion the Corvette had not been taken to the proper place. Why not? My car has been towed away too, but I got it back easily. All I had to do was pay the fine to the officer guarding the yard."

"I was told that the tow truck had an engine problem and ditched the Corvette somewhere along the way."

"You believe that the truck had no engine trouble?"

"Yes, sir. The tow truck's driver and Orang Utan are friends."

"You can prove the relationship?"

"Yes, sir. But both the driver and Orang Utan deny that they were harassing Gustav. Double-parked cars are customarily towed away, and Gustav makes a habit of double parking. Tow trucks are known to have engine trouble at times."

"So how did you manage to arrest Gustav?"

Ketchup held up his hand. "Our report states clearly what went on."

The commissaris nodded. "What didn't the report state?"

"That Orang Utan," de Gier said, "who was riding ahead of Gustav had been warned via the walkie-talkies of our helpful constables that Gustav was following him."

"So the channels of the walkie-talkies were the same as the channel used by the motorcycle cops," the commissaris said, "which is a coincidence, since there are many channels."

"Too much of a coincidence sir."

Jurriaans removed a speck of dust off his sleeve. "Coincidences do happen."

De Gier also removed a speck of dust off his sleeve. "And what were Ketchup and Orang Utan discussing when they met earlier on that same day in the police garage?"

"The weather?" asked Ketchup.

"We are not supposed to provoke," the commissaris said, "but even provocations have to be proved. I spoke to the public prosecutor, who never mentioned the possibility. The lawyer for the defense may speak up, of course, but there's still the heroin found in Gustav's house and the charges that Gustav's prostitutes are pressing against their previous employer. It seems that we did meet with some success after all, but we *were* working on the Obrian case, or am I mistaken perhaps?"

"Gustav is fried," Jurriaans said.

"And there was another suspect. Lennie."

"Are you looking at me?" Grijpstra asked. "Sir?"

"I have to look at someone," the commissaris said. "I can look at someone else if you prefer."

"Lennie," Grijpstra said, "was arrested on a charge of assaulting an officer, Cardozo in this case, whom he tried to throttle and drown. The report was signed by Cardozo himself and the witness John Varé, who is also a policeman, and signed under oath. Lennie was also arrested on a charge of drug dealing. We found two kilos of heroin in his safe."

"And cocaine, one pound," Jurriaans said.

"And hashish," Ketchup said. "Oil, a gallon."

"And some jars filled with speed," said Karate.

"And," said Grijpstra, "on a charge of employing a minor for lecherous purposes, a certain Charlene, fifteen years old."

"A well-formed child," Karate said.

"Overly well-formed," Ketchup said. "If you ignore half, you would still think she is ten years older."

"Gentlemen," the commissaris said, "there's a lady present." He bowed to Adjutant Adèle. He addressed Grijpstra. "The report was not signed by you."

"I signed, sir," Jurriaans said. "I arrested the suspect. Grijpstra and de Gier happened to be visiting the brothel, on the invitation of a friend of mine, Mr. Slanozzel. Trouble arose, someone called for the police, and as I happened to be on patrol in the neighborhood, I entered the establishment."

"Via the waterside?" the commissaris asked. "Since when do you patrol in a boat?"

"We happened to employ a boat, sir, because there had been complaints. Lennie's brothel has a bad reputation, and if we had approached the trouble spot via the quay, we would have been seen. The quay is well-lit."

"So you were on the water, accompanied by five officers, and Grijpstra and de Gier were causing discord in the brothel."

"No, sir," Grijpstra said. "We just happened to be around because we wanted to know what the brothel was like, and also to please Mr. Slanozzel, who asked us to accompany him. It would have been rude to refuse his invitation in view of his friendship with Sergeant Jurriaans."

"Who caused the trouble?"

"Some German," de Gier said.

"And where did he go?"

"He left," Grijpstra said. "We didn't see where he went. There was so much going on, and everybody kept falling into the canal."

"A German," the commissaris said. "I wonder who that could be?" He took off his glasses again and inspected their lenses.

"Sir?" asked Jurriaans.

"Let's have it, sergeant."

"We didn't need witnesses, so Grijpstra and de Gier weren't mentioned in the report either. The charges are clear enough. Naked facts don't have to be dressed up."

"I should say not," Ketchup said. "The girl who I interrogated was shapely enough."

"And did you see the blond?" Karate asked. "Who was taken care of by the Kraut?"

"Hmm," the commissaris said. His small fist hit the table. "That German." He pointed at Grijpstra. "Sublieutenant Röder, Hamburg Municipal Police. He's the only German police officer I can recall who owes us a favor. Did you send for him?"

Grijpstra studied his hands.

"I sent for him," de Gier said. "Röder is a civilian here. He can provoke as much as he likes."

"So you all had a good many drinks first," the commissaris said, "at the expense of this Mr. Slanozzel. I don't know the name."

"Four bourbons," De Gier said.

"Four genevers," Grijpstra said.

"Mr. Slanozzel is an upright citizen," Jurriaans said. "A businessman from the West who likes the quarter. A wealthy man."

"Legally wealthy?"

"I do believe so," Grijpstra said.

"And did you instigate relationships with any of the women?"

"No, sir."

"Although sex was included in the price," de Gier said, "but we couldn't have it anyway. Too much happening, fistfights, fire, cops coming in through the windows . . ."

"If you couldn't extricate yourself from the human situation," the commissaris said to Karate, "and your colleague was unable to influence fate, then we may perhaps excuse the adjutant's just lassitude and the sergeant's rightful ignorance." He rubbed out his cigar. *"If."* He smiled brightly. "But we could still try to analyze the premises." He looked at Adjutant Adèle. "You were highest in rank, so we may assume that you were in charge of the raid. Would you say there was any provocation?"

"I do not always say what I think, sir."

"What would you say?"

"I would say," said Adjutant Adèle, "that we were on patrol and heard citizens shouting for help. We responded. We found what we found."

"Yes." The commissaris shook his head.

"Lennie is stewed," Karate said.

"And did Lennie murder Obrian?"

"He says he didn't," Jurriaans said, "and my report does not mention the Obrian-related charge. We will continue interrogating the suspect, but don't you think we have enough on Lennie?"

"I'm not really thinking yet," the commissaris said. "Yes, Cardozo, you want to say something too?"

Cardozo dropped his finger and smiled slyly. "I too have a theory."

"Which is?"

"I believe," Cardozo said, "that neither Gustav nor Lennie had anything to do with Obrian's death."

"But your theory does include a suspect, I hope."

"Certainly, sir." Cardozo sat up eagerly. His fist pounded the table.

"Who?" asked the commissaris.

27

CARDOZO'S TANGLED CURLS, FRAMING A POSITIVE AND cheerful countenance, amused his peers. The police folk gathered around the table relaxed, feeling at home in the solemn ambience of the room, under solid beams that both supported and adorned the neatly plastered ceiling. Soft light filled the deep windowsills and was reflected in the fresh green of leaves and the muted red of dainty flowers. The station staff's stiff tunics, whose stately blue was set off by the impeccable white of shirts and strengthened by faultlessly knotted black ties, added to the trustful atmosphere. The commissaris' light-colored shantung suit and Grijpstra's neat striped costume contrasted in a dignified manner with the contained frivolity of de Gier's clothing. Cardozo as the lone exception made a comical effect. Lips curled and eyes twinkled.

"You have a suspect?" de Gier asked.

Cardozo tore at his curls. "Yes, sergeant."

"And who could your suspect be?"

"You."

Cardozo dropped his hands on the table and froze. All others moved. De Gier reacted most noticeably: he hid his face in his hands and groaned. Grijpstra crushed a cigar. Jurriaans pronounced a word consisting of consonants. Adjutant Adèle bit the nail of her right index finger. Ketchup veered forward and Karate backward. Reserve Sergeant Varé flattened his nose with the knuckle of his thumb, and the commissaris burped behind his handkerchief.

"Me," de Gier said. "It was *me*. The end is near."

"But, Simon," Grijpstra said. "What's the matter with you? The warm weather perhaps? Some trouble at home?"

"No," Cardozo said. "I feel fine. I've got my facts and I've got my theory. If I fit the facts together in some other way, I get lost in the absurd. Whenever they fit, they point at de Gier as the killer. Is it my fault that de Gier shot Obrian?"

His question wasn't answered.

"It is not," Cardozo said firmly.

"And those facts?" the commissaris asked. "Could we also try to fit them together?"

"I will disclose my facts." Cardozo opened his notebook. "Here is one. We have the report concerning Obrian's murder that was written and signed by Sergeant Jurriaans. My fact is the untruth contained in that report. The report states that the shooting took place at twenty past three in the morning, but Obrian was shot at three o'clock."

"You have witnesses?"

"Three roller-skating young gentlemen," Cardozo said, "who rolled along the Seadike and heard the shots tear through the tinkle of the local church's carillon."

"So I lied?" Jurriaans asked.

"Yes, sergeant."

"But I'm not de Gier."

"De Gier"—Cardozo's voice squeaked and he had to clear

his throat—"is your friend. He shot Obrian at your request. You lied to protect de Gier. If you hadn't lied, he might have been suspected, which would have made you guilty too because of supplying him with the weapon."

"Fact?"

"And the funny clothes," Cardozo said, "No, not a fact, sergeant. Sorry, this part is only a suspicion."

"You're joking," Grijpstra said.

"I'm not joking. Here comes another fact. The murder weapon belonged to Eliazar Jacobs, which I can prove because the experts told me that the bullets that did away with Obrian originated in Jacobs' Schmeisser. Another fact is the actual friendship between Jurriaans and Jacobs. Another fact again—Jacobs lives five minutes' walking distance from the Olofs-alley. Jacobs often drinks too much. The evening before the murder was spent by Jurriaans and Jacobs in one another's company, partly in Hotel Hadde. Jurriaans walked Jacobs home. Now another suspicion. Jurriaans put Jacobs to bed. Took the Schmeisser. Passed the Schmeisser to de Gier. De Gier shot Obrian. De Gier returned the Schmeisser to Jurriaans. Jurriaans took the weapon back to Jacobs' room."

"Jacobs never knew?" the commissaris asked. "We're talking about the Jacobs who works at the morgue?"

"Yes, sir. He was asleep, deeply asleep, because he was also drunk."

De Gier's mouth sagged. He closed and opened it again. "Cardozo, little friend, can I say something?"

"Yes," Cardozo said.

"So why did I later find the weapon in Jacobs' room? Why did I allow everybody to fire it? Why did I ask you to take it to headquarters?"

Cardozo smiled.

"No," Grijpstra said. "You've got to answer those questions. Are you quite out of your mind?"

Cardozo spoke softly. "I'm sane, adjutant. And I'm sad. You know why de Gier forced that situation. You've known him longer and better than I have. You know the bizarre jokes he fancies."

"Me?" de Gier asked. "Don't you think I'm an excellent cop?"

"You're an absolutely splendid cop," Cardozo said. "That's why I admire you so. You're my hero. I'm always imitating you. Your nonsense almost always contains sense. Because you're a good policeman you had the weapon confiscated. It had performed its task in trusty hands, but Jacobs is crazy and you didn't want him armed."

"I'm a bizarre splendid cop?" de Gier asked.

Cardozo caressed the table. He looked up. "I don't know what you are, Rinus. I've been trying to figure you out for a long time, but you never fit my definitions. A policeman who murders a bad pimp—you think that's exaggerated?"

"It seems exaggerated to me," the commissaris said.

"My friend's enemy is my enemy," Cardozo said. "Jurriaans is de Gier's friend. Obrian was Jurriaan's enemy. Sergeant Jurriaans is known was the king of the quarter. Obrian was a mere prince. The prince attempted to supplant the king. I know this station, I served here for a number of years. The sergeants are in charge of the station, and Jurriaans is the sergeants' sergeant. His word is law. He rules by a single gesture at the right moment. He protects and restrains. He's respected."

"You're talking about me?" Jurriaans asked.

Cardozo nodded at Jurriaans. "Yes. Your authority was impaired, a little more each day, and always by Obrian. Divide and rule, that's what you always did; you balanced the princes against each other. Prince Obrian, Prince Lennie, Prince Gustav. Obrian had pushed his brothers out and you could no longer rearrange the balance. Obrian's shadow increased; you couldn't stop the black cloud."

"Pimps can be caught," Jurriaans said, "as you saw."

"So why didn't you catch them earlier, sergeant? You made de Gier grab Gustav because you had lost control. You went all-out, but you could only do that because Obrian had been removed. You were paralyzed when he was still around."

"Why was Obrian so strong?" the commissaris asked.

Cardozo thought.

"Some strange power perhaps? A god?"

"Yes," Cardozo said. "The devil is also a god. Obrian was a man who could make use of the shadow force. I thought so when I saw his wicked dead smile. And then there's the tale about what happened to a woman called Madeleine."

"Yes," Grijpstra said. "No more of her."

"What happened?" the commissaris asked.

Ketchup described the incident.

Cardozo shook his head. "Such a lovely woman, in such a lowly attitude, in public too."

"Please," Grijpstra said.

"It was rather submissive," Karate said.

"Still a bit of a taboo," Varé said, "although it has been common practice for as long as humanity exists. I've seen prehistoric images depicting oral sex. I suppose that the local taboo is of Victorian origin, and local indeed—outside of Western Europe, no eyebrows are raised."

Grijpstra closed his eyes.

"You can open them again," de Gier said. "We'll change the subject. Cardozo, why are you dragging me into your theory?"

"You assisted Jurriaans," Cardozo said, "because you're his friend and because you sympathized with his predicament, and also because the challenge was new to you, for I'm sure you've never shot a pimp before. You're an adventurer and delight in being a hero."

"You make your sergeant sound like a teenage punk," Adjutant Adèle said.

"Maybe I don't express myself well," Cardozo said. "I really admire Sergeant De Gier. He's fearless, and when he thinks he should do something, nothing will hold him back. I always hesitate when I'm about to be courageous, and I usually only succeed in making a fool of myself."

"Courageous?" the commissaris asked. "To mow a man down with an automatic weapon when he's out for a stroll?"

"I think so," Cardozo said. "Not so much the deed itself as the idea that the sergeant did something that went against all the rules."

"So I put up a good show," de Gier said. "Now, what if I tell you that I was peacefully asleep when Obrian reaped his reward? May Tabriz be my witness, for she was stretched out in my arm."

"Who is Tabriz?" Adjutant Adèle asked. "Your girlfriend?"

"His fat cat," Grijpstra said, "that was assembled from the remnants of worn-out Persian rugs. A miserable sod that likes to break glassware and sniggers when you cut your toes."

"A very lovely animal," de Gier said.

"You put up a good show," Cardozo said, "and you're now putting up another. You shot Obrian at night, with a weapon you weren't familiar with. Then you left the burned-out corner house, crossed the Seadike, and entered the police station through a side door. Jurriaans took your weapon and disguise and you left the station again. You drove home, which at that time you could have done in ten minutes. Jurriaans telephoned you. You telephoned Adjutant Grijpstra. You picked him up and drove back to the station."

"And saw some roller-skating gentlemen on the way who would witness against me later on. But because I like to make real trouble for myself, I told you about those jokers so that you could find them and prove that Jurriaans and I had changed the time of my crime."

"That's what you did," Cardozo said, "because you didn't care. I think that's great."

"You do like to create chaos," Grijpstra said. "I've often noticed that tendency. And you often do the opposite of what circumstances seem to require."

"You too?" de Gier asked. "You're also in this scheme?"

"Adjutant Grijpstra plays no part in my theory," Cardozo said, "but Ketchup and Karate do. They contributed to the setup."

"You're not getting personal now, are you, Simon?" asked Karate.

"You wouldn't be slandering your closest friends, now, would you, Simon?" asked Karate.

"Cardozo's quite clever," Jurriaans said, "but some of his theory's details aren't clear to me yet. Why didn't I shoot Obrian myself? Since when do I need others to take care of my problems? I'm a fairly good shot, I don't need movie heroes to take my place."

"I thought we were friends," de Gier said.

"No," Grijpstra said, "you had to make use of de Gier's talents because you were on duty. You had to be on duty so that you could find the corpse, once the crime had been reported."

"And I'm a convenient weapon," de Gier said. "A robot anybody can switch on at the right time. I'll kill Obrian for you, and a day later I'll hunt Gustav down, at the request of the constables here. It's a good thing I managed to hold my temper or that fiend would be stored on ice too by now."

"But what's wrong?" the commissaris asked. "If I listen to you, it seems that everything has been taken proper care of, according to the Argentine method."

"The what method?" Adjutant Adèle asked.

"The Argentine method. The police commandos who drag suspects out of their beds and shoot them at will. The courts do not seem to work very well out there, so the police like to arrange matters themselves. In other South American countries the routine is rather similar. In Colombia bums are hunted down and shot, and even stray children who live on offal and theft. And in Peru the PIP operates. That's also police. If they interrogate a suspect, they undress him first, pull a plastic bag over his head and shoulders, and keep hitting him with truncheons until he confesses."

"I don't quite like that way of behavior," Cardozo said, "even if it does reestablish order. That's why I telephoned the commissaris."

The room became quiet. The commissaries looked at his watch. "A break." He got up. "I would like to see all of you here again in half an hour's time."

28

THE COMPANY GATHERED IN THE CORRIDOR, CALMED DOWN by visits to the canteen and rest rooms, and spread out so that Adjutant Adèle could reach the door. Grijpstra gave her the right-of-way out of everyday politeness, Cardozo because of respect for her rank, and de Gier in view of her beauty. Jurriaans stepped back too and made the delay profitable by watching noisy sparrows in a gutter. Ketchup and Karate joined him at the window.

"That Cardozo, hey? Sergeant?"

"Right," said Jurriaans.

"Will this last very long, sergeant?"

"Depends how strong the commissaris' strings are."

"Which strings, sergeant?"

Jurriaans touched Ketchup's shoulders with his fingertips. "The strings that have been attached to us."

The commissaris had sat down already and was talking to Varé. He got up, nodded at Adjutant Adèle, and pointed at

Varé. "Our colleague has also come up with a suspect, and a theory in which this suspect may fit. He will now elaborate on his findings."

"Ehhum," Varé said. "I appreciate your considering my ideas seriously. As a member of the reserve, I don't really belong to the scene and I often regret being outside, but sometimes I quite enjoy it too. To be able to observe from a distance may afford a better view."

His audience stared.

"Ehhum. Yes. It may also be good that I belong to a minority, since the Obrian case is black, and you're all white, so that you're looking down and I'm looking up. The case is black, yes, as black as Opete, our little angel of death, circling above the alley, and Tigri, the dark spy, sniffing at the corpse and at your legs."

Adjutant Adèle giggled. "You're putting it well."

"I'm glad you think so." Varé allowed a black hand to shoot from a white cuff. "And who are these somber powers, this Opete and this Tigri? They're the extensions of a magician." Varé looked at the commissaris. "This is somewhat of a scientific lecture, sir, and if my expressions are too poetic, you're welcome to restrain me. I'm a sociologist and presently working on research regarding the culture of blacks in the Netherlands. The culture incorporates religion, and the black variety is called the winticult, which is magical, like all religions. We sociologists assume that Negroes are human too and therefore feel the need to tangle with the intangible. If this effort does not work out, an expert is hired. The expert in our case is the magician Uncle Wisi, who I now introduce as our suspect. Uncle Wisi is known to us. Adjutant Grijpstra has called on him. Uncle Wisi was Luku Obrian's teacher."

"A very old man," Grijpstra said. "Neither senile nor crippled, but unable to fire an automatic weapon and make a fast getaway."

Varé nodded. "Indeed. His age makes him innocent of the crime, but he did know Jacobs and lived close to him. Uncle Wisi could therefore obtain the weapon, and anybody can disguise himself. However, I do admit that I don't see him as the actual killer."

"He's still your suspect? You suspect him as the intellectual author of the crime?"

"Yes," Varé said. "I'm familiar with the construction as it belongs to the material that I have to study for my inspector's examination. *He who makes use of another to commit a crime.*"

"Not an easy construction to present to court," the commissaris said.

"Indeed, sir, but easy to incorporate into a hypothesis."

"The motivation?" asked de Gier.

"I'm getting to that, sergeant. I do hope that you won't be upset if I tell you that I did some sleuthing on my own. It wasn't difficult for me, as I speak the Surinam language and I'm a civilian when not in uniform, while you people are cops twenty-four hours a day. My civilian status makes me harmless."

"Where were you?" Adjutant Adèle asked. "In the ladies' boudoirs?"

"The quarter was designed to accommodate the lonely male."

"Yes, yes," Adjutant Adèle said critically.

"Where was I, now?" Varé asked.

"At the winticult?" the commissaris asked.

"Thank you," Varé said. "The city blacks that emigrated from the West—and most of the Negroes now living in Amsterdam belong to that category—never rejected their original religion completely. They may call themselves Christians, and even go to church, but often still rely on the services of their home altar. Sociologically seen, it's good that old habits die hard, since a separate culture often strengthens its practitioners. The cult traveled with the blacks in the slave ships that took them west and made them believe in one single God, the creator of the universe, Massa Gran-Gado, a power that's out of reach of worship, as it exists outside our dimensions. Blacks are practical. If something isn't necessary, they won't spend time on it, and they never built any temples in honor of the original mystery. The cult's sacred buildings are meant for the wintis, and the wintis are the projections of Him who will not let Himself be known—the spirits, or gods, of nature and later also of the cities. The cult worships the wintis that will separate, for our benefit, and also by our choice, into good and bad." Varé kept up a finger. "Originally, however, the wintis are neutral, and separate from any duality. We pray to the wintis and try to make them serve us."

"We?" the commissaris asked.

"They," Varé said, "but I identify with my subject now, to make my lecture easier to listen to."

"I see," the commissaris said. "Carry on, sergeant."

Varé bowed. "I bow to my altar." He mumbled. "I utter sacred formulas." He poured from an imaginary bottle and spooned food onto an invisible plate. "I make offerings." He drummed. He blew a trumpet. He raised his arms and stamped his feet.

"I do all this," Varé said, "to please the winti. If I do that for a good reason, let's say to make somebody else happier or less sad, then the winti will answer by producing positive power. We call that power *opo*. *Opo* may possess objects, or substances, that will change into *obeah*, which is medicine.

"But," Varé said, "I can also make the winti work the other way, to enrich myself, for instance, and that way I manufacture *wisi* that can also turn into something which we also call *wisi*."

"So you're a wisiman," Grijpstra said. "But don't tell me that Uncle Wisi serves the devil. I got to know the man a little, and I think I'm quite fond of the old fart."

Varé clapped his hands. "I'm so glad you said that, adjutant, for I share your feelings. Uncle Wisi is an outstanding old chap, but he nevertheless calls himself Wisi. Now, how would you explain that quirk in his character?"

"I'm not explaining anything," Grijpstra said.

"Then I'll try," Varé said. "How about Uncle Wisi having been converted? And changed into an obeahman who kept his former name?"

"Obrian was bad," De Gier said, "and he seemed connected to Uncle Wisi."

"I do agree. But please remember that I said that the wintis are essentially neutral. The winti provides power, and it's up to us how that power will be directed."

"One moment," the commissaris said. "Didn't you say just now that you made investigations of your own? What can you tell us about Obrian's background?"

Varé frowned. "Luku was once employed by one of the Dutch international lumber dealers, a company that cuts the valuable trees of the jungle without bothering to plant seedlings. Obrian's mother was a whore and his father might have died while doing forced hard labor, but it's hard to believe that Luku knew who his father was, because the children of prostitutes usually do not know their fathers' names. Luku was by no means stupid and his successful thefts from his employer made him an authority among his friends. He was a dignitary of the cult. The company accused him of fraud and he escaped to this country. Luku brought Opete with him, a vulture chick incubated under his arm, of the species which we call streetbird or carrion crow. The streetbird also functions in the cult, for they're supposed to embody a winti, not always but certainly in a case of being born in close contact with an initiate."

Karate and Ketchup scratched under their armpits and looked at each other.

"Wow," said Karate.

"Hup-ho," said Ketchup.

"Silence," the commissaris said. "If you please."

"Obrian arrived here," Varé continued, "and became drunk at once. He stayed drunk for days on end. To be drunk is a form of heightened perception. After three or four days his mental state took its toll and his body began to become paralyzed and he foamed at the mouth. His friends took him to Uncle Wisi. One might say that Uncle Wisi cured his patient, but I prefer to think that Uncle Wisi recognized Obrian as a luku and made use of Obrian's condition to open him up a little further."

"For a beneficial purpose?" the commissaris asked.

"Absolutely," Varé said. "I'm convinced that Uncle Wisi wanted to strengthen Obrian's power so that he would be better able to guide and represent his people here."

"Well, he failed," said Jurriaans. "Obrian became a superpimp, a drug dealer, a slimy sadist."

Varé raised his hands to heaven. "The human being is free. We can always choose."

"Wasn't Uncle Wisi ashamed of what he had brought about?" asked De Gier.

"You've got it," Varé said. "That was his motivation."

"But Uncle Wisi didn't shoot Obrian," Grijpstra said sullenly. "I'll never believe that. That friendly old clown wouldn't point a gun."

"There are injunctions and prohibitions," Varé said. "No adept will pass his power without conditions. Uncle Wisi strengthened Luku Obrian's gift to handle the power, but he must have given him a taboo as well, and when a taboo is broken, the *keenu*, the curse, is triggered off. As soon as the *keenu* is released, the disciple dies."

"Pointing the bone?" Karate asked. "I saw that on TV the other night. With the Papuans, somewhere in New Guinea I believe. There were a couple of dry old chaps huddled around a fire, grunting and grumbling away, and all of a sudden one of them grabs a bone and points it somewhere, and whoever is at the other end, no matter how far away, croaks for sure. He has an accident or gets sick or something."

"You do carry on, you know," Ketchup said. "Obrian got shot. Not by accident. And he wasn't sick either."

"He was, I think," Varé said. "When you're shot, you do have an accident in a way. I would assume that Uncle Wisi set off the *keenu*, weakened Obrian by doing so, and thereby surrendered him to his enemies."

"So Uncle Wisi didn't point a bone," the commissaris said, "but a machine pistol, in someone else's hands."

Varé sat down.

"But what was the taboo that Obrian broke?" the commissaris asked.

"Hmm," said Varé.

"You have an idea?"

"Didn't your female informers tell you?" asked Adjutant Adèle.

"I think," Varé said, "but I only think so, aloud right now, that Obrian's taboo was somehow connected to this police station. Uncle Wisi is on good terms with us. He is, one might say, a special protégé of Sergeant Jurriaans'. Today Uncle Wisi is a respected figure in the neighborhood, but his status was different when he first moved into the quarter. The inhabitants thought that he was some kind of monkey that had escaped from the jungle and could be teased. Sergeant Jurriaans wouldn't let them."

"Aha," Cardozo said, "so Obrian was supposed to show respect to the station."

"Respect?" Karate asked.

"Will we be excused if we laugh softly?" Ketchup asked.

"Interesting," the commissaris said. "Very. What do you think, Sergeant Jurriaans?"

"I have been listening attentively, sir."

"And there's nothing you could add?"

"When Obrian was shot," Jurriaans said, "I was downstairs behind the counter."

"I saw you there," said Karate.

"So did I," said Ketchup. "And never mind the time, that carillon is always off."

"A sergeant's official statement," said Grijpstra, "confirmed by two constables. Even the Supreme Court will bow in silence."

The commissaris checked his watch and stretched. "It isn't getting any earlier. Perhaps we should terminate this pleasant gathering."

His audience moved.

"But even so," the commissaris said, "something still bothers me. There must have been some direct cause, I keep on thinking. Mr. Obrian was a disappointment to Uncle Wisi, but the old man cannot have given up hope quickly. He must have warned his disciple on various occasions until something happened that made the master realize that the disciple had to be removed. At that time the *keenu* was raised by chanting and drumming, *then* the herbs burned, Opete flew over the alley, and Tigri sneaked through it, teeth bare, tail trembling, only *then* the rays of fire flashed and shot Obrian into damnation. But what was the direct cause that brought all that about? What could have been the specific reason?"

The answering silence was oppressive and broken only by

Adjutant Adèle's pink right hand, attempting to squash a black ball-point.

"Adjutant Adèle," the commissaris asked. "Will you permit me to ask you a question?"

The adjutant's lips trembled.

"I have the impression," the commissaris said, "that you know Sergeant Varé well."

"I do," Adjutant Adèle said.

"An affair?"

Adjutant Adèle nodded.

The commissaris smiled helpfully.

Adjutant Adèle unbuttoned the breast pocket of her tunic and inserted the ball point. "I'm fond of black."

The commissaris nodded encouragingly.

"Obrian was black too," the adjutant said, "and particularly attractive to me. I also detested him, especially after he made his request."

"You met with him?"

She smiled ruefully. "Yes, in the street. From then on he was in all my dreams. I knew I would have to give in."

The commissaris' voice was toneless. "On the bridge?"

"Yes, sir. He specified the place." She eyed the commissaris calmly while Jurriaans filled in the gap. "She would have to be in uniform, sir, in full view of everybody."

"You knew?' the commissaris asked.

"Oh, yes, sir. She confided in me. I was aware that something was very wrong. I took the adjutant to dinner."

The ticking of the commissaris' wedding ring on the table broke the tension. Ketchup giggled. "That performance of Madeleine was peanuts compared to what we had coming." Karate crumpled the cigarette he had just rolled. "Imagine this, our very own Adjutant Adèle, in dress uniform, on her knees, on a sunny morning, heeheehee."

"But we would have shot him," Ketchup said.

"And ourselves a little later," Karate said.

"That wouldn't have been necessary," Adjutant Adèle said quietly. "I prevented the final showdown." Her eyes pleaded. "I couldn't have dishonored the service, could I, now? I knew I had to shoot Obrian myself. Without help, without implicating anyone. The weakness was mine, the victory would have to be mine too. It was easier than I thought. Jacobs never knew I borrowed his gun. The time was right, there were no witnesses. I live close by. All I had to do was remove those ridiculous clothes in a doorway afterward and walk home. When Jurriaans telephoned me, I was under the shower." Her mouth hardened as she tried to stare the commissaris down. "I'm sorry."

"We're not playing games anymore, are we?" Grijpstra asked. "What's being said now is nothing but the truth?"

De Gier brushed the left end of his mustache up and the right down. "Will you be arresting the adjutant, adjutant?"

"Me?" Grijpstra asked. His eyelids dropped morosely. "On what charge? The possibility of an impossibility? On the strength of a single statement? Is there any proof? Is anyone stepping forward to provide evidence? All I can see is nothing at all. What sort of a court case would this turn out to be?"

The commissaris waved his cigar. "We aren't quite done. The adjutant said she was sorry. Sorry about what, my dear?"

"That she *didn't* shoot him." Sergeant Jurriaans had gotten up. His hands gripped the table's edge as he leaned toward the commissaris. "I wouldn't allow her to defend the station's honor, sir. I'm all for feminism and equal rights, but we should still defend the better sex. I stepped in before it was too late. She never fired the Schmeisser."

"You?" Grijpstra asked. "You're sure, now?"

"Who else?"

"You confess to having committed the crime?" the commissaris asked.

Jurriaans stretched his back and straightened his shoulders. His hands hit his thighs. "I certainly do."

"One more question," the commissaris said. "I would like to have a verdict." His eyes traveled around the table before they settled on de Gier. "Sergeant?"

"Sir?"

"Would you care to let us have your tentative judgment on all of this?"

De Gier looked away.

"Sergeant?" the commissaris asked softly.

"I have no comments, sir."

The commissaris got up. "My thanks to all of you." He buttoned his jacket and walked to the door. Jurriaans opened it.

"Thank you, Sergeant Jurriaans."

Jurriaans followed the old man into the corridor. "Will you be continuing the investigation, sir?"

"I?" The commissaris sucked smoke energetically before attempting to blow a ring. "No. I'm going home to a late supper."

Jurriaans' hand clasped the commissaris' arm. The sergeant led his superior to the window.

"What do you want me to do, sergeant? Watch the sparrows?"

"Your comments," Jurriaans whispered. "I daresay you have some."

The commissaris looked up. "You require my approval?"

Jurriaans tried to smile.

"You have my *dis*approval."

Jurriaans let go of the commissaris' arm.

"Good evening," the commissaris said.

"Good evening, sir," said the sergeant.

29

THE COMMISSARIS' CITROËN WAS STUCK BETWEEN A PARKED truck and a bundle of bicycles chained to a lamppost. "Shall I get out again?" Grijpstra asked. "Then I can direct your maneuvering."

"No need," the commissaris said. "This superior vehicle is equipped with power steering. Watch this, adjutant." He turned the wheel with one finger and flicked the automatic gear handle with the other. The car responded soundlessly. "Haha," the commissaris said when the Citroën jumped free and slid into the alley. "Modern science knows no restrictions." He braked because the alley was blocked by a van unloading drums, caught and pushed onto the sidewalk by quiet giants. The commissaris switched the engine off and opened the sun roof. "Bit of fresh air, Grijpstra."

Grijpstra looked up and saw a pitch black cloud shot through with red flames and tried to open his door, but the alley was too narrow. He stood on his seat and looked about, and dropped back. "Just a factory chimney, sir, throwing up soot."

"There's no industry in the quarter."

"Must be where they cremate old whores. I always wondered what happens to them in the end."

The van finally pulled away and the Citroën followed. The commissaris grinned as he reached a main thoroughfare.

"Another traffic jam," Grijpstra said, and held on while the commissaris drove the Citroën onto the stone ramp reserved for streetcars in the middle of the street. "It's illegal," the commissaris said, "but my wife is cooking Belgian endives tonight and I don't want to be late. Do you like Belgian endives?"

"With an almost burned crust, sir?"

"Of course."

"Delicious," Grijpstra said, and covered his eyes because the car lurched forward and went through a red light.

"Be my guest," the commissaris said. "I hear that your wife moved to the provinces. You can look now—I wasn't really going through red."

"You're doing it again."

"Never," the commissaris said. "And you should know more about the city's traffic lights. The lights aimed at streetcars have little white dots underneath, and when some of them are on one can still pass."

"This is no streetcar," Grijpstra said. "Shit, sir, that's a gate ahead of us."

"They open when they're pushed," the commissaris said as he slammed through the gate and turned right.

"But, sir," Grijpstra said, "this street is for pedestrians only."

"I know, and I'm driving slowly."

Grijpstra looked back. "The cop over there wrote down your number."

"They'll mail it to me and I'll pay it at once. We're making good time, adjutant, and we're almost there . . . Feel this?" the commissaris asked.

"Feel what?"

"The tickling? Don't you think it exciting? This is the only spot in the city where the sensation occurs. They've used a rough type of brick and it makes the car vibrate. I can feel it in my bones."

"Quite stimulating," Grijpstra said.

"I'll slow down a little, to make it last."

A car behind sounded its klaxon.

"Go ahead," the commissaris said. "You won't spoil *my* pleasure."

Grijpstra had covered his eyes again.

"I know the width of this car exactly," the commissaris said. "Why wear out the brakes if you can easily get through? Here we are. Home. Some cold genever in the garden. I hope we have some time for a quiet drink. I like to have a late supper, but one should have a peaceful half hour to work up an appetite."

Grijpstra looked at the wicker chair that the commissaris indicated. "Too rickety?" the commissaris asked. "It'll hold my weight, but you're a little heavier maybe. Take the other chair, if you like. Thank you, dear." He held up his glass. "I think the adjutant is ready for a refreshening too. I hope you didn't mind that I brought an unexpected guest."

"Not at all," said the commissaris' wife while she served Grijpstra, "because hospitality keeps you at home. I'm glad you did manage to turn up again." She brought a dish of nuts. "You'll have to wait awhile still. The oven is slow. I'll leave the jar here. Don't drink it all. I don't want you to slosh your speech at dinner."

"Health," the commissaris said.

"Your very good health, sir. Shall we drink to the closing of our case?"

"The case was closed when it began." The commissaris looked at the weeds near his chair. "Turtle, do you have to stamp about like that?"

The turtle plodded on and rubbed his shell against Grijpstra's shoe. Grijpstra scratched the hard skin of the reptile's neck.

"Turtle does like you," the commissaris said. "He's the only one of his kind who'll invite petting."

"He's also the only turtle of his kind who has that peculiar light green discoloration on his shell."

"He has?" the commissaris asked, and hung out of his chair. "I see. Maybe you're right. I thought they all came with that imprint."

"They don't," Grijpstra said. "I've seen his species at the zoo and they're much darker all over."

"Is that so?" The commissaris took hold of his glass but didn't drink.

"And," Grijpstra said, "I did happen to meet a turtle, at Nellie's place to be precise, who did have the peculiar light green discoloration *and* who invited petting."

The commissaris emptied his glass and refilled it. "Care for some more?"

"Yes."

"A good woman," the commissaris said, "Nellie is. Why don't you move in with her?"

"Wouldn't everything be the same way again?"

"She's not like your wife at all."

Grijpstra thought.

"Oh, nonsense," the commissaris said. "Nellie'll never get fat."

"Maybe I make them fat," Grijpstra said. "And make them watch TV all the time."

"Aren't you a bit negative?"

"Besides," Grijpstra said, "I've always wanted to live in an empty apartment. It'll give me space to paint. I have to start painting seriously. I've got the ideas, and a little of the technique. In an empty apartment I can work it all out."

"You could visit Nellie more often. By staying away you'll make her unhappy. You may have an obligation."

Grijpstra studied his glass. "You said just now, in the car, before we were vibrating on those rough bricks, that you knew that my wife lives in the provinces now."

The commissaris massaged his cheek. "A slip. I think I'm really getting old."

"Only Cardozo could have given you that information."

"Or de Gier."

Grijpstra shook his head. "Rinus never talks too much."

"Cardozo does?"

"Oh, yes. He also repeats what others have told him."

"Don't underestimate Cardozo, adjutant. He's a most intelligent young fellow."

"An intelligent young fellow does not accuse the innocent."

The commissaris poured more drinks. "He was told to, adjutant, by me, at Nellie's hotel, earlier on today. Cardozo was so kind as to make use of his talent at my request. He had to pretend to be silly, and he managed that very well."

"Good," Grijpstra said. "I'm glad you told me. Did he have to go that far?"

The commissaris smiled innocently. "I only played the game, adjutant. You've been taught to play it yourself. Accuse the wrong person, and the guilty party feels safe. Then switch the attack."

Grijpstra put his glass down, sighed pleasurably, and folded his hands on his stomach.

"By the way, adjutant, when did you know?"

Grijpstra didn't answer. The commissaris waited.

"About the killing, sir?"

The commissaris' silence persisted.

"The possible impossibility, sir?"

The commissaris sipped.

Grijpstra smiled guiltily. "About straightaway, sir. The station was a prime suspect and Obrian was shot in the immediate vicinity. Nobody knew anything. It was quite impossible, sir."

"And de Gier?"

"I think Rinus caught on right away too. We never discussed the matter."

"Too painful?"

Grijpstra's pale blue eyes stared thoughtfully. "Yes."

"Then what? You will admit you allowed yourselves to be misused. Why? To help the station with their spring cleaning?"

"Misused," Grijpstra said. "I wouldn't quite call it that. Shouldn't the city be cleaned? Aren't we hired for that specific purpose? But de Gier did complain a bit. That we were only handed two suspects, for instance, and that they, Gustav and Lennie, hardly fitted the position. He did mention that point, as I recall. We didn't have to be too clear . . . we have worked together for such a long time . . ." His hands waved forlornly. "It isn't always good to say it all."

"You suspected Jurriaans in particular?"

"Didn't you? Why did you leave so suddenly?"

"Did you understand the reason for my disappearance?"

"I thought you wanted nothing to do with the case."

"You could have mentioned the matter to the Ministry of Justice. The ministry employs special detectives who can check on the police."

Grijpstra's hands dropped back on his belly. "You can't be serious, sir."

The commissaris grabbed the sides of his chair. "Let me have your verdict, adjutant. A colleague commits a murder. What's your opinion?

"No."

"Your verdict is negative?"

"I have no verdict."

The commissaris sighed. "De Gier refused too. I provided the opportunity, but we weren't alone then. Here we are together and Turtle isn't really interested."

"Jurriaans may judge himself," Grijpstra almost whispered. "I refuse the choice. We serve the law, but the law may be wrong. Jurriaans chose to ignore the rules we made ourselves, didn't he, sir?"

"Would you have shot Obrian?"

"Hopefully not." Grijpstra watched the ground. "Good and bad, I may not be capable of defining the difference. I wasn't conscious of my stupidity, but this case made that clear." He looked up. "White and black, I may be somewhere in between myself, lost in the gray spaces. De Gier too, but he isn't quite as settled as I. He doesn't care so much. Yes. That's better." His hand rubbed his stomach. "It doesn't gnaw so much then."

"And meanwhile evil is allowed to grow?"

"No, no." Grijpstra's voice dropped even more. "We did do something, didn't we? De Gier found the weapon, he could have hidden it, but he brought it out, all of us fired it even. Cardozo pushed on, we hardly restrained him. I knew he would contact you eventually."

"And if I hadn't come?"

"I thought of that, sir. I planned to ask de Gier and Jurriaans to have a drink with me in that small cafe on the Prince's Island where you take us sometimes."

"You would have made the proper small talk and driven the suspect into a corner? So that there's no way out except straight up?"

Grijpstra tried to smile.

"Good," the commissaris said. "The exercise goes on, it will provide new situations."

The turtle was squashing weeds on his way to a cabbage. The commissaris' wife ran after him and picked him up.

"You know you should stay away from the vegetables. Off to your crate, you monster."

"Poor Turtle," the commissaris said.

"Never mind poor Turtle, and you stop drinking right now. Dinner's ready."

The commissaris got up. "Yes, dear."

She pushed him inside. "Really, no discipline at all. Neither you nor the turtle can go visiting for a while."

30

THE COMMISSARIS LOOKED OUT OF HIS OFFICE WINDOW. THE cars parked in front of police headquarters had changed into smoothly curved snow sculptures and a lone cyclist, tricked by the ice, was trying to pick himself up but lost his footing again. "Nasty weather," the commissaris said. "I'm surprised that you two managed to get here unscathed. I hit a lamppost on the way, but I was almost here by then so I just went on."

"I've read the reports," de Gier said. "Nothing but traffic accidents. If the temperature stays this low, we may as well go on holiday."

A constable brought in the morning mail. The commissaris flipped through the envelopes. "Do we know anyone in Colombia?" He turned the envelope over. "No return address. Marijuana smuggling? Cocaine maybe? Hardly my department, I would think."

Grijpstra flashed his stiletto, turned the knife around, and offered it to the commissaris.

"Do you still carry that weapon? I told you years ago you should surrender it to the arms room. A switchblade does not belong to a detective's official gear."

"But I can throw it now, sir."

De Gier watched as the knife slit through the envelope. "You might try something else, adjutant. Once you've mastered an art, there's nothing more to do. I can get you a blowpipe and some darts."

The commissaris read the signature on the letter. "Erik Jurriaans. So he's come up once more. When did he resign again?"

"Some three months back," Grijpstra said.

"And now residing in Barranquilla, isn't that a port in the Caribbean?" The commissaris scanned through the letter. "Interesting. You want me to read this to you? Are you pouring the coffee, Grijpstra?"

Grijpstra sat on the easy chair for visitors and De Gier on the straight chair for suspects. The commissaris stirred his coffee while he pushed the letter to the middle of his blotter.

The commissaris read:

Gentlemen:

Plural, for I always saw you as a multiple, sir, and Adjutant Grijpstra, and colleague—ex-colleague, I should say now—de Gier, as inseparable parts of your trinity. I still owe you some explanation, and perhaps a word of thanks, and will now try to formulate all that. I'm sitting on a balcony here, called a mezzanine in this country, that has been attached to the inside wall of a tannery, from where, protected by windows and cooled by air conditioning, I can supervise the activity in this huge hall. The tannery only has two walls and the rest is open so that the laborers may enter freely, as most of our workers aren't human but birds, chulos, the vultures that are called streetbirds in Surinam.

They pick clean the skins that have been stretched on frames, and do their work so well that we can unfasten the skins within a day and pack and replace them. I can see palm trees outside the man-high grass, and my assistants are blacks, Spanish-speaking desperadoes, armed with machetes. I'm in Barranquilla, as you'll have seen from the postage stamp, and Amsterdam hardly exists now, but today I have to think of you and the reason that brought me here, and I think I shouldn't put the letter off any longer.

You were right, sir, when you expressed your disapproval. I knew then that I would have to resign. You're the symbol of the service, a patriarch, esteemed by every colleague, admired for your clarity, and when you didn't want to confirm that I saved the honor of the police by doing away with Luku Obrian, I knew that my work had come to an end. I couldn't disappear immediately because the Lennie and Gustav cases hadn't gone to court. As soon as those rascals had been judged, I left, without paying you a visit, and I regret that now. Hence this letter.

What I'm trying to tell you is that I was still thinking then that I did right and that you should have accepted the exception, but I changed my mind yesterday.

Slanozzel was inspecting here. He's the owner of this tannery and many others, the Mr. Slanozzel who may be known to you and who's worth more than I expected when I knew him in Amsterdam, and even in those days he impressed me considerably.

No, Slanozzel is no wisiman, obeahman, incarnate winti, as Varé explained to us so well. I'm not his disciple and don't want to be either. I work for the man, because I have to earn my keep, and because he was kind enough to provide me with the permits that got me into Colombia. I signed a contract—I had to, in order to get the visa—but Slanozzel says he won't keep me to the three-year period. I want to stay, however, to repay the favor, and perhaps also the fine, for the fluttering of a thousand vultures' wings can be unnerving and Colombia is no heaven by any means. Even so Slanozzel has a lot of money invested here, and some exceptionally untrustworthy employees, and when I keep an eye out his profits increase. That I speak Spanish helps. I'll tell Karate and Ketchup to spend their next holiday here. They learned a bit of the language when they came to my class and should practice their knowledge. Your Cardozo would have a good time as well. I taught him too for a while. That boy is an excellent parrot and can repeat even the most complicated constructions.

Slanozzel is a sly fellow, in the best meaning of the word. As sly as the crafty fox from the fable, whom he resembles by the way. Although he must be unimaginably rich, I haven't been able to find fault with his dealings, and I'm familiar with his administration, but he does seem rather opinionated at times, even though he never airs his views, but one can infer his judgments from his behavior.

"So what would you have done?" I asked, referring to my attack on Obrian, and he shook his head.

"Would you have lived in Obrian's shadow?" I asked. He asked if that had been necessary, implying that it hadn't.

That was the end of that conversation. We talked about tanneries and he said that if I had learned all about his leather, a change would be in order and that he intended to transfer me to his scrap-metal business on the Antilles. That division is bigger than what we do here, and the volume here is enormous. Shiploads of skins, all pecked clean by the Opetes. Unbelievable.

Last night I thought, next to the humming air conditioner and a sleeping girl. I'd rather look at her than embrace her beautiful body, for when she makes love she gets too active. You, commissaris, wouldn't have shot Obrian, because you manipulate the wintis and keep yourself free. The gods are in us. I believe that's what Slanozzel meant by not approving my misdeed, like you did before him. Every magic has its antimagic, and a sly man uses the antimagic, but within reason and in modesty, while he steps aside himself, for our deeper being is *free, I really begin to believe that. Adjutant Adèle wasn't as strong as I. I could have restrained her. What seduced me to use the Schmeisser-wisi on Obrian was rage, the so-called legal anger, my frustrated irritation at Obrian's endless teasing. I showed my weakness, which was a pity. The Dutch laws are good enough and our station disposed of sufficient manpower to grab Luku Obrian, on petty charges that, if we had followed up on every one of them (for even Luku made mistakes), could have grown into sizable crimes. I was too busy playing king, so that the prince could push me aside.*

Slanozzel doesn't play king. Yesterday the employees complained that a new chemical that is used on some of the expensive skins hurts their hands. Slanozzel happened to be in my mezzanine and I wanted to tell him to leave me alone, when he asked if he could borrow my overalls. He undressed, got into my work clothes (that are several sizes too big for him), and slaved for hours. I worked with him, so as not to lose face. The acid was indeed something terrible and Slanozzel has discarded the method and is figuring out another, losing money meanwhile, since we can't fill some profitable orders. "What you don't want to be done to yourself do not do to another." I always thought the slogan moralistically childish, but once it's applied, its wisdom becomes apparent.

Not that I want to uphold Slanozzel as the great example. The fellow has taken so much money to the quarter that he could have financed a complete orphans' home and it's a miracle that he isn't diseased to the bone (maybe I should pay some more attention too, the little darlings who share my bed are probably carriers of all the venereal microbes, although they keep saying that they pay regular visits to the hospital). Slanozzel is no socialist and I've always been a supporter of that party. Slanozzel is a capitalist, concerned about profits only. Heaven be thanked, where would I be if he hadn't provided me with work? Still at the station, tortured by a bad conscience? Holding out my hand? (I think welfare is dirty).

As you see, I'm still a long way from answering my questions. What I thought last night is only the beginning, but I know that I should have let Obrian live, and that you were right in not patting my shoulder. Who knows what would have happened then? Karate and Ketchup are ready to roll all pimps and dealers into a mass grave. Those little fellows are in need of a right-minded example. You certainly fill that part, and Grijpstra and our movie hero, if they don't ossify (easy enough in the police) and keep using the wintis proportionally and in simplicity, are your suitable projections. It's good to know that when the vultures squeak around me. They can screech like chalk breaking on a blackboard, but I don't want to complain.

This letter is about ten times as long as I had planned it to be, and some homesickness may have added a sentence here and there. I hear you're having a freezing winter. Here the sun burns into our souls, and when it rains, the streets change into rivers and the street urchins make bridges out of boards and charge a peso before they let you pass. I salute you, commissaris, and the ex-colleagues.

The commissaris folded the sheets covered with cramped handwriting and replaced them in the envelope.

"You're answering?" Grijpstra asked.

"There's no address."

"I can find out," de Gier said. "The Curaçao police can trace him."

"No, sergeant. Jurriaans doesn't expect an answer. But it's good that he spoke up, for him, for you, for me. He who wants to manipulate the wintis consciously should respect them, and any mistake, deliberate or not, should be analyzed and avoided in the future. I suspected as much, and Jurriaans was good enough to confirm my suspicion." The commissaris fetched a watering can from his cupboard and busied himself with his plants.

"How's your rheumatism?" de Gier asked. "I haven't seen you use your cane lately."

"Better," the commissaris said. "Uncle Wisi's obeah works well. He made another supply for me, but it seems the herbs are hard to get. He imported them from Surinam, but there has been some political trouble out there and his shipments get lost or are delayed."

"Maybe they can be obtained elsewhere."

"They can," the commissaris said. "He gave me their Latin names. I also have a recipe for the ointment."

"Won't it be rather troublesome to search for exotic plants?"

The commissaris put his watering can down. "Haven't I been trained to track the elusive?"

De Gier stared dreamily at the overcast sky. "The South American jungle. Tapirs splashing through steaming mud. Colorful birds skimming over the palm trees. Monkeys screeching." He looked at the commissaris. "I would like to join you when you go."

"I have enough for a year."

"I can wait a year," de Gier said.

The commissaris frowned irritably. "No, Rinus. Look for your own herbs. And do some work now. Isn't there anything going on?"

"Our patriarch," de Gier said in the canteen, "our admired archetype. And the coffee is terrible again today."

"What's wrong with the coffee?" Grijpstra asked. "Strong and tasty, I would say. I do believe that you shouldn't be following enlightened teachers anymore. Maybe you should look for your own salvation, all by your miserable self."

"And you, great spirit?"

Grijpstra thoughtfully put down his cup. "Delicious coffee."

"Alone," de Gier said to Tabriz that night, who had clawed herself into his lap. "Not a bad word, really. Rather a good sound, don't you think?"

Tabriz wanted to purr but developed hiccups. She flopped on her back, rowed her short legs in the air, and said something.

De Gier suddenly spread his legs apart as that the cat fell heavily on her back. "You're supposed to turn over when you fall. Real cats do that. What exactly do you mean by 'yoho'?"

The phone rang.

"Marike," de Gier said. "How nice of you to want to visit me tonight, but it'll be impossible, unfortunately."

De Gier listened.

"You have iced champagne and want to share it with me? But I really can't make it."

He put the phone down, carried a chair to his balcony, plucked Tabriz from the carpet, and pulled the cat back on his lap.

"I've got to think," he said to the still-hiccuping cat. "The time has come."

The cat went limp under his stroking hand and fell asleep.

"Don't sleep," de Gier mumbled. "Think with me. About whether I'm going the right way or whether I should perhaps change my direction drastically."

Tabriz snored.

De Gier dreamed. He paddled a hollowed-out tree trunk across a wide river. Luku Obrian sat in the canoe's bow.

Obrian steered the boat by shouting "Port" or "Starboard" so that de Gier might know where to plunge his paddle.

"We're going the right way?" de Gier asked.

Obrian turned around and grinned. De Gier saw the gold gleam in his mouth and the black eyes, flashing from under the brim of his tattered straw hat.

"Yes," de Gier said, "but last time you went completely wrong."

"You've got to do that every now and then," Obrian said, and put all his strength into a single pull. The canoe swished ahead.

"We're going the right way," Obrian shouted, "because that's the direction you chose."

A waterfall gurgled, and sharp rocks rose from the foaming water.

De Gier awoke with a yell. Tabriz leaped off his lap and started a fresh series of hiccups. She sat down and tried to purr again.

"It's complicated," de Gier said. "Whatever was I doing in that wicked fellow's company? And where could we have been going?"

Tabriz raised her upper lip desperately.

"*You* say something," de Gier said.

"Yoho," said Tabriz.

ABOUT THE AUTHOR

JANWILLEM VAN DE WETERING WAS BORN IN ROTTERDAM IN 1931, studied Zen in Daitoku-ji Monastery, Kyoto and philosophy in London, and has lived as well in Amsterdam, Cornwall, Capetown, Bogota, Lima, and Brisbane. In 1975 he settled in a small town on the coast of Maine where he still lives.

The Amsterdam Cops series that features Adjutant Grijpstra and Sergeant de Gier working as extensions of the commissaris, a wily and philosophical Amsterdam Chief of Detectives, was conceived when the author served with the Amsterdam Reserve Constabulary. To date over two million copies of his works are in print in fourteen languages.

His joys are an ongoing study of nihilism, keeping a wooden lobster boat afloat and getting older. His pain is an inability to play the jazz trumpet.

He has been married for a long time, no longer smokes or drinks, and has become allergic to the guru syndrome.

Soho Crime

Other Titles in this Series

Janwillem van de Wetering

Outsider in Amsterdam
Tumbleweed
The Corpse on the Dike
Death of a Hawker
The Japanese Corpse
The Blond Baboon
The Maine Massacre
Just a Corpse at Twilight
The Mind-Murders
The Hollow-Eyed Angel

Seichō Matsumoto

Inspector Imanishi Investigates

Martin Limón

Jade Lady Burning

Jim Cirni

The Kiss Off
The Come On
The Big Squeeze

Timothy Watts

Cons
Money Lovers

Charlotte Jay

Beat Not the Bones

Patricia Carlon

The Souvenir